10/20

SHE WAS
HIS
ANGEL

ALSO BY MIMA

The Fire series
Fire
A Spark Before the Fire

The Vampire series
The Rock Star of Vampires
Her Name is Mariah

Different Shades of the Same Color

The Hernandez series
We're All Animals
Always be a Wolf
The Devil is Smooth Like Honey
A Devil Named Hernandez
And the Devil Will Laugh
The Devil Will Lie
The Devil and His Legacy

Learn more at www.mimaonfire.com
Also find Mima on Twitter, Facebook and Instagram @mimaonfire

SHE WAS
HIS
ANGEL

MIMA

SHE WAS HIS ANGEL

iUniverse books may be ordered through booksellers or by contacting:

iUniverse
1663 Liberty Drive
Bloomington, IN 47403
www.iuniverse.com
1-800-Authors (1-800-288-4677)

ISBN: 978-1-6632-0019-8 (sc)
ISBN: 978-1-6632-0020-4 (e)

Library of Congress Control Number: 2020908553

Print information available on the last page.

iUniverse rev. date: 05/18/2020

ACKNOWLEDGEMENTS

Special thanks to Jean Arsenault for helping with the editing process. Also, thanks to Mitchell Whitlock and Jim Brown for helping with the back cover description.

I also would like to thank all my readers for their continued support but especially Cy Hoselton for always taking the series and its characters to heart.

This book centers on the ideology of powerful women. You don't have to be a superwoman like Paige, Jolene or Maria but then again, why not? In the words of Jorge Hernandez, do you worst!

CHAPTER 1

The world hates powerful women. She can win an election or a beauty pageant; it doesn't matter because, for all the praise and smiles, we already know that she'll be berated on social media before having time to blink. She will get more criticism than respect for everything from the way she answers a question to speculation on whether her tits are real. For every person who encourages women to roar their loudest, many others want to see that bitch burn.

Paige Noël-Hernandez knew this all too well. As a child, her parents made sure their daughters kept in line. Although it was never acknowledged, they were trained as future mothers and wives, not the powerful women that occasionally showed up on television in the 80s, wearing professional attire and speaking with an assertion in their voices. Those were the women that both her parents mocked; her father because he didn't want to think that they existed and her mother because it was a stark reminder of something she would never be and therefore, neither would her daughters.

And it worked. Paige's older sisters fell in line, acting silly and stupid, batting their eyelashes and wiggling their asses until they tied down their high school boyfriends; often the alpha dog types who watched sports and yelled at the television while the women brought them something to eat and grinned like morons. Paige's sisters were good at that because they were well trained however it was the youngest girl who was another story. She was just a little too much, a child that didn't go with the flow, ostracized for not wanting to become one of them.

And she never would be.

And that's why he loved her.

"Paige, your family," Jorge Hernandez couldn't keep quiet. He had remained silent at her father's funeral and on the drive home but was no longer able to hold back. "Why do they not speak to you? I do not understand."

She turned toward her husband with sadness in her blue eyes, causing Jorge to nod and look away. It was him.

"Maybe, you know, I should have stayed home," He ran a hand through his short, black hair, suddenly feeling a mix of Spanish and English jumbled in his mind. "*Tu familia no me quería allí.*"

"No," She immediately moved closer to him, shaking her head. "I don't care what they think and as far as I'm concerned, they're *not* my family. Not anymore. They haven't been for a long time. I regret going. Had I known…."

"But Paige," Jorge abruptly cut in, his dark eyes blazing as his accent grew thicker amid stress. "It is me, they do not like. *Soy el diablo llamado Hernández.*"

"Well, you're not the devil to me," Paige firmly corrected him as she shook her head, causing a tiny strand of blonde hair to escape her bun. "My family can think whatever they want but you, Maria, Miguel, you're my world."

Jorge reached for her hand with the mention of their children's names.

Regardless of what his wife said, he knew the truth. A Mexican who came to Canada to take over the legal cannabis industry, he acted oblivious to the murmurs of his dark past and insinuations that a trail of bodies was carefully hidden as he became one of the most powerful men in the country, even briefly flirting with the idea of running for prime minister. His influence and power were undeniable and those who challenged him, at best, slunk away in silence.

"Paige, I think, if I had not been there today…"

"You," Paige sharply cut him off with a fire in her eyes even though her voice remained calm. "You had every right to be there. You're my husband

and I don't care if they liked it or not. As far as I'm concerned, after today, they're *all* dead to me."

With that, she turned on her heels, her shoes loudly clicking against the floor as she walked into the kitchen. His eyes automatically drifted to her ass in the tight, little skirt causing his thoughts to briefly drift to lust, he quickly looked away and regained himself. This was certainly not the time, despite the temptation but there was something to be said for his wife's fiery disposition, especially when she was usually so calm, so peaceful and balanced.

"Paige," He called out as he followed her into the ultra-modern kitchen, in the soulless house that he was starting to hate. Despite the size and price tag, it lacked warmth. "Paige, this here, it is not about you, it is…"

His words were quickly cut off when she turned around and grabbed him with an unexpected forcefulness, her lips overtaking his, Jorge could feel her hand abruptly sliding into his pants. Quickly distracted by pleasure, he immediately matched her intensity, his heart racing with ferocity. Releasing her lips, he glanced toward the door, then the clock, quickly calculating that the children wouldn't be home for at least another half hour.

"Oh, *mi amor*," Jorge whispered as he gently pushed her towards the cupboard before attempting to pull her skirt up. Feeling his desires increasing, he grew frustrated with the stubborn material and gave it one abrupt tug. A loud rip seemed to temporarily take him out of his cloud of arousal while Paige's head fell back in laughter. His eyes immediately focused on her exposed neck as he moved closer, his tongue and lips met with the smooth skin, gentle at first but quickly showing more forcefulness as he tightened his grip on her body.

Paige's gasp was the encouragement he needed to continue as he slid his hand up her smooth thigh and into the warm place between her legs, causing her to wiggle while letting out a soft moan. He stopped briefly to pull the skirt up to her waist and remove her underwear, before lifting her body to sit on the counter. Jorge looked into her eyes as he unbuttoned his pants and let them drop to the floor. Their lips met again and he wasted no time pulling down his underwear and moving inside her. He felt her legs wrapping tightly around him as he thrust deeper until pleasure became so powerful that their entire world stopped, if even for a moment.

"Oh *mi amor*," Jorge spoke bluntly when he eventually moved away and she slid off the counter. "If only everyone dealt with grief like this, we would have a much happier world, I am sure of it."

Paige giggled as she attempted to fix her mangled skirt. Jorge was pulling up his boxers and pants when he heard her sniff. He quickly pulled up his zipper as the tears began to fall down her face.

"Paige, I am sorry," Jorge whispered as he hugged her. "I did not mean disrespect. I know my words can sometimes be a little too much."

"No," She sniffed and he slowly let her go. "You're never too much for me."

Looking into her eyes, it was a rare moment when he simply didn't know what to say. It was a complicated situation.

"Paige, I…"

"Jorge," She interrupted and shook her head. "I don't even understand. This is so….confusing to me. I haven't spoken to most of my family in years and now…I don't know. If I hadn't gone today, they'd be mad. And I went and…they were still mad."

She began to cry harder and Jorge pulled her into another hug.

Paige took a deep breath and moved away.

"I'm going to…change," She glanced down at her clothes. "Before Juliana brings the kids home."

"I am sorry about the skirt," Jorge spoke sheepishly. "I did not know I was so…aggressive."

"You knew," Paige winked as she headed toward the stairs. "Besides, it's 'fast fashion'. It's not meant to last more than two washings anyway."

Jorge grinned, his eyes sparked a devilish glint as he watched her walk away before pulling out his phone and turning it back on. Regardless of his attempt to step away from some of his duties with Our House of Pot to spend time with his family, the texts and voicemails continued to come in. Whether it be his friend and comrade Diego Silva asking how he wanted to take care of a problem or Chase Jacobs checking in from the club Jorge owned, there always seemed to be a problem.

And with Jorge Hernandez, there was always a solution. Unfortunately, the solutions were often quite messy.

"I put on another one," Paige's voice lacked the passion it held only moments earlier as she slowly walked down the stairs, now barefoot, wearing an almost identical skirt, he met her in the living room. "I was going to switch to yoga pants and hoodie but I didn't have the energy to go through a pile of clothes to find anything. It's like a bomb went off in our room."

"*Mi amor,* I can find it for you if you wish," Jorge suggested but she shook her head. "We had to quickly return from vacation. It was not as if we had time to unpack and organize since then. It has been crazy."

"I know," Paige said as she collapsed on the couch. "I wish today was over."

"Paige, why not go upstairs and sit on your meditation pillow," Jorge suggested as she closed her eyes and he joined her on the couch. "You must have a break to gather your thoughts. I can take care of dinner. You know this."

She smiled and opened her eyes.

"I'm fine, thanks," She regained her usual, calm voice. "But a cup of coffee would be nice."

"I can do this," He replied and winked before standing up. "Thanks to Diego's secret recipe, I now make the best coffee. Maybe next, I will take over the coffee business in Canada."

He let out a laugh as he started toward the kitchen.

"Let's just stick with cannabis for now," Paige gently suggested.

"Hey, the money these shops make," Jorge quickly pointed out as he went to the sink and washed his hands. "Maybe I can combine the two, you know?"

She laughed and he felt his spirit lighten as he went to work.

"You know, Paige," He called out. "It is because I'm Mexican that your family, they don't like me. I was probably the only brown man at the funeral. Remember the time your sister…"

"Ah, let's not talk about that," Paige shook her head. "That was the most disastrous dinner. I can't believe Maria walked in on them saying that I waited too long to get married and had to *settle* for a Mexican…I think that's how she put it."

"I know but your family, they are demeaning and racists," Jorge quickly pointed out. "Although, my reputation, it does not help either."

"If they knew *my* reputation, it mightn't either," Paige reminded him as he reached in the cupboard for the package of coffee.

"If they knew *your* reputation," Jorge spoke abruptly. "They would know better than to piss you off."

He glanced toward the living room and winked, causing her to laugh again.

"Top assassin in the world," Jorge teased her. "You do not fuck around with a lady who can kill you and make it look like a suicide."

"Or an accident," Paige added with a sniff. "And it's not like I do that anymore."

"Well, you know, sometimes, you help out when and where it is needed," Jorge reminded her with his probing eyes before turning on the coffee pot. "This here, it is good. It is…as you might say, a *handy* talent."

"Well, we all have our talents," Paige quipped.

"Ah, but not like yours, *mi amor*," Jorge said with laughter in his voice. "Women, like your sisters, they can, what? Cook a nice dinner? Sew a button? Give a good blow job on their husband's birthday? I do not think they can compare."

Paige laughed and his heart filled with pleasure.

"It is true," Jorge insisted as he returned to the living room. "You know me, Paige, I do not sugar-coat."

"No one will ever accuse you of that," She agreed with humor in her voice as he walked toward her. "Jorge Hernandez is known for a lot of things but sugar coating is not one of them."

"Well, *mi amor*," Jorge said as he sat on the small table across from her as the coffee began to perk in the next room. "There are two kinds of people in this here world. The wolves and the sheep and all you have to do is look out there," He pointed toward the window. "To see we're up to our eyeballs in sheep shit."

Paige gave a knowing smile.

"This is why we must show our fangs," Jorge continued as he touched her leg, slowing running his hand up her thigh. "We must remind them who runs this world and these people, they are ferocious."

"People like you," Paige spoke softly but her eyes flashed dangerously as she leaned forward. "Because no one fucks with Jorge Hernandez."

"Or like you," He moved closer, his eyes staring into hers while his hands continued to gently caress her thighs. "Because it is time the world learns that no one fucks with Paige Noël Hernandez either. It is your turn, my love. Do your worst."

CHAPTER 2

The temporary silence enjoyed by Jorge and Paige abruptly ended when Maria and Miguel barreled through the door, followed by an exhausted Mexican nanny. Pointing toward the floor, Juliana quietly indicated that she was returning to her basement apartment while the couple's 17-month-old ran toward his mother, wasting no time trying to climb on the couch. Paige reached for him and pulled him up.

"*Mamaaaaaaaaaa…..*"

"Oh my God, today was *insane,*" Maria immediately started to complain as she threw her book bag on the floor and sat in a chair across from the couch, her long black hair falling across her face, she quickly pushed it back. "Like these teachers need to talk to one another before they give us a *ton* of assignments. I'm just saying that…"

"Maria!" Jorge immediately snapped at his 13-year-old daughter as he stood across the room, his phone in hand. "What did I tell you about this here new school?"

"But *Papa!*"

"No!" Jorge spoke firmly as he walked toward her while shaking a finger. "May I remind you that it was *you* that wanted to switch schools this fall? You begged and pleaded to go to…"

"Oh gross!" Maria cut off her father and pointed toward Paige who was snuggling her son. "You got a *hickey*. I thought you were going to your father's funeral today."

"We did and.." Paige started to speak in her usual, calm tone but was quickly interrupted by her husband.

"Maria!" Jorge yelled while his eyes blazed. "This stops right *now*. You do not disrespect this family."

"I'm *just* pointing it out," Maria quickly defended herself, her brown eyes widened innocently. "You guys are like *old*. It's gross and disgusting."

"People in their 40s are not old!" Jorge argued with her. "And this here is none of your business!"

"Then maybe you shouldn't make it so obvious," Maria continued to complain, now sitting on the edge of her seat. "I can see it from way over here, *Papa*. You couldn't like, leave her alone on the day of her *father's funeral!*"

"Maria, it's not…" Paige started but quickly had her attention diverted by Miguel who jumped in her face, his dark curls bouncing around.

"*Mamaaaaaaaaaaa…*"

The toddler moved in close and touched their noses together then giggled as he fell toward her and she pulled him in for a hug.

"Enough with this, Maria," Jorge ignored his son's antics and Paige's attempts to speak. "You will show no disrespect and you do not worry about what we do in the privacy of our room. Just like when you are married someday-

"Married?" Maria automatically shot back just as the doorbell rang. "You won't even let me *date!* I'm in a co-ed school now and what's the difference because you won't let me go on a *fucking date!*"

"Maria, enough!" Jorge snapped as he rushed to answer the door. "That language and attitude, that is enough! You are 13. This here is too young."

"Well, other girls in my class date and…"

Jorge ignored her as he opened the door. Diego was on the other side.

"*Amigo!*" Jorge said as he winced and stepped out. "I will invite you in but you know what? Let us go to your house instead."

Glancing past Jorge to see Maria and Paige debating whether she was old enough to date, Diego Silva twisted his lips, narrowed his dark eyes, and nodded.

"Let's go have a drink," The Colombian replied as Jorge shut the door behind him and the two men began to walk next door. "Bet you're glad I live so close *now*."

As usual, Diego spoke in an exaggerated, dramatic tone as he swung his arms around. "I know you, you didn't think I should live so close when I first bought the house but *now* that you see how easy it is to just walk next door…"

"Yeah yeah, you got me on this one, Diego," Jorge reluctantly agreed as he sighed. "This here, it is close, and when my kids are crazy…."

"And that's the other thing," Diego continued as they arrived at his house and he pulled out the key. "You need to get back to work. This extended holiday is over."

"But Diego," Jorge quickly started to correct him as they entered the lavish home. Much too big for one, single man, it was a reflection of someone who wanted the best out of life. Unlike Jorge's own home, nothing was out of place, no toys tossed about, no applesauce on the floor or faded marker stains on the wall but most of all, his house was a quiet sanctuary. "I was retiring and you were to take over…"

"And as you recall, I didn't," Diego stood up straighter and fixed his tie as Jorge closed the door. "And you know why. I told you then, this was only temporary that you would be back by fall."

"It's October."

"It's fall."

Jorge didn't reply but followed him into the living room and past several lime trees. Diego went behind the bar and started to fix them each a drink.

"Let's face it," Diego spoke bluntly and tilted his head in the direction of Jorge's house. "The family you wanted to be around all the time, they're driving you fucking crazy."

"I love my family, Diego."

"Yes, and they're driving you fucking crazy," Diego reminded him. "You're here every day. Remember when I first moved in here and you said, 'Don't be at my door all the time' and well, look at us *now*."

"Yes, Diego, I know," Jorge admitted with some reluctance as he sat on the barstool. "It is *me* at your door all the time."

"Your children are like *you* and that's why," Diego continued as he pushed a drink with a little umbrella and a slice of lime toward Jorge, who looked at it skeptically. "Your son is energetic and wild and your daughter, she's got a mouth."

Jorge gave him a warning look as he reached for his drink.

"And you might not like hearing me say that but you know it's true."

Jorge wanted to laugh but instead took a drink and perked up.

"This here, Diego, it is good!"

"Don't change the subject on me," Diego cut in and nodded. "And of course it's good! What you think, I just make good coffee?"

"I do not need this here umbrella," Jorge pulled out the paper decoration. "But yes, Diego, you are right. I hate like fuck saying it, but you are right."

"And you think you got it bad," Diego continued as he dramatically swung his arms in the air. "What about poor *Paige?* She's gotta listen to the three of you!"

"I do not think my wife minds this," Jorge said and finished his drink. "Juliana is with Miguel most of the time, Maria is in school…"

"Miguel, he is my godson but I see the pure devil of Hernandez in him," Diego continued to speak as if Jorge weren't already talking. "And Maria, she has your attitude."

"It is this new school," Jorge insisted. "I knew she shouldn't go to a co-ed school but she would not let it go."

"Don't blame it on the school," Diego shook his head and curled up his lips. "This here is *you*. She's still your daughter."

"Diego, I…"

"And what happened with her biological mother."

Jorge clamped his mouth shut and the two shared a look.

"That there, it happened months ago…"

"Not that many months ago," Diego reminded him. "It changed her."

Jorge didn't reply but looked away.

"Not that I blame her," Diego continued. "It would change me too."

"Diego, I think….I do not know what to think."

"She seems more hostile but it doesn't make sense," Diego leaned forward as if to confide in him. "Paige saved her life but she's got all this anger toward both of you."

"I know," Jorge nodded and took a deep breath. "I do not understand. I am not sure what to do. Paige has been working with her but....my daughter, I do not think she will ever get over that day. It was....very traumatic for her."

Diego dropped his original intensity and nodded.

"Now that she's in school and started jiu-jitsu maybe that will help."

"I do not know what else to do," Jorge admitted. "I thought me staying home would help but it seems almost as if I made it worse."

"Then come back to work," Diego insisted and leaned in. "Paige is better at this than you. You'll go home later and the entire house will be calm again. You know she's got the ability to create peace and you, you can only create war."

"Don't get me wrong," Diego continued. "That's what you're good at and that's what we need just not in your house."

"I do not mean to..."

"You're an instigator," Diego reminded him. "You stir the pot and that's why you need to come back to work. We can use some of that now."

"Oh yeah?" Jorge appeared intrigued. "You got something for me to deal with?"

"You might say that."

"So what's going on, Diego."

"Everything's going to hell since you left, that's what."

"I thought you said you could handle everything."

"I can," Diego reached for a bottle of tequila and poured them each a shot. "I'm not talking about Our House of Pot. We're fucking flying especially since adding the edibles from that French bakery."

"So, then...."

"It's everything else that's fucked up," Diego shook his head. "You've turned Chase into a killing machine, he's a mess. It takes everything in me to keep him from lashing out at whoever pisses him off from week to week."

Jorge slowly nodded. The young half-indigenous man had once been the least violent of the group but something had snapped in him during the past year and he lost his innocent ways. The group only saw a glimmer of his former self when Maria was present. For some reason, Jorge's daughter brought the frozen man back to life.

"Then there's Jolene," Diego continued to speak dramatically, this time referring to his sister. "She's frustrated with Enrique. Now that she's stolen him from his wife and ripped apart his whole fucking family, she's not sure if she can trust him."

"The challenge, Diego, it is over…."

"But you know Jolene," Diego leaned in. "We gotta keep her preoccupied or she gets out of hand."

"We'll figure out something," Jorge said with a shrug. "These here, they aren't real problems. This is not a reason to get me back to work."

"Jorge, I said you were going out on temporary leave as CEO," Diego reminded him. "People are wondering why you're not back yet."

"Because the temporary part was your idea," Jorge reminded him. "Not mine."

"Admit it," Diego said as he shook his head. "You miss it. I know you're backing that docuseries but…"

Jorge thought for a moment and reluctantly nodded. As much as he dreaded the insanity of constant problems and wanted to keep safely out of the line of fire, there was another part of him that wanted to jump back into the mix.

"Diego, I have talked a lot to Alec Athas," Jorge referred to his regular, secret conversations with the Canadian prime minister, a man he had groomed and helped get elected. "We are working on some plans of our own."

"Yeah, what's that about anyway?" Diego raised an eyebrow. "You're being very secretive."

"Perhaps," Jorge thought for a moment before reaching for the shot that sat in front of him. "It is time we all meet for a….*family* dinner to discuss everything. I may have some surprises in store."

The two men tapped their shot glasses together.

"To the second phase of my plan," Jorge said and hesitated. "And a day no one saw coming."

CHAPTER 3

"I am thinking it is time for the *family* to get together again," Jorge commented as the couple got into bed later that night. Sensing hesitation from his wife, he looked to see the exhaustion on her face. It had been a long day. "I mean, at the bar. In the VIP room. With the food delivered."

"I assumed that but," Paige said as she ran a hand over her face and pulled up the covers. Her blonde hair fell forward and she quickly pushed it back and turned toward her husband as he sat his phone down. "Does this mean you're going back to….everything?"

"Well, in fairness, *mi amor,*" Jorge said as he moved closer to Paige. "I never really left. They were always checking in with me."

"But you had some distance," Paige gently reminded him. "You were home more."

"But is that really going so well?" Jorge countered as he turned on his side and leaned up against the pillow. "Today, with Maria? I know you would've handled that differently than me. I get angry. I do not want her to become an entitled princess like her mother was. This could be a huge problem."

"I know," Paige nodded as she placed her hand on his arm. "But when you get angry, *she* gets angry and nothing is accomplished."

"See, this is what I mean," Jorge shook his head. "I am no good at home."

"It was never about you being home to help," Paige reminded him as she tilted her head. "It was about your staying out of the line of fire since you have a way of being in the wrong place at the wrong time. That's my concern."

"I know, *mi amor,* but this here project with Alec and the docuseries…"

He drifted off and she gave a knowing nod.

"I don't know what to say," Paige said with more confidence in her voice. "I still don't think you should be going in circles like you used to. There has to be some balance."

"I will make sure there is," Jorge spoke quietly as he looked into Paige's eyes. "Meanwhile, this here, it is too much for you."

"Here?" Paige pointed around the room.

"Yes, *mi amor,* this house, these kids," Jorge tilted his head toward the next room where the baby slept. "It is too much. You need a break. Miguel is full of energy and Maria….she never stops complaining."

"We need to do something about that," Paige said and rubbed her eye. "I'm concerned. Since her mother was killed…"

"Leave it to that *puta* to fuck up her daughter," Jorge's eyes snapped as he spoke. "Even from the grave."

"She can't do much damage now," Paige thoughtfully reminded him.

"But yet, she still does," Jorge insisted. "Look at how Maria acted today."

"You know, maybe," Paige started and stalled for a moment. "She's just being a normal teenager. I was doing some research online and it seems like….and this might surprise you, but teenage girls are just assholes sometimes."

"Well, she's got that one mastered," Jorge quipped. "My daughter, today, she was an asshole and this here, it has to stop. One of the issues with parents today is they are lazy and let everything 'run its course'. Remember how they tell us that when we went to the school to register her?"

"And they gave us parenting manuals?" Paige grinned. "Yes, I remember your reaction."

"Well, Paige, it does not make sense to let your kid run the fucking house," Jorge complained. "And someone had to tell them that."

Paige seemed to resist the smile that touched her lips and nodded.

"And you know me, Paige, I am not shy to tell them as much."

"That's a good thing because I'm sure no one else did."

"Lazy parenting," Jorge complained. "Just like the rest of the world, no one wants to do their fucking job."

"Well, at least your employees are different," Paige reminded him. "They go above and beyond."

"This here is good," Jorge insisted. "But that is because I trained them well. That is my point in this whole story."

"As for Maria, you need to talk to her more," Paige reminded him. "Not growl, not yell, but talk. Ask about her day. Try to understand. That's what she needs. Not a lecture."

"I will," Jorge relented.

"Now, when is this family dinner?" Paige switched gears.

"I am going to see tomorrow," Jorge said as he relaxed. "I plan to go talk to Chase in the morning."

"Ok."

"I want to also touch base with Alec before that time to make sure everything is sorted out."

Paige nodded but didn't reply.

"He is…improving," Jorge said and checked her expression but she had none. Knowing that Alec Athas was a man from her past, even though it had been 20 years ago, he felt the need to always watch her reaction when his name was mentioned. After all, the Canadian prime minister was the polar opposite of Jorge Hernandez.

"It takes time," She spoke evenly.

"It is important that a prime minister be cautious when he starts," Jorge repeated what he had told Alec after first being voted in. "People watch more closely in the beginning than fade out later on. This is the time to strike."

"I agree."

"Meanwhile," Jorge changed the topic. "I will need your help too, *mi amor.*"

She didn't reply but it was a topic they had discussed various times throughout the summer.

"We will need your guidance," Jorge reminded her and thought for a moment. "Especially since I will be more tied up in the docuseries for the streaming site. I must make sure it has the right narrative."

"You mean that pot is good and Big Pharma is bad?" Paige said with a hint of a smile on her lips. "The docuseries will show people all the potential of cannabis as well as the myths, the lies…"

"The lies the government tells us," Jorge interjected. "The lies Big Pharma wants us to believe. That is about to come to an end."

"We need to make sure it gets lots of attention in the media…"

"And it will," Jorge assured her. "I'm going to have Makerson write about this 'Canadian produced series' giving it lots of hype."

Paige nodded with a grin. The *Toronto AM* editor was useful when they needed the right slant on a story. Of course, he had a new condo that was proof of his benefits from the relationship, not to mention one of the most popular newspapers in Canada. This was especially impressive considering the industry was, as a whole, dying. *Toronto AM* continued to strive and move ahead.

"I think this can only help make the company grow," Paige said with a tired nod. "Things can only get better."

"They always do, *mi amor,* they always do."

The following morning, Jorge was up before his family. He showered, shaved, and put on a suit and tie before jumping into his SUV and heading out. After grabbing a coffee, he made his way to the *Princesa Maria,* a high-end bar in Toronto's downtown. Over the years, it had grown popular with the elites who worked in the area, especially in the financial sector.

However, the bar didn't open until late afternoon which made it a daytime meeting place for Jorge and his associates. Today, he arrived at the same time as Chase Jacobs, the manager. The young indigenous man was just getting out of his car when Jorge pulled up beside him and gave a quick nod before jumping out of his SUV.

"You're here early," Chase commented with a grin on his face. "You just missed Clara."

Jorge nodded. Clara was the Latina who regularly checked their homes and offices for listening devices and other suspicious gadgets. She was a pro at her job and made certain that they were safe from those who might benefit from listening in to their secret conversations.

"That woman, she moves quickly," Jorge said as he walked with Chase to the club's entrance. "What would we do without Clara?"

Chase merely nodded as he unlocked the door and stepped inside. Turning off the alarm, the two men automatically headed toward his office after locking the door again.

"Maria was telling me something about a hickey…." Chase teased as he turned on the lights as they walked into the office. "She's very dramatic."

"This here, you do not have to tell me," Jorge shook his head. "It was a big…as you say, *ordeal* yesterday afternoon."

"She tells me everything," Chase teased as he went behind his desk, sitting in his chair. "I try to calm her but she doesn't always listen."

"She's 13," Jorge reminded him. "Listening isn't her thing right now. But at least she listens to you more than me or Paige."

Chase shrugged but it was hardly a secret that Maria had a crush on him. Although it made Jorge uncomfortable, it did prove helpful on a few occasions when Maria wouldn't confide in her parents. Jorge appreciated that he always had an extra set of eyes watching his daughter, someone who sincerely cared about her safety.

"I don't think that has anything to do with age," Chase corrected him. "I've known that girl since she was 10. Nothing has changed much."

"Yes, except her life, it is *so* unfair," Jorge spoke dramatically as if to mimic his daughter. "She lives in a big house, has everything a kid could want, and goes to a nice school but still, I am a monster."

Chase laughed.

"At any rate," Jorge changed the subject. "I would like us to have a *family* dinner here sometime soon. We have some things to discuss. I think also, it would be nice to check in with everyone, make sure we are all still on the same page."

Chase nodded and glanced at a book on his desk, shuffling the pages.

"It's free for the next few days," He said and looked up at Jorge. "Want me to check around to see when is best for everyone."

"Sure, as long as it is soon," Jorge commented. "And reasonable. I do not wish to wait a week because Jolene wants to get her nails done or Diego….whatever Diego does…."

"You should know, you're his neighbor now," Chase joked.

"Yes, and although this here is good," Jorge commented but leaned forward as if in confidence. "I had no idea he had so many….boyfriends, you know?"

Chase nodded.

"I guess you used to live with him when you first moved to the city," Jorge replied and leaned back in his chair. "So you know…."

"Yeah, it could be awkward…."

"I always have to look for a strange car before going to visit," Jorge said and looked away. "He puts the 'whore' in hormones, does he not?"

"Probably more so now," Chase reminded him. "With his new house and…"

"And Jolene, she will be next," Jorge cut him off. "She has her sights set on a house near to me too. And you, will you be next?"

"You never know," Chase replied, his dark eyes grew serious. "Anything is possible."

"At any rate," Jorge changed the conversation. "I must stop gossiping. Paige, she tells me that your lessons are going well. That your fighting, it is good?"

Chase nodded. Paige had been preparing him to move up in their organization. She had given him shooting lessons, introduced him to Line fighting which was a brutal form of self-defense and now they were focusing on one of her areas of expertise; how to make a murder look like a suicide.

"This here, it is good," Jorge was impressed. "These are things you must know. You're the younger generation. It is up to you to someday take over."

"It won't be anytime soon."

"No, but that is not the point," Jorge reminded him. "In this world, you either move up or….you die and *amigo,* you have a lot of living to do."

Chase didn't reply. His expression said it all.

CHAPTER 4

"Tell you the truth," Jorge leaned back in the booth of the small, downtown coffee shop. "I never thought I would see you again once you got your money."

Across from him sat a scrawny white kid in his 20s that Jorge once helped when they shared a common enemy.

"I know, I know," Andrew Collin put his hand in the air while a goofy smile appeared on his lips. "You thought I was going to burn through all that money and have nothing to show for it."

Jorge didn't disagree. He had forcefully loosened the reins on Andrew's inheritance but did so with a stern warning to not piss the money away but do something useful with his life.

"And, did you?"

"No!" Andrew appeared a little insulted. "I have a *real* job plus I'm working on projects like your docuseries with my friend, Tony."

"So Tony, he knows his shit," Jorge nodded in agreement. "We've talked a lot about the details and we are on the same page."

They hadn't been at first. That quickly changed.

"Yeah, he said you got lawyers and big-time money involved," Andrew remarked with interest. "You're taking this very seriously."

"Shouldn't I?"

"Yeah, I mean, totally," Andrew nodded with enthusiasm. "Tony is the man. He knows what he's fucking doing or I wouldn't have hooked you up with him."

"I watched some of his other work," Jorge agreed before taking another gulp of coffee. "I like that one he did on ah… GMOs, that is what they are called? Plus, I like the footage for my series that he showed me the other day. This Tony, he's got my attention."

"And he wants to keep it," Andrew reminded him. "He's doing an awesome job, right?"

"Oh, I *know* he's doing an awesome job and he's gonna keep it up," Jorge confirmed with fire in his eyes. "I do not settle for less with my people."

"That's what I told him."

"Did you also tell him that I wanted to help produce this series?"

"I did."

"Then how come," Jorge leaned ahead. "When I talk to him, he seemed to think otherwise."

"He's just careful about who he gets involved….you know."

"Oh, *I* know," Jorge sat back again and took a deep breath. "But for me to have such a huge role, I got to maintain control over the project."

"I see that."

"There's no fucking around with me."

"I know that too."

"So," Jorge decided to change the subject. "You didn't fuck up your life after all?"

"No, I got this new girlfriend, and she…"

"I don't want to hear your drama," Jorge cut him off. "I know your love life, it is complicated. I got a teenage drama with my daughter, I don't need more dramatic stories."

"How old is your daughter?" Andrew appeared intrigued.

Jorge answered him with a glare.

"Anyway, I ah…."

"You were telling me how you didn't fuck up your life?"

"Yeah, I got a real job," Andrew nodded with enthusiasm.

"That right? Flipping burgers?"

"Nah, like a *real* job that requires professionalism and everything."

"Is that so?"

"I work in a crematorium."

"Ah, what?" Jorge asked as if he had misunderstood. "You burn bodies for a living?"

"Yeah, totally."

"You?" Jorge asked skeptically.

"It's true," He nodded. "I'm a cremation technician."

Jorge was stunned.

"I know, right?" Andrew gestured toward him. "That's how everyone looks when I tell them. You should've seen the look on my aunt's…"

"So, you, you burn bodies for a living?" Jorge leaned in and spoke in a low voice. "This here, you know how to do?"

"Yes, I've been doing it for…"

"How does one…...get into that profession?" Jorge was curious.

"Honestly, I asked a guy who did it," Andrew said with a shrug. "I know, everyone is always expecting a big story but really, it's because there was a demand and the pay was decent. I got trained, you know, and here I am."

"And this here, it doesn't bother you?" Jorge was curious. "Burning people."

"Nah," Andrew shook his head. "I mean, it's not like I'm burning them alive."

Jorge raised an eyebrow.

"Its funny, you know, when I started this job," Andrew began to laugh. "I thought of you! I thought, 'if Jorge Hernandez could see what I'm doing now!'"

"Well, I will not lie," Jorge replied. "This here could become more valuable to me than the docuseries. Tell me, do you freelance?"

Andrew began to laugh.

Jorge did not.

"How did I know you were going to ask me that?" Andrew continued to laugh and leaned forward. "Wait, are you serious?"

"Is this the first time we meet?" Jorge countered.

"I got full power over the crematorium," Andrew admitted and grew serious. "But, I mean, I gotta be careful too."

Jorge sat back and pursed his lips.

Andrew interrupted his thoughts.

"It takes a long time, you know."

"What?"

"Burning a body, it takes 2, 3 hours," Andrew said with confidence, sitting up a bit straighter. "Most people don't know that. They think it's like burning paper or something."

"Tell me," Jorge asked while glancing around the room. "You say you never burn anyone alive but this here, it's not *impossible,* is it *amigo."*

"If I've learned anything from you," Andrew quipped. "It's that *nothing* is impossible."

Impressed, Jorge sat back with a devilish grin.

He would later relay this information to Diego at the office.

"Oh, my *fuck!"* Diego's eyes automatically doubled in size as he leaned back in the chair, tapping his fingers on his desk. "Wow! So, that *gringo* got a job burning bodies? And you think..."

"I think that we found an easier way to dispose of our problems, yes," Jorge nodded with a sinister expression on his face. "This here will make life easier for us."

"But is he gonna help?"

"Diego, the price, it will be right," Jorge said and watched his friend twist his lips and nod. "Andrew wants to be a part of what we do. This and the docuseries. I mean, this kid, who knew he could be so useful."

"I never saw it coming," Diego shook his head. "Remember when he tried to break into the warehouse a few years ago?"

"I do, *amigo,* I thought that was his last day on earth but something, it changed my mind."

"You got good instincts, I give you that."

"It's why I am where I am," Jorge confirmed. "Of course, when he got his money, I thought he would party it away but I am....pleasantly surprised."

"But you got Marco checking him out?" Diego referred to the company IT specialist and even more importantly, Jorge's hacker. "Just to make sure?"

"Of course," Jorge nodded. "I may trust my instincts but it is good to always fall back on facts, is it not?"

"He'll go into his emails, text messages..."

"We will make sure but he does not want to fuck with me either," Jorge insisted. "Or it will be his own body cremated, *amigo*. And I will not give him the pleasure of dying first."

Diego gave a smug grin.

"This here, it is my policy."

"I *know* your policy," Diego reminded him. "It's been pretty consistent throughout the years."

"This here," Jorge said as he stood up. "This is true."

"So the family dinner?"

"Tomorrow night."

"Is Athas joining us?"

"No," Jorge shook his head. "Are you kidding me. He's being watched 24/7 since he became prime minister. The media, the spies, they know his every move. He can barely jerk off in the shower without them knowing. But that is fine. I will tell everyone the plan when I see them tomorrow night."

"It will be a whole new day."

"Indeed it will," Jorge replied as he headed toward the door, momentarily turning around and giving Diego a look. "Indeed it will."

CHAPTER 5

"Paige, you know what I always say about people who talk religion too much," Jorge commented as the couple entered the VIP section of the *Princesa Maria* through the back way to avoid the crowded bar. The couple was met by the aroma of Mexican food, causing Jorge's mouth to water. The rest of his *familia* was waiting at the table, while Chase uncovered the many containers.

"This oughta be good," Diego quipped from his seat, causing the others to laugh, Jolene Silva being the loudest.

"Hey, I say," Jorge said while glancing over the many dishes on the table. "That they are not to be trusted. It is a cover, you know? A way to lower people's defenses and make them believe they are a good person. Sometimes to even convince themselves. It works with some…just not with me."

Laughter followed as the couple sat down; Jorge at the end of the table, while Paige took the empty seat to his left.

"What is this about?" Jolene Silva automatically spoke up, her brown eyes expanding in size. "Who talk religion with you? Did those people show up at your door?"

Jorge automatically gave Diego a warning glance. Jolene's older brother had a habit of criticizing her English, which always led to a fight. They had too much to cover in this dinner without the same tired argument erupting.

"It was my sister," Paige shook her head as if to discourage the topic. "She's trying to get in my good graces. We didn't exactly have a warm reception at my father's funeral."

"Oh, this here, it is not right," Jolene shook her head.

"It is what it is," Jorge insisted. "She calls Paige, talks God and forgiveness, such bullshit. The truth is that the women in Paige's family, they resent her strength."

"They resent a lot of things about me," She muttered under her breath.

Jorge winked at his wife before turning his attention back to the table.

"This food, it smells delicious," He gestured toward the dishes and glanced around to make sure everyone was there; Diego, Jolene, Enrique, Chase, and Marco. "Let us eat. Diego, I see we even got some gluten-free options for you."

"*Gracias!*" The Colombian piped up.

The family quickly dug into the assortment of authentic Mexican cuisine and desserts. The food made Jorge nostalgic for his home country. Although he loved his life in Canada, Mexican cuisine always took him back.

"This summer, I started to teach Maria how to cook some of our food," Jorge pointed toward the feast before him as the others nodded while continuing to eat. "It is important that children remember their heritage. I mean, not that she was interested in learning."

Laughter erupted then for a few minutes, everyone fell silent as they ate.

"This is so delicious, sir," Marco Rodel Cruz, the company IT specialist spoke up from further down the table, and beside him, Chase nodded.

"It is good, yes," Jolene commented leaning toward her boyfriend, Enrique, who sat beside her. He was still relatively new to the group but had worked diligently since his arrival.

"We must always give ourselves the best we can afford," Jorge insisted as he chewed. "Otherwise, what is our lives worth?"

Everyone fell silent again but not for long.

"Diego, he tell me that Andrew is back," Jolene said.

"I thought that we were doing that docuseries with him?" Chase cut in before Jorge could answer.

"We are," Jorge quickly answered. "It is, you know, a pleasant surprise."

"So, he gonna help us out?" Chase pushed with a dark look in his eyes. Jorge merely nodded. This seemed to satisfy Chase, if not Jolene.

"Can we trust?"

"Do not worry, Jolene," Jorge reminded her. "Marco, he is always checking these things out. He can find anything about anyone."

The Filipino man nodded with enthusiasm while Enrique listened carefully, although he said nothing.

"This documentary series, we have discussed before," Jorge reminded everyone. "This here is not news but today, I have some more information that is very important."

"First," Jorge continued. "Our original focus with this series was to tell people cannabis is medicinal and can be used for various health problems and not what Big Pharma sells. Now my objective is to not only make people wary of the pharmaceutical industry and make them fall in love with cannabis but to *demolish* their industry."

Everyone stopped eating and looked up at Jorge.

"To...demolish?" Enrique finally spoke up.

"Yes," Jorge nodded. "It is....you know, a challenge but I think it can be done."

"And how are we going to do this?" Chase inquired.

"We got doctors," Diego spoke up dramatically. "Scientists, all sorts of smart people who can cut them down."

"He is right," Jorge agreed. "We are getting lots of people who will bring them down."

"Ahh....I see...." Jolene nodded slowly even though she still appeared confused.

"The goal is to make people wary of Big Pharma," Paige jumped in. "To remind them that despite all the pills they're taking, most people don't feel better and in fact, develop more medical conditions. With all the medical advancements, people should be getting better, not worse."

"One pill," Jorge started with humor in his voice. "Will help your cholesterol but make your dick soft, you know?"

Everyone laughed.

"Then you take a pill for that," Jorge continued with wide eyes. "And it helps you fuck all night, but then your heart races too much...so you need to calm down, so you take another pill for that...."

Everyone continued to laugh.

"It is a vicious cycle," Jorge pointed out. "And this here, is what they want."

"My favorite is the anti-depressant that has a chaser," Diego jumped in. "Like how many fucking pills do you need to not hate your life?"

"Big Pharma, they have a pill for everything," Paige remarked. "After I had Miguel, they tried to put me on antidepressants just *in case* I had postpartum depression."

"Well, of course, a woman who just have a baby is going to be a little crazy," Jorge insisted. "*I* didn't give birth and I was crazy after Miguel was born."

Diego opened his mouth but Jorge quickly cut him off.

"Before you say," He laughed. "A *different* kind of crazy."

Laughter followed as they reached for more food and desserts.

"Anyone want coffee?" Chase asked and started to get up.

"Leave the coffee for the pro," Diego stood up and put his hand up. "I got this."

"The docuseries, when does it start?" Jolene asked.

"We've been filming a few weeks and the first episode will be done soon," Jorge replied. "And as you know, I will be tied up with this project. For that reason, Paige, she will be handling a lot of your...issues from now on."

Everyone turned toward his wife and he noted the respect in their eyes.

"She is as capable as I am," Jorge continued. "If you have something that needs attention, it is her you contact."

"And don't hesitate," Paige spoke evenly. "I want you to treat me the same as Jorge. Don't hold back."

"Yes, it is important you do not hold back," Jorge added. "We do not need surprises because you worry about interrupting her day. We have a full-time nanny so the children, are fine and Paige, she is the best person for the job."

She smiled but didn't respond.

"And also," Jorge continued as the others, one by one, finished their meal. "As you know, I am working closely with Athas on a special project behind the scenes. Together, we are creating new laws that will make Big Pharma squirm."

"How will you do that?" Chase asked with interest.

"New rules," Jorge decided to not reveal too much. "We got some new laws that will come down hard on anyone overprescribing. Athas wants to clamp down on the opiate industry, something we both can agree on."

There were nods of understanding around the table.

"Mr. Hernandez," Enrique spoke up with some apprehension. "You have done so much for me. It is my wish to help with more, so if there is anything…"

"*I* will let you know," Paige cut him off and there was a look of understanding between them.

"Yes, Paige, she will let you know," Jorge replied. "And me, I will be busy with the series but I am never far away. But make no mistake, Paige can handle anything. This here is the most deadly assassin in the world. She can take on anything."

Enrique looked intrigued while Paige blushed and look away as if it was the most intimate compliment.

"She's certainly taught me a great deal," Chase spoke with pride. "I'm still trying to get my shot…

"You'll get it," Paige insisted. "It takes time."

"Yes, you are good," Jolene piped up. "You will get better."

"And these two," Diego spoke loudly as he returned to the table while the coffee began to drip in the nearby pot. "They are the fucking best."

"It is true," Jorge nodded. "Our world, it is one where women, they must be stronger than men, to survive and this, I recognize."

"We are….what is the word," Jolene said and scrunched her eyes. "You know….they assume we cannot do anything."

"Underappreciated?" Chase guessed.

"Yes, but, no.." Jolene shook her head.

"Underestimated?" Paige suggested.

"Yes!" Jolene's eyes widened and her eyes grew in size. "That is it! We are underestimated."

Jorge noted she gave a sideward glance to Enrique before continuing.

"Men, they think we only know makeup and pretty clothes."

"Not everyone thinks that way, Jolene," Diego shot back, clearly not recognizing the underlying message. "Not all men are fucking chauvinists."

"Many are," Jolene muttered and Jorge decided it was time to cut her off.

"At any rate," He began. "We may have some…concerns as we tape this series. We may have some problems crop up. I want you to be prepared because in doing this work, we are making a lot of enemies. We must always be two steps ahead of them."

There was a look of understanding around the table.

"This here is phase two," Jorge continued. "And if you thought phase one, taking over the pot industry was brutal, wait till you see what Athas has in store."

CHAPTER 6

"So you got some more interviews lined up?" Jorge asked Tony Allman almost as soon as he joined the filmmaker at the back of a quiet coffee shop. Tony was a large, white man who seemed awkward because of his size, yet confident in his demeanor. "With doctors or whoever?"

"Yes," Tony shifted uncomfortably in his chair as if it was a tad too small for his stature. "Almost every day next week and everyone is willing to talk."

"This here is good," Jorge said as he reached for his cup of coffee. Taking a drink, he made a face and moved it aside. "I see now why this place is empty."

Tony let out a short laugh, glanced down at his cup, and nodded.

"They ain't no Starbucks, that's for sure," Tony tilted his head toward the counter. "They got a bunch of kids making the coffee, so they don't care. And rumor has it they're selling a little more than coffee."

"Well, this here rumor is probably true," Jorge confirmed, slightly impressed with Tony's observation. "It is my experience that we are surrounded by many that sell more than it seems on the outside."

"You learn a lot when you're in my business," Tony seemed to relax. "You know, about the way the world works. That's why I do documentary shows now. There's only so much you can get out in fiction. People think it's all made up. The characters might be, the specifics yeah but you know, there's always some truth behind every story."

"This is a fact," Jorge agreed and tilted his head. "But only those who want to see it, will see it."

"But to a point," Tony spoke thoughtfully. "It's the same with what we're doing too. People only will see what they want."

"Our job, with this series," Jorge spoke boldly. "Is to make sure everyone is talking about it and pissing on Big Pharma. We're starting a revolution."

"Hey, you know I'm all for that," Tony nodded and studied Jorge carefully. "I got into this work to shake things up."

"And remember, if you run into any issues…"

"I know, you'll take care of them," Tony nodded. "Hey, when I first got this idea and Andrew suggested you might be interested, he said, 'Jorge Hernandez is your guy. He will make people listen and if you got problems, he'll handle them.'"

"Well, I am pretty good at handling these things," Jorge confirmed without giving further details. "But you do know, this here will make a lot of people say that you do not know what you are talking about. They will try to give you a bad name."

"I already dealt with that when I did my first docuseries on GMOs," Tony confirmed. "I had threats. I had so-called experts saying I was crazy, that I was full of shit. But when I wanted to talk to them face to face, on camera, they wouldn't do it."

"Ah! Yes, I do know about such people," Jorge confirmed. "It is my experience that they tend to step back when confronted. As my associate Diego often says, the world, it is full of sheep. And for that reason, we must always be a wolf."

Tony didn't reply at first but laughed, giving an enthusiastic nod.

"I like your associate already," He finally replied. "He's got that right."

"I make a point of surrounding myself with good people," Jorge clarified as he briefly considered taking another drink of his coffee but decided against it.

"You gotta if you want to succeed in this world," Tony spoke thoughtfully. "If you got the wrong people around, they have a way of holding you back."

"I did not take over the cannabis industry in this country by letting anyone hold me back," Jorge reminded him. "So you got new footage for me to see?"

"There's a lot."

"Send me the strongest."

"I'll get it to you later today. You can give me your feedback. Sometimes I start a project with one idea in mind and it takes a different direction right away."

"Is that so?"

"Yes," Tony nodded and finished his coffee. "Like the GMO series? I was originally just going to talk about pesticides in foods. Then I came across how they're taking over the industry and that became my focus."

"That will not be the case with our series," Jorge spoke sternly. "We are here to talk about Big Pharma, opiates, and how they ruin lives."

"I agree" Tony spoke nervously. "It's just in the future if we wanted to expand on this further, I've been doing some research and I find it interesting that there are some of the same people who manufacture food also got their hands into Big Pharma. Some of the food they are selling us with pretty boxes and addictive flavors actually contain questionable ingredients. Ingredients that make us sick."

Jorge raised his eyebrows and sat back.

"So you create the disease," Tony continued with a look of despair in his eyes. "So you can then create the cure."

"Except, it is often not the cure," Jorge added.

"No, of course not," Tony shook his head. "To think so is naïve. They don't want us to get better. There's no money in healthy people. But sick and dying people, now that's another story."

"You know, Tony," Jorge took a deep breath. "in my business, I am often the 'bad guy' because I sell cannabis but yet, these people, who sell us poison, it is ok. These people give us medicines that are making us sicker. These people who sell children food full of sugar and artificial colors…."

"A chemical shit show," Tony cut in.

"Yes," Jorge nodded. "This here, it sounds about right. A chemical shit show. I will not allow my children to eat it. My wife picks our food carefully. My son, he did not eat store-bought baby food. My wife, she bought organic, locally made. Organic milk. It is scary what is in some food."

"That's exactly my point," Tony smiled and the two men shared a nod. "But it ain't gonna make us popular when we start shaking some trees."

"Well, Tony, as you probably already guessed," Jorge grinned. "I'm all about shaking people's trees. But they do *not* want to shake mine."

Satisfied with the conversation, Jorge ended the meeting and headed for his SUV. Turning his phone back on, he automatically saw a message from Paige. He called her after he was on the road.

"Hey, *mi amor*," Jorge spoke with a smile in his voice. "My love, I just had a productive meeting. I will discuss it with you later."

"Oh that's great," She spoke calmly although he noticed an echo behind her. "I'm at the warehouse."

"At the warehouse?" Jorge asked while hiding his surprise. "Is something going on?"

"You might say that," Paige was vague. "Jolene had a little problem she needed help with."

Jolene never needed help with little problems.

"Is that so?"

"Yes, but nothing we can't handle."

"Maybe I will stop by?"

"If you wish," Paige said with a yawn. "We should probably go over a few things here anyway."

That was a sign. His wife was trying to say she needed him, despite the boredom in her voice. This was in case anyone tapped into the call. You had to be two steps ahead.

"I am on my way," Jorge said and ended the call.

The next call he made was to Diego.

"I will be a bit late," Jorge confirmed as soon as the Colombian answered. "Something came up."

"With the film guy?"

"Nah, actually, this here is good," Jorge confirmed as he drove through traffic. "He has more interviews set up for next week and it seems, we are on the same page. I am more excited about this documentary series now, *amigo*. It is, as they say, going to blow the roof off a few people's houses."

"Yeah, well, if there's one thing you like to do," Diego confirmed. "Is blowing up people's houses."

"You know me," Jorge replied. "I am all for the betterment of the people. It will be a revolution. A much-needed revolution."

"So, what's up now?" Diego spoke abruptly.

"I am going to the warehouse," Jorge replied and simply added. "Paige called me."

"Paige?" Diego's voice immediately turned emotional. "Is she ok?"

"Of course she is ok," Jorge spoke with laughter in his voice. "You know, your sister, she is also there. No worry for her?"

"So what's going on?" Diego ignored his question. "What you got?"

"Nothing," Jorge tried to sound casual. "Just a *little* problem that needed solving."

Silence.

"So, I'm headed there now," Jorge calmly added. "You know, it is good to look in from time to time, to see how things are going."

"I got you."

"You got *me?*" Jorge had humor in his voice.

"I gotta go."

Diego immediately ended the call.

He would be at the warehouse.

Jorge was sure of it.

CHAPTER 7

"Where the hell are you?" Diego's voice rang through the SUV. "I had time to get from the office to here and you were already on the road…"

"I know, Diego, I know this," Jorge sighed loudly and glanced from side to side. "I am stuck in fucking traffic. I think there is construction or some shit ahead but I will get there. Do me a favor, check things out."

"I will."

"And Diego," Jorge added. "Be calm."

"I'm always calm," Diego replied in a frantic voice.

"This here," Jorge quickly reminded him. "It is *not* calm."

"Don't worry, I got this," Diego insisted.

"Somehow, this does not make me feel better."

"I'm going in."

"To be continued."

"Adios."

The call ended and Jorge took a deep breath. Glancing around, he felt trapped in the insanity. He had a love/hate relationship with Toronto. As much as he enjoyed the cultural aspects of the city, he was sick of beings stuck in endless traffic and lineups, everywhere he went. Paige always said it was because when we're young, crowds excited us but as we grow older, they seemed to suck away time that we simply didn't have anymore.

His mind returned to the warehouse. Paige could take care of herself and he did feel some comfort that Diego was there too, but it didn't stop the anxiety from creeping in. Life had many unwelcoming surprises. He knew this too well.

The traffic started to move ahead but he wasn't encouraged. His stomach turned, his neck felt stiff and his chest was heavy. When Diego didn't call back, Jorge tried to call him. It went directly to voicemail. When he tried to call Paige and Jolene, the same thing happened. They had their phones turned off.

His anxiety only grew as traffic finally broke up and he was able to get to the warehouse. He shot into the parking lot and flew into a VIP space before jumping out of the SUV and rushing toward the door. Reaching for his gun, he took the side entrance where select employees were authorized to enter. He walked inside to find no one was around.

Walking into Jolene's office, he found it empty.

Glancing toward a door behind Jolene's desk, he automatically knew they were in a private room in the basement. It was the place they used for when certain situations arose, somewhere soundproof, cut off from the hundreds of employees packaging and shipping products elsewhere in the building.

Opening the door carefully, he slowly made his way down the stairs with a gun in hand. Unsure of what he would find, Jorge felt his heart racing as he carefully crept down each step, his legs feeling weak as if they couldn't complete the journey. Was this a sign that something was very wrong? It was much too quiet.

What he found, stopped him in his tracks. An attractive, black woman was tied to the chair with tears streaming down her face. In front of her stood Paige with her arms crossed in front of her chest, a blank expression on her face. Jolene stood nearby, a gun pointed at the woman's head while Diego was holding a baseball bat.

"What the fuck is going on here?" Jorge automatically asked. "Who the fuck is this one?"

"This one," Jolene automatically piped up. "She comes here to kill me."

"Well, we don't know that," Paige calmly began to explain. "She's not talking."

"Wait....I do not understand," Jorge tried to comprehend the story. "She tried to kill Jolene?"

"I get back from lunch and this woman, she has a gun to my head when I walk in the office," Jolene spoke dramatically, her eyes narrowing on the woman. "She demands some information that I will not tell her."

"What information?" Jorge felt like he was slowly getting up to speed.

"She want to know about a documentary of some kind?" Jolene said and shook her head. "I do not know of such."

She did.

"She want to know these things that I cannot answer," Jolene continued. "I do not know about any documentary, do you?"

Jorge exchanged looks with Paige.

"She won't tell us nothing," Diego jumped in. "Who she is, who sent her, nothing."

"But how did you," Jorge turned to Paige. "How did you get involved?"

"You say if any problems, we call her," Jolene answered for his wife. "So, I did. I tell this one here," She stopped to gesture toward the woman on the chair. "I tell her I know nothing. That I just take care of the warehouse that I must call Paige. She allowed this and when Paige got here, she did this fancy move and knock the gun out of her hand."

Impressed, Jorge turned and winked at his wife.

"Then we put her on chair and now, she won't talk," Jolene continued.

"Who sent you?" Jorge spoke calmly and walked toward the woman, "The problem is that the docuseries, it is a secret. If I tell you, it cannot leave this room."

"She mightn't be either," Paige spoke evenly causing the woman to cry harder. "Because we aren't getting anywhere, so I might have to up the ante."

"And you, you don't talk no more?" Jorge addressed the woman on the chair. "What the fuck you doing here? Who sent you? Why you come to Jolene? How did you get into the building?"

"I got Marco working on that now," Diego piped up. "If someone let her in…."

"If someone, they let her in," Jorge jumped in. "We will throw their dead body on top of this one's if she don't start fucking talking."

"She's not being very corporative," Paige gently replied as the woman continued to sob.

"Lady, less crying, more talking," Jorge snapped. "Do not piss on a dog then get mad when he pisses on you too."

"She wasn't crying originally," Paige calmly explained. "There may have been some…torture involved."

"It turns out," Jolene jumped in. "That taser thing that Diego has, it must really hurt."

"I wouldn't use it if it didn't," Diego quickly added with a satisfied expression. "I hadn't tried this one before, so at least, now I know."

"Ah! I see," Jorge nodded. "So lady, you got something to say now."

"You're fucking animals!" She suddenly found her voice. "All of you."

"First of all, why you pick Jolene?"

The woman clamped her mouth shut.

"This has been the last hour or more…" Paige pointed toward her. "Other than insulting us, she won't talk. My guess is she thought Jolene would be the easiest to get to because she's kind of secluded. The office would be too difficult. The club…well, probably not much better. If she came to any of our houses, she would be dead in a heartbeat, so that left the warehouse…."

Jorge nodded. The woman stopped crying.

"Unfortunately for her," Paige continued. "I've dealt with this kind of situation before and I have a way of making people talk."

"She only wants to ask the question," Diego complained. "She don't want to answer them."

"Well, as I always say," Paige replied. "There's more than one way to skin a cat."

"This cat here," Jorge gestured toward the woman. "She is about to be skinned."

Paige grinned.

"*Mi amor,*" Jorge continued. "Do your worst."

Paige merely raised an eyebrow as Jorge stepped aside, while she moved closer to the woman in the chair.

"I'm listening."

"No," The woman shook her head. "No, I'm not telling you a thing. You're only going to kill me."

"Is it worth it?" Paige continued to speak evenly. "Whoever sent you, are they worth it? What did you think would happen when you stuck a gun in one of our faces? Did you *really* think that would work? This doesn't make sense to me. What do you get out of this?"

"Money," The woman replied. "I need it for my family. My daughter is sick and…"

"Save it for the fucking Hallmark movie," Jorge snapped from across the room. "We don't believe that shit here."

"Sure she's not a cop?" Diego spoke loudly, causing Jorge to jump.

"We checked her carefully before you arrived," Paige replied. "No wires."

"She was asking about the docuseries," Jorge reminded them. "Maybe, you know, Big Pharma send her?"

The woman said nothing.

That's when it happened. A devil broke through Paige's angelic demeanor, as she abruptly slapped the woman across the face, almost knocking her over. A loud whimper escaped the black woman's lips as terror filled her eyes.

"Still not talking?" Paige asked but before the woman could answer, she moved behind her and grabbed a handful of her long hair, and roughly yanked it, pulling the entire chair back, slamming it on the ground, causing the captive stranger to let out a painful cry. Paige fell to her knees behind the woman's head. "Because I might have a solution for that."

"Stop!"

Paige ignored her cries and turned toward Jolene.

"Get me the machete you have in the office," She instructed and watched Jolene nod and rush toward the stairs. "I'm going to start by cutting off all her pretty hair, then I'm going to…..should I cut through her skull, or should I just go for her throat?"

Jorge stood back, delighted by what he watched. There was something incredibly sexy about his wife taking charge, her strength, her power, it was intoxicating. He felt his heart race in excitement as he watched her victim cry, beg for her life while his wife, she wasn't affected by the pleas.

Jolene rushed downstairs with a gun in one hand, a machete in the other, and held it over the woman's skull.

"Me, I would do it right there," She suggested. "It would be like cutting a watermelon."

The woman on the floor had sheer terror in her eyes.

"Oh, how the tables have turned," Paige spoke sympathetically, even though she showed no compassion in her eyes. "To think, Jolene, only an hour or two ago, this situation was very different. She had a gun to *your* head."

"This here, it was not a smart life choice, you know?" Jolene spoke to the woman on the floor. "You, you should start making better *decisions*."

"Ah, yes, or your life can go so terribly... *terribly* wrong," Paige replied.

"I was hired," The woman cried out as she gasped. "But I don't know by...by who."

Paige listened.

"I...I work for this woman...."

Paige sat up straighter.

"She...she sends me on assignments but I..."

"You're an assassin?" Paige suddenly asked as she pulled back slightly.

The woman didn't speak for a moment while the two shared a look. Jolene stepped back and appeared unsure.

Paige stood up and stared at the woman for a moment.

"Can someone help me with her chair," Paige asked and Jolene sat down the machete and gun but Diego was already there, lifting the chair up. The woman stopped crying, appearing to calm down. She relaxed.

Paige walked behind her, reached for the gun Jolene had placed on a nearby table, pausing for only a moment before swiftly shooting the woman in the head.

CHAPTER 8

"....the body in the bad end of town, so the cops won't bother putting much work into the investigation," Paige spoke quickly from the passenger side of the SUV. "Whoever sent her will find out and be warned."

Jorge quietly drove, his mind so clouded by lust, he could barely focus on her words. Seeing his wife in such a powerful position always brought out his most primal desires and yet, he managed to keep it together to take care of the details. The body would be left in a park that night with no ID, no evidence, and no connection to their group. There never was.

"Paige," Jorge put his hand up as traffic slowed down. He felt himself grow calm when faced with her rare moment of anxiety. "You must relax. This here, we will take care of as we always do."

"It's not the body I'm worried about," She spoke nervously. "It's everything else. Who sent her? She got in so easily..."

"She snuck in behind an employee who was too busy looking at his phone to notice," Jorge cut her off. "Jolene is back there now, firing him then warning the others to be more vigilant."

"I didn't see it at first," Paige shook her head as lines of worry wrinkled her forehead. "She's an assassin. How could I miss it?"

"*Mi amor,* how could you miss it?" Jorge asked, confused by her observation. "Me, I still do not understand how you see it in the first place. She was just some woman hired by..."

"Trust me," Paige cut him off as she turned to make eye contact as traffic started to speed up again. Her face was flushed. "It's not something most people would see but I *should* have and I didn't until the last minute."

"I do not think…"

"It was the way," She took a deep breath and began to calm. "It was the way she attempted to manipulate us. She went from furious to crying in the chair."

"Maybe because you scare her?"

"Nah, that's not it," Paige shook her head. "She switched too quick, it was manipulation. We were supposed to feel bad for her especially when she started to talk about a sick kid. She mentioned that earlier too before you arrived."

"Yes, well, that don't mean anything."

"It was her tactics," Paige continued as she stared ahead. "She chose Jolene because she's the easiest target."

Jorge didn't reply but nodded.

"We might want to move her around," Paige thought out loud and Jorge continued to nod. "She's secluded."

"But Jolene, she took care of it," Jorge reminded her as traffic stalled again. "I still, I am not sure she was an assassin. She never did answer your question."

"She was," Paige confirmed. "I could see it in her eyes when I asked. She did everything I was trained to do….not *well*, but she did it; stalling, not talking, most people would sing like a bird as soon as Diego got the taser out, let alone zapped them."

"Leave it to Diego," Jorge couldn't help but laugh. "But yes, I do see your point. This was not her first rodeo."

"It was her first rodeo with me," Paige seemed to slowly ease back into herself. "And it didn't go so well."

"You know Paige," Jorge hesitated. "I do think you have a point but at the same time, why would they send an assassin? She just wanted answers."

"She's new and they were testing her," She said with a slight pause. "She made a lot of amateur moves but there are other things, like how she got in the warehouse…"

"Well, *mi amor*, no one pays attention anymore."

"She waited for the right person," Paige rolled her eyes. "But she didn't do anything to the cameras."

"Again, my love, maybe she is not an assassin."

"But it was also how she crept up behind Jolene," Paige added. "Let's face it, Jolene is not a new kid on the block. You can't sneak up on her that easily. She knew what she was doing. Even in how she grabbed her…the questions she asked, everything."

"But you, you got the better of her, *si?*"

"But barely," Paige reminded him and they made eye contact. "I had to move fast to get the gun away from her but it was another amateur mistake. I'm telling you, Jorge, I'm sure she was an assassin. She mightn't have been there to kill but she was trained well enough to get answers. That's what they do when you start. If you can do the job and live through your original assignments, then you move on to the real work."

Jorge felt his desire grow as she spoke. Nothing turned him on like her powerful side and watching his wife deal with the woman from the warehouse was like an aphrodisiac to him. He fell silent. Focused on traffic, he just wanted to get her home.

"I guess she didn't pass the test," Paige purred and Jorge felt his heart racing while his body grew warm. "Such an interesting situation we find ourselves in."

"Well, *mi amor,* I am finding myself in an interesting situation right now," Jorge spoke up as he began to loosen his tie and cleared his throat. "All of this…"

"You don't look right," Paige's eyes were full of concern. "Maybe you're sick.."

"*Mi amor,*" Jorge couldn't help but laugh. "I am not sick. I am horny as hell but I am definitely *not* sick."

This caused her to laugh. The girlish giggle only increased his arousal as he suffered his way through traffic. Even when it started to move, it wasn't quite fast enough.

By the time they finally arrived home, Jorge wasted no time jumping out of the SUV and heading toward the door.

"You go to the office," Paige instructed him. "I will meet you."

"*Mi amor,* I…"

"I just want to check the baby," She insisted. "I won't be a minute."

He didn't reply but simply nodded as the two headed into the house. He went directly to his office just in time to hear a secure call coming through. Seeing it was Alec Athas, he cringed as he collapsed in his chair.

"Don't you have prime minister work to do?" Jorge snapped when he answered. "We got a....situation to take care of."

"I have a bit of a situation myself," Alec chimed in hurriedly.

"I am sure it is nothing like mine," Jorge insisted as Paige quietly entered the room and locked the door. "I cannot talk long, what is it?"

"The opposition started a huge campaign stating that I've done absolutely nothing since I was voted in."

Jorge thought for a moment.

"Have you?"

"These things, they take time."

Jorge didn't reply but watched as Paige began to remove her clothes as she walked toward him.

"They certainly do," Jorge replied, distracted by his wife. "But you are a big boy, I am sure you can take care of it."

"That's the thing," Athas continued. "They keep holding up everything I try to pass through and..."

"Alec," Jorge cut him off as Paige moved closer. "I have an urgent matter that I must take care of. We had a problem earlier today that needs my....prompt attention, so I will call you back shortly."

There was some hesitation on the line.

"Yes, ok, but I have a meeting in half an hour..."

"I will get back to you before that time," Jorge reached to undo his pants. "This here, it shouldn't take too long."

Jorge had barely ended the call when Paige was straddling him on the chair, their mouths roughly joined together as his hands pulled her close. Although the couch was merely steps away, his intense arousal made it impossible to pause even for a moment as he devoured her, their bodies quickly fused causing him to gasp in pleasure, after the long anticipation of that moment. Paige moved quickly, her breasts rising and falling in her bra, making him lose his mind as he escaped into a world of pleasure. She finally collapsed against him, both their hearts racing as Jorge pulled his wife into his arms.

"I did not think sex got better with time," Jorge whispered. "That is what they say, no? That marriage makes it boring."

"Nothing is ever boring with you," She whispered back as she held him tight.

"When you were with that woman today..."

"I know, it turns you on."

"What can I say," Jorge laughed. "I am one sick fuck when it comes to what gives me pleasure."

"There are sicker," Paige reminded him as she pulled away slightly. "Much sicker."

"This is true," He agreed. "I just get turned on when I see my wife killing someone."

"Or when you kill someone."

"It does, it brings out my primal natures and desires," He reminded her. "I do think the cavemen would say this is perhaps, normal?"

"What did Alec want?"

"I...I dunno," Jorge replied as his wife slowly got off his lap. "This here, I do not care about. I am not here to hold his hand."

Paige merely grinned as she started to fix her thong and reach for her clothes.

"It is always the same with him," Jorge rose from the chair and zipped up his pants. "The opposition, they will undermine him every time they can."

"Should we tell him about today? After all, it's kind of connected to what you two are doing," Paige suggested.

"I do not know," Jorge spoke honestly. "But I do see problems ahead. We only started working on this docuseries a few weeks ago and already, we have issues. Why is that?"

"Who knows about it besides us?"

"The people we are set to interview," Jorge replied as he stood awkwardly by his desk. "Let us hope someone out there is not making roadblocks."

"We will unblock them if they do," Paige replied as she finished dressing. "We always do."

CHAPTER 9

"I only have a few minutes," Alec reminded Jorge as soon as they started their conversation. "Do I want to know what was so urgent earlier?"

"You probably do not," Jorge grinned as he leaned back in his chair.

"You sound calmer so whatever it was, it must be taken care of."

"It was taken care of."

"One less dragon to slay," Alec muttered.

"Well, Athas, you know me," Jorge replied abruptly. "I *do* enjoy slaying a dragon from time to time but today, *amigo,* it was Paige who carried the sword."

"I see," Athas paused. "Does this have anything to do with…"

"I believe so," Jorge replied. "This docuseries, it has barely started and already, it seems word has somehow gotten out."

"Interestingly, the opposition is also turning up the heat all of a sudden," Athas replied. "But tomorrow I plan to announce that we're looking into regulations around opiates and how casually they are being given out."

"It is a white man's world," Jorge reminded him. "So it is ok. Me? I have maintained that those who *choose* to use whatever it is I sell, have made a *decision.* But how is one making a choice when your doctor is pushing a prescription in your face and saying 'you need this'. This here is very different."

"I plan to look into how often this is happening."

"*Amigo,* Big Pharma, they will not like this," Jorge reminded him in a sing-song voice. "You are not playing the game."

"I'm playing a game," Athas reminded him. "It's just not with them."

"And, you have made the right choice," Jorge confirmed. "We will talk."

He ended the conversation and sat with his thoughts. Jorge was getting his ducks in line but there would always be some that might go astray. It was important to keep a close watch.

A knock at the door interrupted his thoughts.

"*Si?*"

It was Maria.

"*Papa,* can I sit in your meeting?" She stood tall in the doorway.

"Maria, what is this?" Jorge shook his head. "Where is this coming from?"

"This is my family business, I think it's time I start to learn what you talk about," She spoke bravely causing Jorge to suppress a grin. "I want to know."

"Maria, your only job is school," Jorge reminded her. "But I do appreciate your interest."

"But *Papa,* what if something ever happened to you and Paige?" She spoke with sorrow in her eyes as she approached the desk. "Then I would have to…"

"Maria," Jorge shook his head and gestured for her to come closer. "This will not happen. We are ok. And even if something terrible were to happen, I have a lot of people in place who would look after this company and you."

"I don't mean the company, *Papa,*" She said and tilted her head as she stood by his chair. "*You* know what I mean."

"Maria, I *do* appreciate this," Jorge affirmed and reached out to touch her arm. "I do, *chica,* but this meeting, it is to talk about….some issues we had earlier today at the warehouse. I think I might move Jolene elsewhere."

"Where?"

"Can you keep a secret?"

"Of course," Maria said as her eyes widened.

"I am buying a crematorium," Jorge replied and she made a face. "I would like Jolene to oversee it."

"Really?" Maria looked a bit startled.

"Yes."

"Why?"

"I thought it would be a...good business move," Jorge shrugged casually. "People, they always die, right?"

"That's gross."

Jorge laughed.

"That's it?"

"That's it, *bonita,*" Jorge reached out to touch her long, black hair. "It is boring, you know, these meetings. We talk about the company, changes, problems."

"What are the problems?"

"Personnel issues."

"What was the personnel issue?" Maria's eyes widened. "I promise it will be a secret."

"A man who works for us was so busy with his phone, he allowed a bad person to come into the warehouse."

"Really?"

"This is why you can't have your eyes glued to a phone all the time," Jorge shook his head. "You miss a lot of things going on around you."

"But *Papa,* couldn't they do that anyway? Even if you weren't looking at your phone?"

"It makes you more vulnerable."

"But aren't you safer if you have a phone because if someone grabs you..."

Jorge let out a loud sigh just as he heard Diego and Paige approaching, their voices getting closer.

"Ok, Maria," Jorge reluctantly admitted. "You have a point."

She nodded knowingly.

"Maria..."

"I will be careful," She giggled and gave him a quick kiss before rushing out of the room and past Diego and Paige.

"Where are the others?" Jorge automatically asked with a yawn. "Chase? Marco? Jolene?"

"On their way in," Diego gestured as he took his seat. "Jolene is talking to Miguel. I think Marco and Chase are talking about his new car."

"Chase got a new car?"

"It's kind of...*plain*," Diego made a face. "For me, you know."

Jorge merely grinned.

"It's not exactly a clunker," Paige remarked as she sat beside the Colombian.

Diego shrugged as the others made their way into the office. Chase closed the door and Jolene's voice echoed through the room.

"He grow up so fast!" She said while heading for her usual seat. "So much energy, that little boy!"

"Tell me about it," Paige shook her head. "Getting him to bed at night is a challenge."

"This is good," Jorge replied as he turned to Marco who was nodding and laughing. "Me, I wish I had some of that energy."

"We all do, sir," Marco replied.

"He's practically climbing the walls," Paige said as she shook her head.

"He will rule the world one day," Jorge insisted. "Him and my Maria. Do you know, she comes in here earlier to ask if she can join our meeting to learn the family business?"

Diego and Jolene both showed expressions of horror while Marco laughed and Paige looked touched but then started to grin.

"She more likely wanted in the meeting to spend time with Chase," She suggested and everyone laughed.

"I don't do anything to encourage her crush," Chase put his hands in the air.

"My daughter, she needs to worry about being a kid for now," Jorge said with a sigh. "But we must get to business."

Suddenly the door opened and Miguel stood in the doorway.

"Ah, so cute!" Jolene spoke up. "He wants to join us."

Juliana suddenly showed up behind him with a look of concern on her face.

"Julianna," Jorge shook his head. "This here, it is ok. He can come in."

"To our meeting?" Diego asked. "Are you sure?"

"Diego, he is what? 17-18 months?" Jorge shook his head. "I do not think he will be traumatized by what we have to say."

Juliana nodded, closing the door behind her as Miguel made his way across the room, suddenly looking shyly at the others who watched him.

"Miguel, *ven a Papa!*"

Following his instructions, the little boy laughed and rushed toward his father, who immediately lifted him, placing the child on his lap.

"This here, Miguel, will be your first meeting," He said as the little boy snuggled close to him. "Do not tell Maria, she will be jealous of you."

The mood in the room lightened.

"Now, we must get to business," Jorge immediately jumped in. "Today, we took care of a problem as you know by now. Paige, she believed it was an assassin."

"She was going to kill me!" Jolene ranted.

"No," Paige assured her. "When you first start, you don't kill. They send you on these kinds of missions as a test. See what you can do before they put you in more dangerous situations."

"I do not think she would have a more dangerous situation than today," Jorge insisted with a grin.

"I don't think she anticipated that," Paige admitted. "Although, someone wasn't doing their research."

"Apparently not," Jorge replied.

"So, you've only been working on this series a few weeks," Chase jumped in. "And already, people are trying to get information."

"They are scared," Jorge insisted. "As they should be because me, I will fuck up a lot of people with this."

"Jorge!" Jolene snapped. "The baby!"

"Jolene," Jorge glanced toward his son. "He's sleeping. Do not worry."

"So, we think that Jolene," Paige looked past Chase, who sat between them. "That you're a bit too secluded at the warehouse. Maybe it's time to switch you around."

"Where? The club?" Jolene squinted. "But we already have two there…"

"No," Jorge answered. "I'm buying another business that we need someone to oversee."

"New business?" Jolene asked skeptically.

"A crematorium," Jorge replied and noted the shocked expression on almost everyone's face. "I thought, this here, it would be a good business move."

"You want me to work in a crematorium?" Jolene made a face.

"Jolene, it's not like you haven't dealt with messy situations before," Diego shot back and Marco began to laugh.

"I do not want to burn bodies…"

"You won't be doing the work," Paige automatically corrected her. "You'll be overseeing the business."

"With people? Like customers?"

"No," Jorge shook his head. "You will run it but someone else deals with the customers and another person burns the bodies…"

"That's the thing," Paige added as Jolene started to seem more accepting of the idea. "The guy burning the bodies, it's Andrew Collin."

"What?" She made a face.

"You know, the guy you once kicked in the…"

"I know who it is!" Jolene shook her head. "No, I cannot work with him."

"Jolene, you will be his boss," Jorge reminded her. "We need someone strong in case….of dicey situations."

"Oh….*oh!*" She paused if suddenly understanding what Jorge had in mind for the business. "I see now."

"We must make sure someone we can trust is there," Jorge continued. "You will be trained on how to do everything by the current owner before he leaves. What you need to know, this kind of thing."

"Ok," Jolene seemed to put it together. "The warehouse, we are not sure."

"Enrique?" Chase asked. "Me?"

"Yes, this is a good question," Jorge replied. "Paige?"

"Well, I was thinking that secret room came in handy today," Paige replied. "Plus, Enrique is doing ok with the club."

"But can he work alone yet?" Diego asked. "Can we trust him?"

"Yes, you can trust!" Jolene defended her boyfriend.

"*You* do because you're fu…."

"Ok, you do not need to say," Jolene cut off her brother. "The baby, he does not have to hear this vulgar talk."

"I'm just saying…"

"We can trust!" Jolene insisted.

"Chase?" Paige turned to the man to her right.

"I see no reason not to leave him alone at the bar," Chase replied. "Plus, I can log into the cameras from the warehouse and see what's going on."

"Ok, so this is what we will do," Jorge nodded. "Paige, anything else?"

"Nope," She shook her head. "That covers everything for now. We have to figure out where that woman from today is from."

"Once her name is on the news," Marco said. "I will find out."

"Until then….." Jorge nodded. "We will see."

CHAPTER 10

"It's going to be a revolution, baby," Jorge said with a sinister grin on his face. "We are going to make Big Pharma squirm in their panties."

Across the desk from Jorge, Alec Athas looked less convinced. Although historically, the two men were careful about when and where they met since everything with the prime minister was public, this time was different. They were purposely making sure what appeared to be an irrelevant meeting to most, would set off bells for others.

"What?" Jorge shrugged as he glanced around his office. "You do not look so convinced, *amigo.*"

"Let's not throw that word around too much," Athas suggested. "It makes people nervous."

"Me? I think it is exciting," Jorge replied. "Does the Greek *God* not want to fight?"

"I do," Athas agreed, ignoring Jorge's sarcasm. "But I prefer we say that we're….working hard to improve the health and safety of Canadians."

"Fair enough," Jorge agreed. "This here you are probably right about."

"But we have to start slow."

"Of course," Jorge nodded. "You deal with this here study on opiates prescriptions and shake a few trees and I will work on my docuseries. You change the laws, I poke the fire with this series and Makerson will give us the press we need."

"Your media guy," Athas smirked. "He creates an interesting spin on things."

"That is why he works for me," Jorge reminded him. "This is the true key to success. You must have someone in every corner who will work with you."

"You have that covered."

"And you," Jorge asked and leaned forward on his desk. "Any more issues with your staff?"

"Not since earlier this year," Athas shook his head. "I guess when people start dying, everyone pays attention."

"That is perhaps a smart decision, *si?*"

"I did question your methods at the time," Athas admitted as he glanced at the clock and rose from his chair. "But now, I see that you were on track. I've had full cooperation since we took care of those problems."

"As I said you would," Jorge reminded him as he stood up and reached for his phone, turning it back on. "Now, I must go to another meeting. I bought a new business and I have to sort out some details."

"Oh really?" Athas appeared interested as the two men headed toward the door. "What's that? Something pot-related?"

"A crematorium."

Athas stopped in his tracks and gave Jorge a wide-eyed look.

"Why is it," Jorge started, "that everyone looks at me funny when I say this?"

"Because they know you?" Athas suggested in a quiet voice.

"What can I say?" Jorge replied as he opened the door. "Death, it is one of the few guarantees in life."

"Especially when you're around," Athas quipped as the two men walked out of the office.

Shortly after the prime minister left his home, Jorge jumped in his SUV and headed downtown to meet with Andrew Collin. On the way, he made a few quick phone calls.

"Tony,"

"Good morning Mr. Hernandez," The filmmaker's voice echoed through the SUV. "I was meaning to check in with you."

"Are things going well?"

"Yup, I have an interview this morning and I think another lined up for either tonight or tomorrow."

"No problems?"

"Nope."

"Very good," Jorge relaxed slightly. "If I were you, I would hold that footage close."

"I have a safe deposit box," Tony admitted. "I make copies to take there. I have to do that with all my projects for safety reasons."

"If you have *any* safety issues," Jorge reaffirmed. "You talk to *me.*"

"Not yet but I prefer to be cautious."

"This is wise."

"I was thinking about the title for the series." Tony admitted. "I usually don't worry about that much until the work is done but this time, it hit me. Since it centers on how Big Pharma is out to make money despite the collateral damages to the consumer, I thought we could call it *Eat the Rich before the Rich Eat You.*"

"Tony!" Jorge exclaimed. "I love it! This here, it is *perfecto!*"

The producer could be heard laughing.

"In more than one way," Jorge thought about it. "This here, it is perfect and catchy!"

"That's what I'm thinking."

"I love it!"

"I will let you know how the interviews go."

The call ended.

Satisfied with the results, Jorge phoned Makerson, the editor for *Toronto AM.*

"Hey Jorge," Tom Makerson's voice rang through the SUV. "How's the series going?"

"You knew we started?"

"A little bird told me."

"It is going well," Jorge thought out loud. "I plan to give you the first details, first clips, first everything."

"I can't wait," Makerson replied. "If you're involved, I know this is going to be big."

"It will ruffle some feathers," Jorge insisted as he drove along, getting closer to the coffee shop. "But you know me, I do enjoy ruffling a feather from time to time."

Makerson laughed.

"We will be in touch."

Jorge ended the call as he arrived at the coffee shop. He parked his SUV and headed inside.

Andrew sat at the back of the room with two coffees on the table. He perked up immediately as soon as he noticed Jorge.

"What is this here?" Jorge pointed toward the second cup of coffee. "Do we have another person with us?"

"No," Andrew appeared insulted. "I got it for you."

"Oh," Jorge said as he sat down. "Thank you. I did not expect that."

"I'm not always a moocher, you know," Andrew spoke sheepishly.

Jorge didn't reply but grinned as he reached for the coffee. Grabbing a creamer, he stirred it in.

"You're lucky I trust you," Jorge said and took a drink. "Or I wouldn't drink this coffee."

"What? Like I'm gonna put something in your coffee," Andrew appeared humored. "I don't wanna rape you."

"There are other things," Jorge said as he laughed. "You can put in one's drink that is a little more…well, maybe not *as* disturbing as what you just described."

"Yeah yeah," Andrew rolled his eyes with a humored expression on his face. "I got you. I'm not used to this, you know, criminal shit."

"So," Jorge changed the subject. "You got a new boss."

"Yeah, you," Andrew perked up. "I know, they told me yesterday about the sale."

"Oh, I'm the owner, but I am not your *boss.*"

"Ha?" Andrew looked nervous.

"Jolene, she will be your boss."

"What?" Andrew's mouth fell open. "She hates me!"

"She doesn't hate you."

"Remember the time she kicked me?"

"Ok, that there," Jorge reminded him. "That there was because you broke into the warehouse."

"And I like, looked at her ass or something…"

"Yes, this here, you may not want to do when she's your boss," Jorge grinned.

"Oh fuck!"

"Do not worry, it will be ok," Jorge insisted. "Remember, she is new to this business. She will be counting on you to help her out. *I'm* counting on you to help her out."

"I will."

"And you got problems…and you know the kind I mean," Jorge leaned in. "You call Paige."

"Not you?"

"I am busy with this docuseries, *amigo,*" Jorge reminded him. "If it is related to that, otherwise, call Paige."

"No matter what?"

"Me as a second person but I prefer it is Paige."

After going through a few more details, the two men ended their meeting and soon, Jorge was back in his SUV and heading home.

He called Chase on the way.

"Are you at the warehouse?"

"Yup."

"Jolene show you what you need to know?"

"Yup," Chase replied. "Paige already checked in this morning."

"Jolene there now?"

"She was but she left to go to the crematorium to meet that guy who's going to train her before it switches hands."

"I don't know why I checked," Jorge shook his head. "Paige, she is all over this."

"We got this."

Jorge ended the call and drove the rest of the way in silence. It was hard to let go of control but he was doing it, although somewhat slowly.

Arriving home, he noticed an unfamiliar car in the driveway. Driving into the garage, he checked for his gun before walking in the door. He found Paige on the couch with an older, Latino lady. His blood ran cold.

CHAPTER 11

"So, what is this here?" Jorge tried to seem causal despite the tension he was sensing. His gun within quick reach as he entered the living room. "You part of a religious group trying to save our souls or selling makeup door to door? People, they still do that?"

"Jorge Hernandez," The woman spoke with a heavy Argentina accent as she glanced over his body, purposely avoiding the question. "How did you survive all these years? Most people in cartels, they end up in prison or dead, how is it you are here…living the good life in Canada?"

"Lady," Jorge automatically grew defensive. "I don't know what the hell you are talking about. I am CEO of Our House Of Pot. In case you are not up to speed, this here is legal in Canada. There are no cartels."

The woman's eyes narrowed, the lines on her face deepened as she gave him a cold stare.

"Jorge, we should probably take this conversation into your office," Paige suggested in a calm voice.

He agreed, knowing that if things got messy, the children wouldn't be exposed to anything unsavory.

The three headed toward the office and Paige shot him a warning look that he didn't understand. Who was this woman and why was she in their house?

"Ok, lady," Jorge automatically took on his usual sharp tone after the door was closed, causing the stranger to stop, turning quickly, her cold eyes studied his face. "Who the hell are you and what you doing here?"

"It does not concern you *who* I am," The woman met his abruptness. "I am not here for you, I am here for Paige."

"Yeah, well, what the fuck does that mean?" Jorge felt his anger build and noticed Paige stepping between them, almost as if she was a barrier.

"Let's calm down," Paige said with her hand in the air as if to indicate for both of them to stop. "Please, let's sit down and I'll explain."

Jorge didn't reply but sent the woman a warning look before heading behind his desk.

"Ok," His wife spoke up as they all sat down. "Jorge, this woman is the person I used to work for...when I was an assassin. She prefers no one knows her name. It's better that way."

"So you," Jorge pointed at the lady as he leaned back in his chair. "You are the one who would call her, tell her the assignment, this kind of thing."

"Yes, that would be me," The woman replied with a slight nod. "It is me who contacted her when there was a problem that needed....fixing."

"Ah...." Jorge managed a grin and relaxed slightly. "I see, I see. So, this here, it is a social call? You get us a late house-warming gift?"

He was served a glare while Paige raised her eyebrows. Jorge automatically began to laugh.

"This, it is a joke," Jorge raised an eyebrow. "What, they do not have jokes where you come from?"

"I'm here," The woman started with some reluctance. "Because I wanted to see with my own eyes who it was that took away my best assassin. And you, I can't believe you're still alive."

"We back to this again?"

"It is unusual for a man in your position to survive many years in the cartel," She reminded him. "Unless you ended up in prison and yet, you escaped that *and* death. You must have been very well protected."

"Lady, if this is some kind of threat..."

"It is not a threat, just an observation," She finally smiled. "I'm impressed. I know your world well and I know, it's rare. I wonder, who it is that gives *you* your instructions. There are many rumors..."

"I would not worry about those rumors," Jorge insisted. "Those days, they are over."

"Ah, but with the cartel, those days are never over," She reminded him. "You're doing it from a different place, a different way, but I know that you're still making money for the cartel. You are in a very…unexpected position."

"As I said if this is a threat…"

"It is not a threat," The woman seemed sincere this time. "I wouldn't do that to Paige. She was my most loyal employee at one time, my *best* girl. I don't understand why she left all that, something she was so good at, for this."

Jorge was confused for a moment as the woman swung her hand around in the air to indicate the room.

"My wife, she has a pretty nice life," Jorge said and glanced at Paige for reassurance. "We have a nice home, family. I do anything for my family."

"This is also unusual for a man in your position," The woman commented with suspicion in her voice. "Most that are in the cartel, they would throw their mother under a bus to get ahead…or should I say, under a train…"

Jorge felt his heart race and he reached for his gun. Pulling it out, he pointed it toward the Argentinian woman.

"Jorge!" Paige automatically jumped up but spoke calmly. "Put the gun away. She's not suggesting you did it."

He reluctantly followed his wife's instruction while continuing to glare at the woman, who appeared unconcerned with the weapon.

"I'm sure you did not do it yourself," She continued.

"His mother committed suicide," Paige calmly clarified as she sat back down. "No one pushed her."

"Are you sure about that?"

"Yes," Paige shared a look with the woman.

"Can we please get to why you're here?" Jorge snapped.

"I am here," The woman replied and turned her attention to Paige. "Because I haven't been able to replace Paige. No one else was as efficient as her, no one else can do the job as well. I need her back."

"I can't take those chances anymore," Paige spoke up with assertion in her voice. "I have a baby. I have a family."

"Do you not already think you take a chance being married to this man?" The woman asked while shaking her head. "You didn't exactly pick a doctor or a lawyer, you picked a man who surrounds himself with violence. And don't tell me that you're not also involved. You may have sold the bakery but you haven't stopped making the cookies."

Jorge ran a hand over his face and raised an eyebrow.

"So you are here to persuade my wife to kill for you again?" Jorge decided to get right to the point. "This is it?"

"Originally," The woman replied as she returned her attention to him. "But I also wanted to see her new life. And now I also see you, Jorge Hernandez, with my own eyes."

"Now you have," He shrugged. "And she told you she does not want to work for you."

"You know," The woman turned her attention back to Paige. "That night, when you called me and said you had the wrong man. I was surprised because you normally did not make mistakes. But it was an unusual circumstance and everything had been very rushed."

"I remember," Paige spoke in a small voice.

Jorge also remembered. He had woken to a stranger in his hotel room, who held a gun to his head. After some persuasion, he managed to convince her that she had the wrong man. He remembered the call she made, the hesitation in her voice. Jorge would never forget the night he met his wife.

"Do you remember what I say to you in that call?"

"Yes," Paige stiffly replied.

"I said," The woman turned her attention back to him. "Jorge Hernandez is one of the most dangerous men in the Mexican cartel and you have a gun to his head? I said either kill or fuck him or you'll never get out alive. But I do not recall suggesting you *marry* him."

Jorge laughed in spite of himself while Paige seemed less amused, if not slightly annoyed.

"Again, this here, it happened a lifetime ago," Jorge said with a shrug. "So now, you show up at our door?"

"There is more," The woman insisted, causing Paige to appear surprised. "You killed another one of my girls."

"From the warehouse?" Paige spoke up. "That was *your* girl? You sent her to kill one of *my* people"

"Paige, you know this is not true," She shook her head. "It was to get information from you. That is all. No one was *supposed* to be killed."

"You had someone put a gun to one of *my* people's heads and you hadn't considered that an option," Paige snapped. "I might be out of the game but I still play by the same rules."

"I suspect both of you do," The woman glanced from Paige to Jorge. "But to answer your question, she was not supposed to do this either. I did not give her specific instructions. I had a nervous client wanting to learn about the docuseries."

"He should be nervous," Jorge shot out. "If he is in Big Pharma, I will fuck up his world."

The woman didn't reply but nodded.

"Your assassin...or spy, whatever she was," Paige cut in. "She was terrible. A complete amateur who shouldn't have been let out to work."

"That is why I am here," The woman continued. "It reminded me that there has never been anyone as professional as Paige Noël."

"Hernandez," Jorge automatically corrected her. "She's a Hernandez now."

"So, what? She can no longer work?" The woman asked. "I want her back. I want her to work for me."

"I have enough work here," Paige insisted.

"Wiping a baby's ass?" The woman rolled her eyes then pointed toward Jorge. "Cleaning up *his* messes too?"

"When I was with you, there were a lot of great assassins," Paige reminded her. "Who made sure no questions were asked. They always slipped under the radar. You don't need me."

"But this is where you are wrong," The woman turned toward her. "*You,* you could get to the *ones* the others could not. You were more skillful. When I say you were my *best girl,* it is because there are no other women on my team who come close. And as we both know, there are some places that only women can go....successfully."

Jorge sighed loudly and glanced at his wife who considered these words.

"I will think about it," She finally replied. "But if I do this, it can't be often. I'm not willing to travel."

"The farthest you will travel will be within this country," The woman seemed to soften. "And it will be rare."

"I need assurance that a situation like the other day," Paige quietly added. "Won't happen again."

"If anyone is lurking around you, your family, your business," The woman spoke confidently. "You will be the *first* to know. I will tell you who, what they want and it will be immediate. But you have to work for me."

"There can't be any conflicts of interest."

"This is reasonable," The woman nodded. "I am not here to steal your life, Paige. I am here to make my clients happy and as with before, you will be paid incredibly well."

"I'll think about it," Paige replied.

Satisfied, the woman stood up to indicate the meeting was over but Jorge wasn't ready to let it end.

"One last thing," Jorge spoke abruptly and he slowly stood up, his dark glare fixated on her. "If anything, *anything* happens to my wife while she's on the clock, I am coming after you lady. And your team of assassins, they will not be able to protect you."

His threat seemed to sober her. She merely nodded as she stepped back.

"No one hurts my family."

The woman's expression softened but she didn't reply.

CHAPTER 12

"Because that's how the biggest criminals and psychopaths work, Paige," Jorge ranted after the Argentinian woman left. "They don't do the dirty work, *you* do."

Paige looked away as if to ignore the fact that Jorge was pointing at her.

"And how's this any different from what I was doing before?" Paige reminded him in a calm voice. "In fact, how is it any different from what I do for *us*. She wouldn't be here if she didn't need me and it gives us some leverage. She has information that we don't always have access to."

"I thought, you know," Jorge spoke hesitantly. "You had contacts from your old life you could ask."

"I do, but they don't know as much as she does," Paige shook her head. "If there's something we need, *she* can find out. I think this could be a win-win situation."

"I do not like the fact that you will be in danger," Jorge calmly reminded her. "It is not because I am a chauvinist who doesn't want you to work but it is like me with the cartel. There is more at stake now than before…"

"I know," Paige nodded and moved closer to touch his arm. "I know, believe me, I don't want to put myself at risk either but it's going to be fine. She said *within* Canada. When I used to work, it was usually outside of Canada so there probably won't be many times she'll call and if I don't want to, I can still say no."

"Can you?" Jorge asked, unconvinced. There was something in her eyes that troubled him.

"Yes," Paige insisted while a smile. "Trust me on that. She's not trying to get me killed. We talked about this before you got home. Remember, I worked for her for a long time. She made me who I am today, so regardless of what you think of her, that woman did bring us together."

Jorge reluctantly nodded.

"I know I rarely talk about my life back then," Paige offered nervously. "Maybe if I did, you'd understand better. There's a reason why I became an assassin. Something happened to put me on that path."

"What?" Jorge asked with a smooth grin. "How does a nice white girl become one of the best assassins in the world? You must tell me."

Paige looked down and shook her head.

"Once violence is introduced to your life, it's hard to go back."

Without saying a word, Jorge led them to the couch where they sat in silence. It was clear that Paige was hesitant to continue but she finally did. Looking up, their eyes met and he knew it was important for him to be patient.

"I was working at a store in my 20s and it was robbed," She spoke quietly. "My..supervisor was shot in front of me. He was killed. It isn't the blood or the sounds that I never forgot, it was that look in his eye. The desperate look that said he knew he was about to die. It was as if he was trying to communicate with me in his last seconds."

There was emotion in her voice and Jorge was surprised to see Paige look away and blink back a tear.

"*Mi amor*, I had no idea," He reached for her hand. "You did not tell me this."

"I don't like to talk about it," She replied. "It was traumatic. I didn't realize at the time but I had PTSD and it was almost as if I couldn't function. I kept seeing him being shot, over and over. It was in my nightmares. I couldn't sleep. I didn't know what was normal anymore and I was frightened all the time."

Jorge nodded. He remembered the first time he saw someone shot. It felt surreal but each time after, something changed in him. He grew detached. His conscience was no longer rattled. He compared every death to when his brother Miguel died at the age of ten, which made each victim much less innocent by nature. He never considered that they too were someone's brother, he wouldn't allow himself to think in that way.

"To be an assassin," Paige explained. "I think a part of you has to die for this darker, more dangerous side to be born. A part of me *did* die that day and something had to fill that space and at first, it was depression. I was miserable. I wanted to die. I wondered why *him*. Why did he choose to kill him and not me?"

Jorge opened his mouth to speak but fell silent. He squeezed her hand and they shared a look.

"But eventually, I couldn't live like that anymore," Paige continued as a spark lit up her eyes. "I couldn't wake up another morning with a sense of dread, almost like a huge weight was on my chest and I couldn't breathe. I got angry. I was furious because the man who did this, he pretty well got away with it. He was arrested but got a slap on the hand. The judge didn't care. Everyone made excuses for him. He barely got prison time. It was a joke. I realized that these people, police….judges….a life means nothing to them. *My* life would've meant nothing to them if I was killed."

"The police, *mi amor,* you know how I feel about them," Jorge was quick to agree. "They do as little as possible to get a case closed. And the judges, they are no better."

"Exactly!" Paige spoke enthusiastically. "In my mind, if they could be desensitized about violence, then why couldn't I? If *my* life didn't matter to them and they were supposedly important, powerful people, then why should the lives of other important powerful people matter to me? I began to get a picture of reality, I was no longer naïve enough to believe that any of this, the entire system was there for the people. It was a joke."

"Can you imagine me?" Jorge said as he leaned closer to her. "Growing up in Mexico where it is so…blatant that the police are corrupt? At least here, they try to hide it a bit."

"It changed my perception forever," Paige nodded. "It's like a loss of innocence, I guess. Even my family, they'd tell me to 'get over it' or 'move on'. Which made me think if I had been killed that day, would they have had the same attitude about me? 'Oh, she's been dead a year, we've moved on'. It made me view life, my life, very differently."

"It does give you perspective," Jorge agreed. "This was me when my brother died. I saw, with my own eyes how they mourned him and made me the devil. It is then that I saw that they wished me dead too."

"I doubt they wished you dead."

"They did not wish me to be alive, *mi amor,*" Jorge insisted. "To them, I kill my brother even if it was an accident. An eye for an eye, they would say. This here, it changed me in much the same way you described. I no longer trusted anyone to take care of me. It had to be me against the world. But that mentality, made me survive as long as I did. It is as the lady today say, not many in the cartel keep their freedom or their life for long."

"I guess….that's why we connected that night in the hotel room," Paige observed and tilted her head. "When we met. Maybe we sensed that from one another."

"Definitely *mi amor,* I know."

"It was like I had this painful wound that grew into a fury," She continued her story. "Next thing, *I* was taking self-defense and learning how to shoot a gun. The weapon that gave me nightmares, made me empowered. It wasn't logical but it worked. I felt safer. I felt stronger. I was full of anger and refused to be a victim ever again and the woman you met today, she saw that in me."

"She saw this in you?" Jorge nodded in understanding. "Much like the man who gave me a chance, saw it in me."

"Just like you saw something in Chase…."

Jorge nodded. It wasn't something that could be described. You just knew. Your senses grew stronger, like those of an animal. Your awareness was a whole other level that most couldn't understand.

"I am wondering," Jorge was curious. "How you were discovered?"

"Not in a way you might think," Paige began to laugh. "I was actually at a nightclub with some friends. Some guy grabbed my ass. Without a second thought, I swung around and twisted his arm behind his back and shoved him against the wall."

Jorge joined her in laughter as he pictured it.

"It was as if someone else took over my body," Paige continued. "I felt powerful and enraged at the same time. I threatened him. Of course, I got thrown out of the club, not him. I didn't know it but the woman you met today was there. She saw me. She recognized how quickly I reacted, my strength, the look in my eyes, and saw the savage I had become and she followed me outside."

"She followed you?"

"She tried to tell the bouncer that I had a right to defend myself but we live in a misogynistic world especially back then, so I was told I created the problem by *overreacting*."

Jorge widened his eyes as he listened with interest.

"After the bouncer left, she asked me where I learned to do that move on the guy," Paige's voice seemed to relax. "I said I had taken self-defense because of this situation I was in…she asked what, so I told her about the robbery. Since my friends deserted me after my incident, she suggested we go talk at a nearby diner. We talked about what I was doing to protect myself and she suggested that maybe I needed to consider using these abilities in a career. I thought she meant the police…"

"Ah, the *policia!*" Jorge laughed.

"She said no," Paige shook her head. "But she didn't exactly come out and say I should be an assassin either. She talked like I would be involved in…security…investigating….that she would train me, as long as I was willing to travel."

"Did it ever occur to you that this woman, she might not be someone you want to get involved with?"

"You know at that point, my entire life was falling apart," Paige offered. "My family, dating, work, my emotional state….I was desperate to start over and she was the first person who seemed to listen to me, to understand, and saw something in me. No one else did."

"Plus, I had time to think," Paige continued. "She suggested I learn Spanish and tell friends and relatives that I was going to Latin America to teach English. She insisted I continue to take shooting lessons, that I start training in various forms of martial arts….she even wanted me to meditate, she said I needed to be balanced to do this job right. I had to be centered."

"And that's how you became the greatest assassin in the world?" Jorge teased and she blushed and shrugged.

"It didn't happen overnight," Paige admitted. "But she gave me an opportunity. She monitored my progress and eventually, I left Canada to 'teach Spanish'. But what I was really doing is training with ex-marines, people who were navy seals, people who knew every way to kill someone and how to be clean about it. You know, where to stab someone so there's less blood, how to shoot someone smoothly in a crowd….how to get into their hotel rooms in the middle of the night…"

Jorge laughed at the memory of her doing the same to him.

"Everything that could prepare me for that world," Paige continued and took a deep breath. "And I was a young and eager student. I *did* start in security but it quickly turned into something else. *I* turned into something else. I said I wanted to do more….and here I am."

"*Mi amor,* I feel that I knew so little until now," Jorge admitted as he leaned against the couch. "But I do see why you did not talk about it. You had a very traumatic experience….I can see you not wanting to tell this story."

"It became something…I wanted to leave in the past," Paige admitted. "Telling that story is like walking on a spider's web. Once you're in, you get stuck. I don't know how to logically explain becoming an assassin other than to say it was a series of….phases, of craziness, that led me down that path. You don't see it until you're there and once you're there, you feel like you've taken back your power and if you step away, you may never get it back."

"You are talking to one who knows," Jorge reminded her and looked deep into her eyes. "My path, it was not so different. But *mi amor,* I must ask, can we trust that woman who was here today?"

"Yes," Paige replied. "Look, I know you were taking swipes at each other but if you were to drop your weapons, you'd see that you aren't so different."

He considered her words and didn't reply.

"I was hesitant," Paige continued. "The more I think about it, the more it makes sense to have her on our side. And trust me, we would rather her with us than against us. She's one hell a friend but she's also one hell of an enemy."

CHAPTER 13

"This place here," Jorge spoke loudly as he joined the others in Chase's new office, at the warehouse. "It is bleak. You need something to brighten it up. Maybe a plant? Maybe one of Diego's lime trees, no?"

"Hey," Diego automatically swung around in his chair and made a face. "My lime trees, they need lots of sunlight which is a struggle enough without putting them in this dungeon."

"You know what would be pretty?" Jolene spoke excitedly as Jorge sat down beside Paige. "We could redecorate this office, Chase. It is dark and depressing since I remove my lamps and I had that little fountain thing, with the water and lights..."

"Why do I not remember any of this?" Jorge shook his head.

"Jorge, you were never here, how would you?" Jolene reminded him. "We did not meet here."

"I don't know but Chase," Jorge gestured around the office. "You need something. A little light. Maybe some music, some alcohol...."

"I'll put it on my grocery list," Chase quipped and everyone laughed.

"I just say....it needs...something in here."

"You just miss the bar," Diego sniffed.

"We can still meet there," Jolene reminded them.

"But this place is a little more off the grid," Paige insisted. "It might be better."

"Plus there's a lot of people doing maintenance at the bar lately," Chase added. "It might be smart to stay away."

"Enrique, he must watch these people closely," Jorge thought out loud. "We tend to have problems at that bar."

"He's watching....I promise," Jolene insisted.

"Clara is in every morning and yes," Chase replied. "I've been very clear on the importance of keeping an eye on people. But even from here, I check the bar with the cameras, just to see."

Opening his laptop, Chase hit a few buttons to show the others a screen that displayed various views of *Princesa Maria*.

"I have this open and use my other laptop," Chase continued as he closed it again and moved it aside. "I feel better keeping an eye for now."

"You do not trust Enrique," Jolene accused but Chase automatically shook his head.

"I know how fast things can go down."

"I think this is good," Jorge nodded. "This is good. Keep an eye."

"Besides, if I recall," Chase nodded toward Jolene. "When you were training me and I showed you this, you were watching him too.....you didn't have a problem then."

"I just want to see…"

"You wanted to spy on him," Chase cut her off. "Except, I'm doing it for work reasons and you're not."

"I….was curious what he do."

"Ok, this here soap opera," Jorge cut them off. "We don't got time for. We have a lot to discuss. Where's Marco?"

"Shit, I forgot to tell him…" Diego started and reached for his phone.

"No," Jorge shook his head. "This here is fine. I do not think we need him today."

"He found out who that woman was," Diego gestured toward the door that led to the secret room in the basement.

"It does not matter," Jorge shook his head.

"What do you mean it don't matter?" Diego scrunched up his lips. "The other day you said…"

"We found out who sent her," Paige cut in, automatically calming Diego. "It's been looked after."

"By who?"

"I do not think she said," Jorge turned to Paige.

"She indicated it was Big Pharma," Paige gently reminded him. "She's going to tell them it's a dead end."

"For that woman, it was," Jorge laughed at his joke.

"What the fuck are you guys talking about?" Diego jumped in. "Who said all this?"

Jorge continued to grin as he turned to Diego.

"We got a surprise visitor yesterday," Jorge told the others. "It was Paige's former...boss, is that how you say?"

"I don't know if 'boss' is the accurate term," Paige replied. "But it's the easiest to explain. It was the woman who used to connect me to the.... work I used to do."

"As an assassin?" Jolene asked. "She the lady who set up things?"

"Yes," Paige nodded. "She showed up at our door."

"Oh...that is strange, right?" Jolene looked confused.

"The woman we had here not long ago," Jorge pointed toward the door leading to the basement. "She sent her which, you know, originally pissed me off because she worked against us."

"She didn't exactly send her strongest girl," Paige muttered. "So it wasn't a concern to her either."

"Maybe this was on purpose to find a way to get to you," Jorge suggested as if they were having a private conversation. "To let you know that she could easily work against you as *for* you."

Paige didn't reply.

"Ok, back the fuck up here," Diego shook his head and dramatically swung his arms around. "What are you talking about? Paige's old boss sent this woman for information?"

"And to kill me!" Jolene shot out. "What? We are working with the person who sent her to murder me?"

"She wasn't sent to murder you," Paige quickly assured her. "She wasn't supposed to threaten anyone but snoop around and find information."

"But she work against you?" Jolene asked and shook her head.

"This here, it is what I'm saying," Jorge agreed.

"You have to understand that if she *really* wanted information, there's no way she'd send her," Paige insisted. "She knew this woman would get nowhere and it was also a test supposedly to prove she wasn't able to do this kind of work, that she needed more training. To scare her. It backfired."

"She did not seem too concerned, you know," Jorge muttered to Paige.

"The person she sent was weak. She has no compassion or use for weak people."

"Who is *she* exactly?" Chase showed interest. "This boss or whatever you call her, what's her name?"

"Oh, this here, it is the best part," Jorge spoke boldly. "We cannot know."

"We can't know?" Diego shot out and made a face. "Why the fuck not? She got a name or what?"

"She doesn't want people using her name," Paige clarified. "She refused to even tell me and I've known her for years."

"So we call her *Senorita* No Name," Jorge joked and everyone laughed, while Paige merely smirked.

"I know it sounds strange," She calmly injected. "But you have to know our world. We usually went by agent numbers, we didn't use names. It was better that way. So obviously, with that in mind, it makes sense that she wouldn't reveal hers either. Even when I met her, she basically told me that people *referred* to her as t*he queen*."

Jorge rolled his eyes.

"Still, she send a killer for me," Jolene complained. "Maybe not on purpose but still, it is unsettled."

"Unsettling," Diego corrected her English and was given a dark glare.

"Look, I know this probably doesn't make sense to anyone," Paige attempted to explain. "But you have to trust me here. She's a valuable person to have in our corner. She has information. Her point in allowing this to happen was to remind me that she makes a good ally. I have contacts that know some information but she knows much more. She's aware of any professional hits on anyone in the world. She knows about underlying problems that aren't even on anyone's radar. She *is* the underworld. Rather than having Marco searching for hours on the dark web, we can call her. She might save us some time plus she will let us know if anything comes up, like the other day with that woman….who again, I want to be clear, wasn't sent here to kill anyone. She was sent on a mission to find out what the series was about. She could've chosen many ways to find something out but instead, she made many errors."

"Wouldn't a woman like…this *queen* lady be," Chase paused for a moment. "Wouldn't she be better at picking someone for this kind of assignment? She got way off track."

"I agree," Paige nodded. "But you can never really know until they're out there. Realistically, it sounded like a simple task. One that the person she sent would pass or fail."

"So, now, what?" Diego asked. "She's gonna help us just because?"

"Well," Paige said. "There are conditions."

"She wants Paige to work for her again," Jorge jumped in. "And this here, I'm not happy about."

"I told you," Paige insisted. "It's only in Canada and it won't be often."

Jorge wasn't convinced and shared a look with his wife.

"But hey, if she can help us," Diego shrugged. "This might be good."

"We will see," Jorge said. "I am not completely convinced yet."

"Me neither," Jolene spoke loudly. "She does not sound like we can trust…"

"I wouldn't introduce her to the group if we couldn't," Paige assured her. "She's careful and for a reason. She's put out some really *big* hits. Some that would blow your mind."

"We gotta be careful," Diego replied while appearing conflicted.

"We must move on," Jorge decided to change the topic. "Anything else?"

"My new job," Jolene started. "The crematorium, it is creepy."

"Just stay in your office," Jorge reminded her. "You don't got to be down there burning bodies."

"It is creepy," She repeated. "But at least, my office, it is nice."

"It's going ok?" Chase asked.

"It is fine," Jolene seemed skeptical. "I do not always have things to do."

"Well, that's good," Jorge reminded her. "It's better to not be tied up. It frees you if we need help elsewhere."

"Same here," Chase added. "I mean, I got work to do but the supervisors got it under control unless there's an issue. I keep an eye on the numbers, staff…"

"That is what you do," Jolene reminded him.

"So transition went well," Paige nodded.

"Enrique, he's doing ok at the bar?" Jorge asked Chase. "No problems?"

"Nope.

"And the docuseries?" Chase asked back. "How's that going?"

"According to plan," Jorge nodded. "And Athas, he is about to make an announcement that's going to blow the top off Big Pharma. He will tighten the rules for opiate drugs and *suggest* alternatives that of course, include cannabis as *safe* options."

"Big Pharma," Chase muttered. "They ain't gonna like that."

"Let the fuckers squirm," Jorge said with a shrug. "Me, I hardly care about hurting their feelings."

"But if we put pressure on them…." Paige started.

"Then they will have bigger problems to worry about," Jorge reminded them. "While they're trying to put out a fire and reason with Athas, I will be making a series that will put the final nail in their coffin."

"Tap tap!" Diego mimicked as he pretended to use a hammer while the others laughed.

"Tap tap motherfucker," Jorge added with a smirk. "Tap tap."

CHAPTER 14

"A psychotic baby?" Jorge shot back and shook his head. "I'm being blamed for a psychotic baby? This here, it can't be true."

"It's not you directly," Paige corrected him from the other side of the desk while the muffled sound of Maria's music could be heard from upstairs. "It's the entire cannabis industry."

"I *am* the cannabis industry," Jorge reminded her and let out a loud sigh. "So, this here lady smoked pot *before* her pregnancy and now she has a little monster and it's somehow my fault? This here is fucking unbelievable."

"It's obvious propaganda," Paige calmly reminded him. "But you have to remember too, you shot the first bullet with Athas and now, they're going to shoot back."

"But this here is crazy!" Jorge complained. "So what? Miguel, when he acts wild, it is because I snorted coke years ago? Because we smoked a joint once in a while before your pregnancy. This is complete fucking bullshit."

"It's based on a study from…"

"I don't care," Jorge quickly shot back. "The fact that anyone believes it…"

"One of the major networks in Canada is all over the story," Paige reminded him with a shrug. "But they're always going for any attention they can get."

"Fuckers," Jorge muttered as he glanced toward the darkened windows. "So, what I think we should do…"

"Nothing," Paige put her hand in the air. "This isn't for you. Remember, I'm the problem solver now, so you can focus on the docuseries. I got this."

"But *mi amor*…"

"I told you so you're in the loop," Paige insisted. "You don't need to worry. I got the PR department on it."

Jorge thought for a moment.

"This is a PR situation," She continued. "We know it's bullshit but it's up to them to say that in the nicest way possible."

"But I could…"

"No," Paige shook her head. "I got this plus, if you get involved, you won't handle it as tactfully as necessary. This is a delicate situation. It involves a baby. You know how people feel about anything with children."

"Yes, well, if you ask me, her baby is psychotic for other reasons."

"Probably loaded up on sugar," Paige muttered. "When I see how some people feed their kids, it makes me sick."

"Well, Paige, not everyone is a good mother like you," Jorge commented and watched her beam. "Miguel, he is lucky because you are careful about what he eats. But he will be king of my empire someday, so this is good. He needs the best start."

"King of your empire," Paige grinned as the mood lightened and he winked at her.

"Paige, you know this here, it is an empire," Jorge reminded her as he sat forward in the chair. "And one day, it will be our children who inherit it."

"Hopefully they don't have to go down some of the same roads as us."

"Paige, that is why I do everything I do," Jorge reminded her. "By then, it is my wish that cannabis is more accepted, used, and trusted for a great many things, and that this here is automatic. My goal is to remove the skeptics to make it smooth sailing in the future. We own all these retail operations around the country and online plus develop products with various businesses. Athas changed the laws so we got the monopoly. It will be ready for the kids in the future or if they decide they do not want this, for them to sell and follow their dreams."

"I doubt you'll be that ok with them selling everything and following their dreams."

"I will be dead by then Paige."

"Don't say that!"

"Paige, we are in our 40s, Miguel is a baby. It is not that unlikely."

"Can we not talk about this anymore?" Paige appeared saddened.

"I am not saying this to upset you," Jorge reminded her. "It is a fact. But hey, either way, eventually, I may retire."

"I've been hearing that for the last year or more."

Jorge grinned and winked at her.

"So, what I'm thinking…"

Paige halted when the phone rang.

"Ah!" Jorge leaned forward. "My secure line. It's Athas."

"Want me to leave?"

Jorge shook his head while answering it.

"Athas, Paige is here, should I put you on speakerphone?"

"Sure," Athas sounded out of breath and frustrated.

"Ok," Jorge said after hitting a button and sitting the phone down. "What has got you all out of breath, *amigo?*"

"I was just running from the fucking vultures outside," Athas spoke abruptly before sighing loudly. "You know, my biggest enemy is the media. And if they told the truth but they spin things."

"You do not have to tell me," Jorge reminded him. "My company *apparently* has contributed to someone's baby being psychotic."

"I saw something about that," Athas commented. "But was it directed at your company specifically?"

"It was directed at my industry and that is enough to declare war."

"We're not declaring war," Paige corrected him. "PR will come up with some facts that make her look like…"

"She's a fucking idiot?" Jorge asked.

"There might be some other research involved," Paige said with a shrug. "If science doesn't do it, her questionable past might be the nail in the coffin."

"Well, *mi amor,* we do not have to worry about coffins now," Jorge muttered and winked, "with the crematorium."

She grinned.

"I'm getting a lot of push back from Big Pharma," Athas spoke up. "The regulations I'm introducing for the industry aren't going over well."

"Of course not," Jorge replied. "It affects their bottom line."

"They want to fight it," Athas continued. "But even if they do, it will be tied up in court and we have the doctors and facts behind my concerns about addiction."

"People who work in rehabs or anywhere dealing with addicts will tell you opiates are the biggest problem now," Paige spoke elegantly. "Not the old-fashioned street drugs. People are going in hooked to a pill their doctor prescribed."

"Right," Athas piped in over the phone. "Except now, Big Pharma has propaganda on social media saying that the Canadian government wants to take patient's pain medication away. They're making it sound like I'm ripping it out of the system and no one is interested in looking at how the problem started in the first place."

"It's because they want someone to blame," Paige reminded him. "No one wants to take responsibility if they can blame the government."

"Well, the fucking media wants to drown me with this story," Athas insisted. "They're making it sound like I'm going to take away cancer patient's pain medication and that's not what I'm saying."

"Ok, so this here," Jorge cut in. "You need to talk to Makerson. He interviews you and you can bring out these facts. But Athas, you must be strong, you must bring numbers that show all the people dying of opiate overdoses, comparing it to other addictions."

"Point out how it is putting an unnecessary strain on the health care system," Paige suggested. "That people are suffering needlessly while patients are backlogged."

"Maybe we need to find," Jorge thought out loud. "Someone who was addicted to opiates that Makerson can also interview along with you, Athas. He can talk to them about how they got addicted and maybe how casually these here pills are handed out."

"A lot of people have a medical plan that pays for everything too," Paige said. "So, if they aren't costing you much or nothing, people often don't give it a thought. Plus if your doctor is giving them out, you assume they're safe."

"There's no reason to say no until it's too late," Athas said and there was a silence. "I might have someone who can talk."

"You do?" Jorge asked. "About drugs?"

"Remember, I used to be in social work," He reminded them. "I was downtown, I saw it all. There's someone I know who struggled with drugs that were prescribed. She thought they were safe and didn't even realize she was addicted at first."

"Get her," Jorge suggested. "Find her and have Makerson ask all the right questions."

"That would be ideal," Paige agreed. "Say that you saw this many times when you were doing social work..."

"Yes, *do* remind the people of this career," Jorge suggested as he moved closer to the phone. "They must know this is something you saw in your work. Maybe this was an issue that brought you to politics."

"Because you wanted to make a change," Paige added and Jorge nodded. "You wanted to help these people and now that you have a chance...."

"But bring up pot too," Jorge added. "Just say you see cannabis as a more natural solution to some concerns, that you have seen the studies... work it casually into the interview."

"I'll tell this to Makerson," Athas agreed. "Good points. I have people here to help me deal with this kind of thing."

"These people," Jorge reminded him. "They go to their problem-solving book that tells exact answers that sound fake. You have to talk like a real person, not a politician."

"Right," Athas sounded calmer. "Ok, I'm going to call Makerson and take care of this now."

"*Perfecto.*"

The conversation ended and the couple exchanged looks.

"I think we need to do more," Paige suggested.

A grin formed on Jorge's lips and he nodded. He knew exactly what she was thinking.

CHAPTER 15

"Of course it will take some time to adjust," Alec Athas stated in the interview between him and Tom Makerson which streamed the following morning. "All changes are the same but in the end, we feel this will ensure the safety of Canadians when dealing with such powerful drugs. Opiates have damaged and destroyed lives and it's our job to make sure that we protect the vulnerable and in this case, we're all vulnerable if these medications aren't distributed with absolute caution and care."

Jorge grinned and reached for his coffee as the voices on his laptop rang through the house. Paige was at the company's office with Diego, Maria was at school and Juliana had taken Miguel to the playground. It was nice to be home alone, if even for an hour.

"You've indicated in the past," Makerson began and glanced at the tablet in his hand. "That doctors have been caught prescribing large quantities of pills in exchange for sexual favors…"

"We know for a fact that this is happening," Athas quickly jumped in. "Plus several cases are waiting to go to court where doctors have taken advantage of people struggling with addiction. This is unacceptable and a disgusting abuse of power."

"Would you go so far as to call them drug dealers?" Makerson gently pushed. "In the past, you've compared these doctors to people on the streets, selling illegal substances."

"We tend to walk on eggshells because of their education and status, however," Athas shook his head and fell silent for a long, dramatic moment, "these people *are* no better than the drug dealers on the street. They might be worse because they've taken an oath to take care of people."

Jorge raised an eyebrow and heard his phone beep.

Did you see that??

This was Diego.

Yes, he is right.

But it's gonna cause a scandal. Paige agrees.

Before Jorge could reply, his phone rang. It was Tony.

"Good morning, how is filming going?"

"Perfect," Tony replied, much to Jorge's relief. "But I was just watching the live stream and I'm wondering, what are the chances we can get the prime minister to speak about these changes in the series?"

"I am wondering," Jorge thought for a moment. "If it might be better to use footage like this in the docuseries and perhaps show some of the push back he gets. Maybe if we look into who is pushing the hardest, we can make a connection between them and Big Pharma."

"Follow the money."

"Exactly what I was thinking," Jorge replied. "Any issues?"

"Nope got lots of footage," Tony admitted. "It's going better than I expected. I think the formula I originally had might be changing."

"How so?"

"I'm talking to some doctors who want to remain anonymous," Tony paused for a moment. "They're being blackmailed or pressured by Big Pharma to push their drugs."

"This here is interesting," Jorge perked up, "*very* interesting."

"I thought you'd feel that way," Tony went on to explain. "Sometimes when it comes to a project like this, we start with one idea but it expands. I was going to add in food as a major topic and how it makes us sick so we need all these pills, however, now, it's looking like it will be one episode of the series, if at all. It might be a whole other season in itself."

Jorge thought for a moment.

"I think we must stick with opiates for now and perhaps, at the end of the season, have a teaser for the audience," Jorge suggested. "Something that suggests that if you thought Big Pharma was fucking with your health, wait to see how it's in bed with the food industry."

"I was kind of thinking the same," Tony replied. "I still want one episode to focus on pot but I gotta tell you, we're collecting footage fast. I'm trying to wade through and put these episodes together."

"And Andrew? He will help?"

"Yup, he has access to some people I didn't," Tony replied. "And he got some great interviews. It's not bad."

"I'm on my way out to meet him shortly," Jorge noted the interview between Makerson and Athas had ended and closed his laptop. "I have some ideas of something extra he can do before the series comes out but I want to run it by him first. I noticed on YouTube, people have channels and build subscribers. We should look into doing the same thing before the series comes out, perhaps something that leads up to the topic."

"Oh?"

"I have not worked out the details," Jorge stood up from the chair and reached for his keys. "I do not know what. Behind the scenes, maybe?"

"I like that," Tony sounded intrigued. "You guys talk it through and get back to me. I got my channel too so we can link it. It'll pique interest until we can release the series."

"This is my hope."

They ended the call as Jorge walked out of the house and headed for his SUV but something stopped him. Glancing toward Diego's, he noticed a car at his house.

Amigo, are you expecting company? There's a pricey car in your driveway.
No!
I got this.
I'm on my way.

Slipping his hand inside his leather jacket, Jorge felt his gun before taking a shortcut through his yard and walking around the fence that divided them. He noted two men were in the car. He abruptly tapped his fist against the window causing them to jump.

The window slowly opened and an older man wearing a suit appeared alarmed.

"What you want?" Jorge abruptly shot out.

"Are you…do you live here?" The man gestured toward the house.

"Just call me the neighborhood fucking watch," Jorge shot back. "Now what you want?"

"We were here to talk about the Bible…"

"Really?" Jorge cut him off. "I don't see no Bibles in there…"

Gesturing inside the car, Jorge noted that both men appeared nervous.

"Well, we don't necessarily use them all…."

"Plus, you and your people would be roaming through this here street with your literature…"

"Well, we…"

"Get out of the car."

"We just…"

"Get out of the fucking car," Jorge demanded and pulled his jacket open to show his gun. "And tell me why you're really here."

The man on the driver's side turned white as a ghost while his passenger quickly followed his instructions and jumped out of the car.

"We…we don't want trouble…" He stuttered as the man on the driver's side slowly opened the door, putting his hands in the air before getting out. "We're here…"

"Don't give me that Bible shit," Jorge insisted as they both exchanged sheepish looks, as if not sure of what to do. "I don't see no Bibles. Tell me what you're actually up to."

"We're looking for my son," The second man quickly spoke up. "I had someone investigate and I was told this was where he was last seen."

Jorge stared at him without saying anything.

"Your son, he ain't here," Jorge replied as his brain raced.

"Please, it is important," The man continued while the other man continued to hold his hands in the air. "We must find him."

Jorge didn't respond and grabbed his phone.

Diego, do you got one of your boyfriends at the house?

What? No.

This man is looking for his son and said this is the last place he was seen.

I don't got no one's son.

"The man who lives here," Jorge spoke calmly even though his mind was racing. "He just move here. So it may be the wrong one."

"I was told my son was here."

Diego, he says this man was here recently.

I dunno Jorge. I had a lot of guys over lately.

Whore.

"Well, if your son was here," Jorge insisted. "He ain't here now."

"You are in contact with the owner?"

"I told you," Jorge gestured around the quiet street. "I'm neighborhood watch. We keep an eye out for one another."

"I promise, we aren't here to cause trouble."

Jorge wasn't convinced.

His phone rang. It was Andrew.

"Where are you? I thought we were supposed to meet?"

"Something came up," Jorge replied. "I got two suspicious people at Diego's place. I might have some business for you later."

"Ah....live chickens or already slaughtered?"

"I haven't decided yet," Jorge confirmed. "But we, we will meet later. I got something else for you."

"Tony said something about a YouTube thing..."

"We'll talk."

"Till then, I'll keep the home fires burning."

"You do that."

Jorge ended the call just as Diego shot into the driveway with Paige in the passenger seat. He wasted no time jumping out of his car.

"What the fuck is this?" He yelled gesturing toward the strangers. "And who the fuck are you?"

"Apparently, they're here to talk Bible with you," Jorge smirked and exchanged looks with his *hermano*. "And now, they say something about a missing son."

"I don't got your fucking son," Diego directed his comment at the wrong man, who gestured toward the other, shifting everyone's attention. "I don't got your fucking son either."

"Maybe we should take this conversation elsewhere," Paige pointed toward the garage and glanced at Diego and Jorge. "This seems...private."

Jorge didn't reply but Diego hit the garage door and gestured for everyone to go inside. Once behind closed doors, he became infuriated.

"I don't got time for this bullshit," Diego yelled at the two men and pulled out a gun. "What the fuck is really going on here? Why are you hanging around my house? Who *are* you?"

The men exchanged looks.

CHAPTER 16

"Please, we don't want any trouble," The man who had been in the passenger's seat quickly insisted. "My son is missing and we had someone check his phone somehow and traced him to here."

"Ok," Paige calmly intercepted. "Your son is missing. Has he been gone for long?"

"Just a day but…"

"*Senor,*" Jorge interrupted. "Your son, he is an adult, no? He can do as he pleases."

"He's 16," The man shook his head.

Jorge and Diego exchanged looks.

"Ok, nah nah," Diego automatically piped up as his face turned red. "I do not deal with teenage boys, ok? Why does everyone think gay men are pedos too? I only…"

"Diego," Jorge automatically began to laugh at his friend's assumption. Shaking his head no, he continued. "I was not thinking this but obviously, they have the wrong house."

The two men seemed to stiffen their positions as they listened to the conversation and exchange looks, something that didn't go unnoticed by Diego.

"What the fuck?" He snapped at them. "You got something to say?"

"My son," The man continued. "Can I show you a picture?"

"Yes, please do," Paige replied and shot Diego a warning look.

The older man reached for his phone and hit a few buttons before turning it around for the others to see. It was a photo of a kid that would barely pass for 16 and Jorge merely shrugged. He noted Paige studying the image closely while Diego backed away and dramatically swung his hands in the air.

"I don't know that kid," He said with certainty. "The men I have here, aren't children and if anyone..."

"Diego, calm down," Jorge said and took a deep breath as if it would somehow make his friend relax. "This kid, he could've been walking down the street when they track him. He may have been in a car nearby, lots of things."

"I....I don't exactly know how this phone tracking thing works," The old man shook his head while the other man stood in silence. "Someone from the church was helping us when he went missing."

Jorge grew frustrated. His phone beeped again. Glancing at it, he saw that Andrew was checking in again.

"You have a meeting," Paige reminded Jorge. "Go."

"But, *mi amor..*"

"We can handle this," Paige insisted. "You go, we'll talk later."

Jorge reluctantly followed her instructions but turned before reaching for the door.

"Text me."

"I will," Paige assured him.

With that, he went outside and started down the driveway. Glancing into the car, he now noted some religious materials on the seat as well as a cross hanging on the mirror. Perhaps they called themselves religious but that gave him little comfort.

After sending Andrew a message, he jumped in his SUV and headed out. On the way, he decided to check in with Marco at the office. The company IT specialist was working on a few projects and Jorge wanted to see if he had any new revelations.

"Mr. Hernandez," Marco greeted his call with enthusiasm. "Good morning, sir."

"Marco," Jorge automatically felt his mood lighten. "How are things today?"

"Well, sir, I have a few projects on the go but the day, so far, is looking promising."

"Is that so?"

"Yes, Tony and I, we will talk later."

That meant he had some tips that would help him out with the docuseries.

"*Perfecto.*"

"Also, I have found that Enrique, he is speaking to his wife…or is it ex-wife in Mexico."

Jorge didn't reply.

"I see several calls in recent days."

"This here, it does not matter to me," Jorge said as he got closer to the coffee shop where he was to meet Andrew. "He has children, so that is why I assume they talk regularly."

"That is my assumption too."

Jorge thought for a moment.

"May I ask, Marco, why is it you are looking into Enrique's phone activities?"

"Jolene, she asked me…"

Fuck.

"…and I thought it was because maybe you had concern that he…"

"Jolene, this was her idea?"

Marco paused for a moment before answering.

"Yes, I thought you approved this."

"Marco, I don't know nothing about it," Jorge spoke honestly. "If Jolene approached you to spy on her boyfriend, it is for her. So, unless you see something suspicious…."

"No, sir," Marco assured him. "I am sorry, I thought this was your instruction."

"Marco, do not take instructions from Jolene," Jorge advised him. "It is rarely to anyone's benefit other than Jolene's."

"Sir, it did not seem like he was doing something wrong," Marco admitted. "But if he is, I do not want to tell her."

"Just say," Jorge thought for a moment as he looked for a place to park near the coffee shop. "That you see him carrying out regular business. Talking to his kids. That kind of thing."

"Please, do not tell Jolene I tell you this."

"I won't," Jorge grinned as he glanced around. "In the future, if she asks you to do something, you call me first."

"I will, sir."

"We will talk more later."

He parked the SUV and headed into the coffee shop. It was busier than he would've liked but fortunately, Andrew was at the back, away from the others. Playing on his phone, he almost didn't see Jorge arrive at the table.

"You hungry?" Jorge asked and Andrew shook his head. "That would be a first."

"I can eat though."

Jorge caught the waitress's attention and ordered them each breakfast.

"It has been a crazy morning."

"That's what I gathered."

"Some old men were at Diego's looking for their son? I dunno, Paige and Diego are handling it."

"Weird. Sure it's not like the cops or something."

"These guys are old as fuck. I don't even believe that they would have a son that's as young as they say, let alone be cops."

"Super weird."

"Some religious types."

"Ah, well some of those religions, they have like a hundred kids with every woman in their fucked up churches. Like, they screw around with teenage girls and everything. I was watching a documentary on it. Totally creepy."

"Sounds it," Jorge replied. "So I got a question for you."

"Shoot," Andrew said then stiffened up. "Not literally."

Jorge merely grinned.

"So, you want to be a YouTube star like we started to talk about earlier," He finally asked. "Go on there, do some things that will make people interested in this series before it comes out."

Andrew thought for a moment. "Sure, but how were you thinking?"

"That's for you to figure out," He replied as the waitress brought their food. After she left, the two started to dig into a plate of eggs, toast, and bacon. Jorge made a face.

"I'm a little disappointed. I thought it would have those little potato things."

"Hashbrowns?"

"Sure, whatever they are," Jorge shrugged and began to eat. "So, you got any ideas for something you can do? Just short little videos, nothing serious."

"Well," Andrew thought for a moment. "You know, some guys go on there and just talk but I don't know if I can do that…."

"Well, we are trying to talk about the dangers of opiates in the series," Jorge considered. "Maybe find some druggies to interview? Check out the people on the street, see what they got to say…"

"Hmm….I like that idea," Andrew considered. "I know some people who will talk."

"Make sure it's about Big Pharma, not the cocaine they got from some Latinos, you know?"

"I know."

"You got any sources," Jorge asked. "you know, not someone we can use in the series but someone talking about what they see?"

"Yeah, I do," Andrew admitted as he chewed. "Like a lot of people out there. One buddy of mine, he works construction and fell at work, fucked up his back and they put him on these pain pills…like fucking strong shit and he got reliant on them then they suddenly pulled them away."

"Yes," Jorge thought. "But this here new law, it will give out fewer pills so that might not work for us."

"Nah, not like that," Andrew shook his head then shoved a forkful of eggs in his mouth and chewed for a moment. "He got a lot of drugs before they pulled them away and we're talking like fucking morphine strong."

"Is this so?"

"Yeah man," Andrew nodded his head. "His doctor, he got in shit for making girls suck him off to get more pills, so my friend, he was left high and dry 'cause his new doctor wouldn't give him nothing."

"That's quite a story," Jorge thought as he chewed. "This here is perfect. If you can talk to people like that."

Andrew didn't reply but glanced around the coffee shop for a moment.

"I got an idea," Andrew leaned in. "I watch this guy, he talks about illegal shit on his channel. He covers his face and people eat it up. What if I do that? I cover my face, try to disguise myself and maybe the others do too. Tony will share them on his channel."

"He said he would," Jorge nodded, intrigued with the possibility. "Earlier."

"Then that's what I'll do," Andrew spoke excitedly. "Create some hype."

"And remember, we are trying to make Big Pharma look bad…. not me."

"Obviously," Andrew nodded fast. "I know the hand that feeds me."

"Remember that."

Jorge's phone rang and he saw it was Paige calling.

"*Mi amor*," Jorge said as he glanced at Andrew who watched with interest. "The old men, are they gone yet?"

"Gone," She replied. "And mystery solved."

"That did not take you long."

"I had a feeling."

"Ah…Diego?"

"No," Paige replied and paused. "You might want to talk to your daughter about this one."

"Oh fuck!" Jorge said loudly causing someone nearby to turn his way while Andrew giggled. "Now what she do?"

"I'll explain when you come home," Paige replied. "But don't freak out. It's not what you think."

"Paige, you do not want to know what I'm thinking."

"Trust me," Paige replied. "You'll see. Juliana is bringing her home now and…I'll explain when you get here."

CHAPTER 17

"Maria, this here better be good!" Jorge snapped at her as the two of them walked into his office while Paige caught up, giving him a warning glance as she entered the room. He ignored this and continued to rant as he closed the door. "I do not need the *policia* at my door looking for that kid."

"He texted his dad to say he's fine," Maria insisted, turning around just before sitting on a chair. "It's not like we're kidnapping him."

"Maria!" Jorge felt his temper rising as he walked behind his desk and sat down. "You do not understand, this boy, he is a minor. His father had every right to be looking for him as I would do the same if you were missing."

"Maria, he does have a point," Paige insisted as she eased into the chair next to her step-daughter. "But, Jorge you're going to have to hear the whole story. She did help him for the right reasons."

"You hid a boy in your bedroom all night for the *right* reasons?" Jorge started to yell but quickly noted the look on his daughter's face and took a deep breath. "Maria, you better have one hell of an explanation or you're back to a girl's school *mañana,* do you understand?"

"*Papa,* come on!" Maria shot back as she leaned forward in her chair. "He's *obviously* gay so we *obviously* weren't having sex if that's what you're worried about."

Jorge immediately looked away as his heart continued to race. He said nothing.

"I had to help him!"

"Maria, it is not for us to get involved in whatever issues are in his family," Jorge said in a calmer voice. "If his father does not accept that he is gay, that is unfortunate however, this is not something we can help with."

"It's not that, *Papa,*" Maria countered with wide eyes as she glanced at Paige before continuing. "Cameron's father is super weird about all this and because of their religion, he wants to send him to conversion therapy!"

"What?" Jorge paused for a moment and let the words float through his head. "What is that? I do not understand?"

Paige jumped in.

"It's a therapy that supposedly changes someone's sexual orientation," She calmly explained, as if choosing her words carefully "So, his family wants to send him away to this program hoping to make him straight."

"This here," Jorge was confused. "This is possible?"

"No!" Maria shot back. "They want to torture him into being straight. It's so messed up."

"Their particular religion believes that being gay is like a disease," Paige continued. "So they want to *cure* him by sending him to some weird, underground conversion therapy group. He was scared and that's why Maria had him here."

"How long has he been here?" Jorge attempted to process this information. "How did you get him in here?"

"It was just one night," Maria assured him. "They wanted to send him today so he texted me last night and I said to come here and I'd hide him."

"Maria, I do not like the idea of you hiding anyone in our house," Jorge explained before taking a deep breath. "However, I do understand."

"So he can stay?" Maria's eyes brightened up.

"No, of course, he cannot stay," Jorge explained. "This here is not for us to say. He is their son. We cannot keep him here."

"He's 16," Maria reminded him. "Lots of kids leave home when they're even younger."

"Maria, no," Jorge spoke sternly. "I do not like the idea of you hiding him here in the first place."

"I thought you understood," Maria began to whine, causing Jorge to wince.

"I say I understand," Jorge reminded her. "Not that he could move into my house."

"But what is he supposed to do?"

"Does he not have other relatives?"

"Yeah, but they'll just go along with his family."

"Maria, I am sorry for your friend," Jorge began. "But we cannot do anything. We cannot get involved."

"But you always say we have to be loyal to our friends!"

"I do, Maria, this is true," Jorge agreed. "But how long have you known this boy?"

"It doesn't matter," She attempted to brush it off. "We're very close."

"Maria," Jorge shook his head. "I do not know."

"How about…" Paige cut in, "You let me handle this one."

Jorge felt relief wash over him.

"Paige, are you sure?" Jorge was skeptical.

"We will talk, see what we can come up with," Paige said. "Diego is out there with him now, trying to come up with a solution."

Jorge considered her point and nodded.

"Whatever you wish," He said. "But Maria, you cannot do something like this again. You must be honest with us."

"But you wouldn't have let him stay," She insisted. "That's why I didn't say anything."

"Maria, you did not know this," Jorge argued. "But I do not want anyone else showing up at my door looking for their kid."

"Well, technically," Maria quickly reminded him. "it was Diego's place."

Jorge gave her another warning look before the three of them headed back to the living room, where Diego was having a lively discussion with the skinny, white boy. He looked as young as Maria and for someone about to be sent off to conversion therapy, much more relaxed then he should've been.

"*Papa,* this is my friend, Cameron," Maria spoke in her usual bubbly voice. "We're in the same dance class."

"Hi!" The young man beamed from his seat beside Diego. "Thanks *so* much for letting me stay here…I mean, even though, I guess you didn't know."

He let out a high pitch laugh while exchanging looks with Maria, who quickly followed his lead.

Jorge grimaced, forced a smile, and nodded.

"Nice to meet you, Cameron," He turned to his wife. "I believe Paige, she is going to help you find a solution."

"I have a solution," Diego spoke up abruptly. "Make this public! There's no way the LGBTQ community will let this shit happen, let me tell you!"

"Maybe, see what you can come up with," Jorge suggested just as his phone buzzed and he reached for it. "If necessary, perhaps I can make a call to Makerson."

"Ohh!! I like that," Diego nodded excitedly. "But we gotta be careful, this is a sensitive situation…"

"I must go," Jorge said as he held his phone up. "I got some stuff to take care of."

Noting that his daughter's face was full of appreciation, he winked at her before heading outside. Relieved to be away from the house, he headed for his SUV while checking text messages. The first was from Andrew.

I talked to Tony. He has some people for me to interview.

How soon can you start the channel?

Tonight. And I might have my friend I told you about.

Perfecto.

The next text was from Tony confirming this same information.

I'm sending Andrew the slush pile that I'm not sure about.

Perfecto.

He can decide on the keepers.

Gracias.

The last message was from Marco.

Will you be by the office later?

I can go right now.

Thank you, sir.

He thought about Makerson.

Can we meet sometime soon?

Sure.

I got some stuff related to the series.

About that, we got to talk.

When is good?

Tomorrow morning?

8?

Sure.

See you then.

Makerson had his ear to the ground so chances were good, he might have something that would be helpful for the docuseries. Also, there was a chance that he would help them promote it in *Toronto AM*. Jorge was pleased that things were finally coming together.

Just as he started the SUV, another text came in. This one was from Chase.

I got a problem. Are you around or Paige?

At the warehouse?

Nah, not here. The bar.

What's going on?

Jolene and Enrique.

Chase, are you watching live porn as we speak?

Not that kind of problem.

Want me to meet you there?

It might be a good idea. If we don't get there soon, there mightn't be anything left of the bar.

Fuck.

Jorge called Marco as he flew out of the driveway.

"*Amigo,* I got to go to the bar," Jorge apologized. "I may be late."

"Sir, did you want me to meet you there?"

Jorge thought for a moment.

"Yeah, you know, maybe this here will be good. I might need your help."

He had no idea what kind of mess he was about to walk into.

CHAPTER 18

"What the fuck?" Jorge shouted when he entered the empty club to find broken glass on the floor, scattered fragments almost to the door, jagged pieces on the tables while a red-faced Jolene stood across the room with a wild look in her eyes. It took him a minute to notice Enrique looking like a trapped animal in the corner of the bar.

"She did this!" Enrique managed to mutter as he pointed toward Jolene. "She has gone *loco!* I don't know what to..."

He didn't finish his sentence before having to jump back from another glass flying in his direction. Barely missing his head, it smashed against the wall and shattered everywhere while Enrique turned away, covering his face. Jorge noticed a tray of clean glasses sitting on a table beside Jolene and immediately put his hand up and rushed toward her.

"Enough with the glasses, Jolene!" He barked at her only to be met with a dark glare as she reached for another and threw it at him. Automatically dropping his head, he heard the glass whiz by and smash on the floor behind him. With his hands out to protect him, Jorge carefully lifted his head to see that nothing was flying in his direction.

"You Mexican men, you are all the same!" Jolene shot out with the devil in her eyes. "You selfish pigs! It is only about you and to hell with everyone else!"

"Ok, this here," Jorge automatically regained his stance while taking on a harsher tone, one usually reserved for his daughter. "This here stops, NOW! I do not know what the fuck is going on between you but you are not going to destroy my bar. This here, it ends NOW!"

He saw Jolene take a deep breath, pushing her breasts out, she stood taller and her face continued to show signs of fury. Jorge managed to walk around the pieces of glass until he was able to reach her weapons, removing them from her reach.

"Enough, Jolene," Jorge insisted as he picked up the tray of glasses and moved them away. "This here soap opera, it fucking ends now. I don't know what is going on with you and I don't fucking care and..."

Just then the door opened and Jorge heard a gasp. He turned to see Marco walking in with his bicycle, which he quickly placed beside the door while Chase followed, his face full of disbelief which quickly turned to anger.

"What the fuck happened to *my* bar?"

"It is not *your* bar anymore!" Jolene informed him, only causing Chase to glare at her while Marco grabbed a broom and began to sweep up the broken glass. "So do not worry."

Chase didn't respond but met her eyes with a quiet fury. Jorge took a deep breath just as his phone beeped. Sitting the tray of glasses down, he reached for it to see a message from Paige.

I think we resolved things here. Are you at the office?

I'm at the bar. Jolene has gone loco.

What?

Will tell you later.

Do you need me there?

No, I got this one.

Taking another deep breath, he looked up to see Marco sweeping up a dustpan full of glass as Enrique rushed from behind the bar holding a garbage can, also being careful to not walk on anything while giving Jolene a skeptical look as he scurried out of the line of fire.

"Now," Jorge spoke up in a slightly calmer, yet irritated voice. "What the fuck is this about? Why are you destroying the bar, Jolene? What the fuck is wrong with you?"

Now appearing shameful, she glanced at the floor and didn't reply.

"I do not like this drama, Jolene," Jorge reminded her as he gestured at the broken glass while Marco continued to sweep. "Thanks to you, my top IT guy is sweeping fucking floors. You know how much I pay Marco and how important his work is? And he's cleaning *your* fucking mess. Think about *that* Jolene."

Marco was grinning as he continued to work while Chase started toward her with no signs of compassion in his face, despite Jolene's pained expression.

"This is just how she is," He automatically attacked her. "Things don't go how she wants, she has a fucking fit. It's *not* the first time."

With that, Chase spun around and headed for the closet that contained cleaning products. Jorge ran a hand over his face and shook his head.

"Jolene, what the fuck?"

"He," She pointed toward Enrique. "He was disloyal."

"To me?" Jorge glanced toward Enrique who automatically put his hands up in the air and shook his head.

"No, sir!"

"No, to *me*," Jolene spoke boldly. "He was disloyal to *me*."

"You?" Jorge looked at her with disdain. "I don't give a fuck about you."

She automatically shrunk back with a pained expression on her face.

"Jolene, I don't got time for this fucking drama," Jorge snapped as Chase joined Marco cleaning up the mess while Enrique looked as if he wasn't sure what to do. "Did he fuck another woman? Flirt with another lady? What?"

"He talk to his ex-wife!" She spoke accusingly. "I catch him."

"They *do* have children," Jorge remind her.

"They were *not* talking about children," Jolene automatically regained her strength.

Jorge shook his head, showing little interest.

"I see him," She continued. "All the time, he is on the phone."

"When she spied on me!" Enrique shot back. "She was spying on me."

"Good thing!" She countered and pointed in his direction. "This is how I see something was wrong. Then when I invite you to move into my house with me..."

Enrique didn't respond and shook his head.

"Nothing you say," Jorge cut in. "Explains why you destroyed my bar."

"I catch him on the phone," Jolene complained. "He was talking to *her*. He wants to go back to her."

"I did not say that," Enrique attempted to reason. "I just...it is hard when you have children in another country. I never see them, why can't you understand this?"

Jorge noted the sympathetic look on Chase's face. He knew all about that.

"So, you what?" Jolene gestured around the bar. "Leave this, leave *me* for them?"

"So, this is what it's about?" Jorge cut in, his brain already spinning. "Ok, this here it will end. I want to speak to each of you, *separately,* in the office."

Walking toward the room behind the bar, he gestured toward Enrique to follow him. Once behind closed doors, he automatically began to speak.

"Is this here, what you want?" Jorge asked as he went behind the desk and sat in the chair. "To return to Mexico?"

"Sir, I do not wish to disrespect you," Enrique automatically began to plead as he fidgeted. "I...I miss my family. And Jolene, she is..."

"Crazy?" Jorge asked and pointed toward the door. "Yes, this is obvious."

"*Si,*" Enrique relaxed. "But you have done so much for me, I was not sure what to do."

"Enrique, if you want to go back," Jorge shrugged. "Go back. Me? I am not stopping you. I may have an opportunity for you down there."

"Oh?" Enrique perked up.

"Between us, I need someone in Mexico to be my eyes and ears. I will find an official job for you but really, you will be my spy. You will be ready if I need you to check out anything. I have others, of course, but when the cat is away, the mice will play. I need you to make sure everything is on the up and up."

"I can do this sir," Enrique assured him. "Anything you need."

"*Perfecto.*"

"But sir, Jolene..."

"Do not worry about Jolene," Jorge insisted. "I will tell her to back off and she will listen."

"Ok, sir," Enrique appeared skeptical. "I am concerned..."

"I will ask Chase to oversee the bar until I figure out other arrangements."

"Are you sure, Mr. Hernandez?"

"Enrique, I have a family so I understand," Jorge insisted. "I know that this here is difficult and you try but you know, in the end, your children are what is most important. If it is your wish to move, then please do so. I will have something for you and quite honestly, this might be of more value to me than having you run a bar."

Enrique nodded.

"Are you certain this is what you want?"

"It is, sir, I am sorry…"

"Do not be sorry," Jorge shook his head. "This here does not bother me."

"Thank you."

"Now, if you can," Jorge pointed toward the door. "Please send in Jolene."

"I will," Enrique stood up and suddenly stopped. "And if you ever need anything…"

"I will give you a call."

Jolene appeared exhausted when she entered the room, shutting the door behind her. The look of defeat weighed on her face but he knew how to deal with her.

"Jolene, Enrique is going back to Mexico," Jorge ripped off the band-aid before she even had time to sit down. "But this here is good because he wants to be with his family…the one, I must remind you, *you* broke up."

"You cannot break up something that is not already broken," Jolene insisted as she plunked down in the chair across from him. "he did what he want at his free will."

"But Jolene, you saw the vulnerability.….new country, new job, he was homeless for some time, scared," Jorge pointed out. "But again, I do not want to be caught up in a *telenovela*. He has made his decision and you must accept it."

She didn't reply but he could see tears in her eyes. He ignored this.

"Meanwhile," He thought for a moment. "I will find something to keep your mind preoccupied. Until then, why not take a little vacation?"

"A vacation?" She appeared surprised. "But…

"Jolene, you have this new house you will soon be moving into," Jorge reminded her. "Is this not a good time to plan for such…"

"But it will be alone," Her voice sounded small this time, unlike the roaring lion she was earlier.

"Your brother, he also said the same thing to me," Jorge informed her. "When he moved earlier this year but now, he is happy. It is ok."

Jolene didn't reply.

"Jolene, I cannot figure out your life," Jorge spoke bluntly. "This is up to you but for now, this is all I can tell you."

She didn't reply.

"Go home, Jolene," Jorge suggested. "Take this day to think and meanwhile, send Marco in."

She stood up in silence, appearing to be in shock as she headed toward the door. He ignored her reaction and welcomed the end of the insanity. Marco swept in with a smile on his face, closing the door behind him.

"Oh sir, I did not expect this," Marco spoke in a low voice, pointing toward the door. "That was *crazy!*"

"Welcome to the world of Jolene," Jorge gestured toward the chair and Marco sat down. "so what you got for me?"

"Well, sir," Marco replied as he leaned forward in the chair. "This might make your day!"

Jorge grinned as he leaned back and listened.

CHAPTER 19

"Right about now, *mi amor,* I would like to send her on a permanent vacation," Jorge ranted as he crawled into bed beside Paige that night. Placing his phone on the nightstand, he ran a hand over his face and yawned. "This week, it was fucking exhausting between dealing with Jolene, Maria and the psycho baby situation..."

"Oh, I hear you!" Paige chimed in. "I had my own *psycho baby* screaming half the day plus dealing with Maria's friend the other half. Maybe it's a full moon."

"But *mi amor,* Jolene, Jolene is always crazy," Jorge complained as his wife moved closer to him. "Unfortunately, if she does not have a distraction, she goes *loco* and I am tired of this nonsense with her."

"Well, we can't kill her because she threw a glass at you," Paige appeared amused. "So, I hope that's not what you're suggesting."

"I did not say *kill,* Paige, I just think that she is a ticking time bomb," Jorge paused for a moment. "Although she does sometimes help, most times she is out of control."

"That's just Jolene," Paige reminded him. "She's very erratic at times."

"Yes, well, throwing glasses at Enrique and wrecking my bar is beyond erratic," Jorge fell back on his pillow, welcoming the comfort. "Maybe she needs some medication."

Paige laughed.

"Funny thing to hear from you since you're going up against Big Pharma."

"Well, *mi amor,* maybe not that kind of medication," Jorge grinned and turned her way. "Although, I am willing to make an exception so I do not have to deal with her insane temper tantrums anymore."

"She was hurt and upset but yeah," Paige slowly nodded. "That was hardly the rational way of dealing with it."

"I point out to her that *she* had a part in breaking up this marriage in the first place," Jorge shrugged. "But she did not seem to understand that perhaps, she made this mess herself."

"Enrique's children is a pretty powerful reason to move back," Paige thought for a moment, her eyes lit up. "Unless, what if she moved to Mexico with him, or is he getting back together with his wife?"

"You know, this, I do not know," Jorge said and hesitated. "That is an interesting point, Paige."

"It depends on how badly you want to get rid of Jolene."

"If you had asked me that earlier today," Jorge replied and shook his head. "I would have packed her suitcases myself."

"That's what I thought," Paige quietly replied. "Maybe I'll put the idea in her head tomorrow, see where it goes."

"You know, this here might work."

"But can we afford to *not* have her here?"

"The problem, Paige is that she is always a grenade about to go off," Jorge considered. "And when grenades go off, they destroy everything around them. I do not want to see this one day."

"I'll talk to her tomorrow."

"You, Paige, can work your magic," Jorge flirted with her as he moved closer. "Now, about this boy...Cameron?"

"His father backed off," Paige replied. "I reminded him that a lot of people wouldn't look very favorably if he put his son in conversion therapy. He's well known in the Toronto area so he doesn't want his name tarnished. I assured him that's exactly what would happen if he even thought about sending Cameron away."

"This here, will it work?"

"Well, considering Cameron is very close with Maria, I'm certain," Paige said as Jorge eased in closer to her. "Let's just say your daughter is pretty savvy so if anything seems unusual or he stops showing up at school, she'll be on top of it."

"I must admit," Jorge began. "This here was another dramatic event that I did not want to be part of but I guess my daughter, she made a good point. Loyalty is everything and if we are disloyal to our friends then who are we?"

"But are we being disloyal to Jolene if we send her away?" Paige wondered.

"If we were disloyal to Jolene," Jorge said as he ran his hand under the sheets and over her stomach. "She would have been dead long ago. No, *mi amor,* we are being forward-thinking."

With that their conversation ended.

The following morning, Jorge was up early and planning his day. Glancing over the news highlights at the kitchen table, he turned to see Maria walk into the room and head for the coffee maker.

"Oh, thank God! I *so* need a coffee!"

"Maria, don't drink too much of that," Jorge reminded her. "You are young to be hooked on coffee."

"There are worse things I could be hooked on, *Papa.*"

Jorge shot her a dirty look and she giggled and poured her coffee.

"Maria, so your friend was ok?" Jorge asked as he closed his laptop. "I did not see you last night.'

"I was hanging out with Cameron at his place."

"I am not sure you should be at his house, his family…"

"It's fine," Maria swung her hand in the air as she walked toward the table with her coffee in hand. She sat beside him. "His parents are never home anyway. They live and breathe religion. It's so *weird.*"

"What do you mean?"

"I don't know, I guess they study the Bible a lot."

"So Cameron, he does not like this?"

"Are you nuts, he hates it."

"It is good he can think for himself," Jorge mused. "Many people cannot."

"I know, I know," Maria spoke dramatically. "Always be a wolf, don't be a sheep. You say it all the time."

"I am happy you are listening, *chica.*" Jorge nodded. "This is important."

"But that's why I like Cameron," Maria insisted. "He's himself. He doesn't care what anyone thinks."

Jorge nodded.

"His brother told him to just go along with the conversion therapy thing to make them happy," Maria wrinkled her nose. "That's so gross."

"Well, Maria there are a lot of gross people in the world but your friend, he is smart to not be bullied into something he knows is wrong."

"That's what I said."

Glancing at his phone, he stood up from the table.

"Maria, I must go," Jorge reached for his coffee cup and took it to the sink and rinsed it. Heading back to the table, he kissed the top of the head. "Please give *besos* to Miguel and Paige for me."

"I will, *Papa.*"

"And Maria," He hesitated before heading for the door. "I'm very proud of what you did for your friend. What you said, this is true. Loyalty, it is most important and helping him, this is also good, you know?"

She beamed as he turned and left.

Outside, he jumped in his SUV and flew out of the driveway. Hitting a button, he called Andrew.

"Hey, I got the YouTube set up."

"Good morning to you as well," Jorge grinned to himself. "I saw your message this morning."

"I sent you the link."

"I will subscribe later today."

"I already have some guests that Tony threw my way," Andrew added. "Tony said after I have some videos, he will include them on his channel. It'll get people thinking before the series comes out."

"Excellent."

"He's also looking into not putting it on the streaming site all at once but dropping an episode weekly. That way we can release it sooner."

"This here, it is smart."

"He's already completed an episode and well into the next."

"*Perfecto.*"

"I'm sure people will love it. If not, you'll persuade them."

"No, me," Jorge shook his head as he moved through traffic. "I gotta stay in the background if possible."

"True."

"I'll keep you posted."

He ended the call.

Lost in thought, he was stuck in autopilot when he parked the SUV outside the coffee shop near Makerson's office. Going inside, he was relieved to find it almost empty. People were in line but most were picking up something and leaving. He saw Makerson at the back of the room.

"Good morning," Jorge sat down, immediately noting the apprehensive look on Makerson's face. "At least, I think it is?"

"I got a problem."

"You do?"

"We got Big Pharma as a huge advertiser for the paper now and I was told that I can't do anything that might ruffle their feathers."

"Fuck!" Jorge cringed. "This here, you realize it is on purpose."

"Maybe there's a way around it."

"This is too bad because I have a story for you," Jorge leaned in. "The psychotic baby situation? I got proof that it was propaganda from Big Pharma."

"You got proof?"

"I got proof," Jorge confirmed. "I believe it falls under their 'PR expense' which is what that lady received a cheque for."

Makerson looked troubled.

"Fuck, my hands are tied!"

"What if," Jorge thought for a moment. "Our House of Pot bought more advertising?"

"More than you have now?"

"You name your price."

"I can't see how they can go against you then."

"Consider it done."

"I'll bring it up," He hesitated for a moment. "You really got proof?"

"I got a great IT guy."

"Ok, then we can work around *how* I got the info."

"You make it happen," Jorge insisted. "And if you don't, *I* will."

Makerson didn't reply but nodded. He knew.

CHAPTER 20

"The going away dinner is tomorrow night," Paige confirmed a few days later as the couple sat together in the office. "In the VIP room."

"And just like that, we are getting rid of Jolene?" Jorge grinned as he leaned back in his chair. "This here is good. Who knew it would only take a man to lure her out of town? I would've found someone to charm her long ago."

Paige gave him a mischievous grin.

"But I guess," Jorge hesitated and moved his chair forward. "She has been helpful at times but I find her...a little too much sometimes, you know?"

"She has been," Paige agreed. "But I think this will be good for everyone."

"Is she planning to sell her house before she even moves in?" Jorge wondered.

"No, she wants to save it for now," Paige answered and thought for a moment. "which might be smart, all things considered. I wouldn't be surprised if she returns."

"The Mexican atmosphere, it may not agree with her," Jorge suggested with a raised eyebrow. "So, what else is on the agenda for today, *mi amor?* Perhaps, you should take the day off and stay home?"

"No thanks," Paige shook her head. "Miguel is having another crazy day so I need a break from the house."

"Ah! *Mi amor,* remember when he wasn't saying 'Ma' and you worried?"

"Yeah and now he says it all the time," Paige laughed. "Non-stop, actually, he's usually screaming it at the top of his lungs and throwing his toys around."

"Perhaps, Jolene has already had too much influences on him?" Jorge suggested and the couple laughed. "So, today, what is the plan?"

"I'm going to the office to make sure Diego is *really* ok with his sister leaving town," She paused for a moment. "I might check in on Marco too."

"He did good work, *mi amor,* when he found out the truth about that psycho baby story. Once Makerson revealed proof that the company paid off the lady to make these claims, they were shut down."

"When I saw the footage online," Paige shook her head. "My first instinct was that she just had a kid with temper tantrums."

"They were not unlike Miguel's. I wonder if this means something is wrong?"

"It's a phase," Paige shook her head. "I did the research and I'm keeping him away from sugar and gluten."

Jorge laughed.

"Being the top advertiser for *Toronto AM* seemed to make it easier to get this story out," Paige observed. "But I also heard that Big Pharma is moving its way into the television world more and more."

"This is the thing, Paige," Jorge mused for a moment. "Do people watch television as much as they used to? It is all online now, especially with young people. They stream, they go on YouTube, they listen to podcasts. Television? Not so much."

"But it's usually the older people who watch TV," Paige reminded him. "And they're the ones most likely to vote so if they see any anti-pot propaganda, it could cause an issue for the next election."

"We will cross that bridge when we come to it."

"True."

"For now, we must focus on this docuseries," Jorge pointed toward his laptop. "It will be launching soon."

"Yes, I like the idea of releasing one episode at a time," Paige nodded. "It creates more anticipation."

"I have already viewed the first one and it is perfect."

"Eat The Rich Before the Rich Eat You?"

"It is a catchy title that will pull people in," Jorge insisted. "There is already a lot of buzz. I made sure of it. People are talking."

"What's the first episode about?" Paige asked.

"The first, it is about how greedy corporations took over," Jorge reached for his tablet and turned it on and glanced over an agenda before turning it toward Paige. "He will talk about how these corporations got out of hand and how they use people as collateral damage."

Paige nodded as she glanced at the tablet.

"After that, we will talk to different experts who discuss say, addiction to pills, or why certain drugs are so dangerous. We will talk to scientists, people who worked for these places and know all the secrets. It will be massive."

"Andrew's channel is getting a lot of attention," Paige commented as she moved the tablet aside. "I've been watching his shows when I can. He mentioned an upcoming interview with Tony about the series."

"Tony is also sharing his videos," Jorge pointed out. "it is a win-win for everyone."

"So where does that leave you?" Paige asked. "It sounds like everything is ironed out.

"I would love to believe this but you know how it is," Jorge reminded her. "The calm is always before the storm."

She nodded slowly as a chill crept into the room.

"I am going to meet Andrew," Jorge said as he glanced toward the window. "He's got some ideas for me and you know, that is about it…"

"That's it?" She spoke in a flirtatious voice.

"That is it, unless," Jorge leaned forward. "You have something for me?"

"I might."

"Let us go do our work," Jorge said in a quiet voice. "And maybe, we can meet back here a little later…"

"Don't even say it," Paige warned as she started to stand. "Every time you do, something happens."

"This is true," he laughed and stood up. "We will talk…later."

She nodded and they headed for the door.

He found Andrew waiting for him at a dumpy café that wouldn't have been his first choice but it was almost empty.

"Good morning," Jorge said as he sat down and Andrew looked up from his plate of food. The smell of bacon caused his stomach to growl. "I may have to get one of those."

"It's good."

After ordering his grease ladened plate of bacon, eggs, toast, and hash browns, Jorge sipped his bitter coffee and pushed it aside.

"So, what you got for me?"

"Well," Andrew said after swallowing a mouthful of food. "My viewership is rising every day. Lots of weirdos commenting but I delete them."

"Tony and you working together?"

"Yup," Andrew nodded and reached for his coffee cup. "Last night I talked to some homeless people about the fentanyl crisis."

"Oh?" Jorge raised an eyebrow just as his food arrived. After thanking the waitress, he quickly dug in. "What they say?"

"That's the thing," Andrew muttered and leaned ahead. "They talked about how word was that it was put on the streets with the intent of killing them."

"Oh yes, this here," Jorge nodded. "That happened earlier this year."

"You knew?"

"I helped expose it," Jorge talked through his mouthful of food. "It was their way of 'taking care' of the homeless situation."

"Well, this guy talked about how he lost some friends and he made accusations about Athas…"

"Nope, we can't smear Athas," Jorge shook his head. "Not that he knew, it was his staff."

"His staff?"

"His now *deceased* staff."

Andrew nodded and made a face.

"Anything else?"

"Nah, just that," Andrew paused for a moment. "Well, something else but it might be nothing."

"What's that?"

"This lady's saying that it's Big Pharma that had a hand in creating some kind of super virus and then made the vaccine or whatever…"

Jorge stopped chewing and stared at Andrew.

"But I don't know if it's true," He rushed to continue. "The lady, I don't know her."

"Let me….let me see if I can find anything," Jorge said and started to chew again. "I will talk to Marco and meanwhile, you and Tony see what you can learn."

"It wouldn't surprise me."

"This is the kind of bomb we want to put in this series."

Andrew didn't reply but thought for a moment.

"Do you know the name of the virus?"

"I think one of the older ones," Andrew wrinkled his nose. "I forget which one. They always have such fucked up names."

"That's cause they are created by fucked up people."

"Allegedly."

"In my business," Jorge reminded him. "Allegedly often is a fact more than it is not."

With this thought at the forefront of his mind, he swung by the office after breakfast to look for Marco. Instead, he found Diego and Paige in the conference room.

"Big meeting in here?" He asked as the two looked up.

"I gotta tell you," Diego put his hand up in the air. "Getting Jolene out of town, this is perfect timing."

"What do you mean?"

"See this here," Diego pointed toward a piece of paper on the desk. "Not only did she spy on Enrique, but she also had someone investigate him and charged the company!"

"She was sneaky about hiding it," Paige pointed out. "It doesn't look good on our books either."

"Take it off the books, charge her!" Jorge automatically shot out as he sat down. "We aren't paying for this here."

"Well, there's more," Diego added with an irritated expression on his face. "We were also paying for fine dining and everything else. I guess she thought since she was in charge of the warehouse, she could charge everything as an expense."

"Who found it?"

"Chase," Diego replied. "He came here to see me this morning."

"Why did he not call me?"

"Probably afraid you'd kill Jolene before she had a chance to leave," Diego automatically shot back then calmed. "Not that I'd blame you."

"He wasn't even sure," Paige jumped in. "He popped in earlier with what he found and asked if we knew anything about it."

Jorge took a deep breath and shook his head.

"How many other things was she hiding?"

"We need to find out."

"Yeah, but the party," Diego automatically jumped ahead. "I don't know if I can sit through that fucking going away party knowing she was pulling this shit."

"You know what?" Jorge finally decided. "A few dinners, let it go. But remember, we may not have a job for her when she returns."

"Well, if…" Diego trailed off.

"Diego, do you think this is an *if* situation?" Jorge countered.

"So we let it go?"

"We let it go," Jorge confirmed. "We let *her* go *too*. She just does not know it yet."

"Can we trust Enrique?" Diego wondered.

"What did our investigation say?" Jorge pointed toward the piece of paper on the table.

"Just that he was talking to his wife," Paige replied.

"We will have them watched," Jorge said and turned toward Diego. "I know she's your sister…"

Diego gave a sad shrug. His loyalties were clear.

CHAPTER 21

"Why would I say her personality? I did not know her *personality*. I knew her ass and that is what attracted me to her." Jorge shot out as if he were asked the most absurd question. "Why would you ask this, Jolene?"

Everyone around the VIP table laughed while Jolene Silva waved away Jorge's reply and shook her head.

"Men, you are such perverts sometimes," Jolene insisted before snuggling up to Enrique. "Why can you not say her *eyes* or her *pretty face*....anything but her ass!"

Jorge turned toward his wife and noted that she was laughing, not offended by his comment.

"Because it is true, *Jolene*," Jorge replied with humor in his voice. "When I meet Paige, the first thing I saw was her ass so when you ask what was the *first* thing that attracted me to her, this is it."

"Come on, Jolene," Diego jumped in. "Who the fuck you think you're talking to here? Some pretty boy in a movie or what?"

"Some pretty *white* boy in a movie," Jorge cut in as he put his arm around Paige and pulled her closer. "Me, I do not think this way."

"But your kids, if they ask, you aren't going to say..."

"Jolene, I assure you, my kids," Jorge shook his head and leaned in her direction. "They do not care about such things. And there are other things

I, of course, notice about Paige when we met, but you did not ask me that. You asked the *first* thing and I answer."

Appearing to give up, Jolene shook her head before staring dreamily into Enriques's eyes, causing Jorge to glance in Diego's direction to catch him rolling his eyes. Across the table sat Chase who was stoic and taking it in. Jorge pointed toward the drink in front of him in hopes that it would relax the youngest member of the group. He didn't want Jolene to be suspicious.

"In fairness, it does sound like something Maria would ask," Paige countered and gave a little shrug when he turned her way, causing him to relent.

"Maria, she asks a lot of questions that I do not always care to answer," Jorge replied and reached for his Corona. "But I admit, I hate to see her grow up."

"I think we all feel that way about our children, sir," Marco replied from the end of the table. "It is not easy."

"But I think Maria is a little more…difficult…" Paige suggested.

"Yes, with her, what does she call it, Paige?" Jorge turned to his wife. "*Gay* boyfriend?"

Paige nodded while Marco appeared confused. Meanwhile, Enrique and Jolene were in their own, little world, making the conversation awkward.

"But would you prefer that or a *straight* boyfriend?" Paige reminded Jorge, causing him to cringe.

"*Mi amor,*" Jorge shook his head. "I think we both know the answer to that."

"I do not understand, sir," Marco spoke up. "What is a *gay* boyfriend?"

"It means," Diego automatically jumped in to answer. "Her friend who's gay. Someone to go shopping with, go to the movies…"

"Why not just say a 'friend'?" Marco appeared confused. "Is that not the same thing?"

"Women are closer to their gay boyfriends than they are their female friends," Diego insisted and pointed toward Paige. "I'm her gay boyfriend."

"Yes, Diego, you're her *gay boyfriend,*" Jorge spoke sarcastically. "Let us make sure that you get the gay part in because we never would've guessed otherwise."

Everyone laughed except Diego who attempted to fight a grin by jumping in to retort.

"Hey, not everyone thinks I'm gay!" He reminded him, leaning in, his eyes widening. "I'll have you know that lots of women hit on me too."

"They smell the money, Diego," Jorge pointed toward his suit.

"Yeah, well no one hits on you," Diego shot back and pointed toward Jorge's suite. "And you wear...some pretty expensive suits."

Jorge shot him a mock glare and changed the topic, noting that Enrique and Jolene were still unengaged in the conversation.

"So you two," Jorge attempted to break up the lovefest. "What is the plan when you go to Mexico?"

"I have a place that we are moving into," Enrique replied. "It is not far from my children so I can see them pretty regularly."

Jorge noted the fake smile on Jolene's lips.

"Well, this here is nice," Jorge replied. "Family, you know it is everything."

"Oh and I will miss Maria and Miguel so much," Jolene automatically jumped in. He noted the sincerity in her eyes. "Especially that baby! My godson."

"Well, you can always visit," Jorge spoke casually and glanced at Chase who continued to look tense. "He is going through a crazy stage right now so it is probably not an exciting time to deal with him anyway."

"Oh, is he ever," Paige shook her head.

"The odds weren't good with him as a father," Diego pointed at Jorge. "He got crazy written all over him."

"Unlike you, Diego? The *gay* boyfriend?"

Everyone laughed but Jolene laughed especially loud which caused an unsettling feeling in Jorge's stomach.

"So Chase," Jorge glanced in his direction. "You will be a busy man, looking after everything."

"I can handle it."

His response was abrupt and to the point, something that Jorge appreciated.

"I'm only a phone call away," Paige reminded Chase, which seemed to soften his disposition. "That's what I'm here for."

"Unless your queen boss with no name, she calls you with a job," Jorge reminded her of the Argentinian lady who had recently dropped by the house.

"I don't think that's going to happen too often," Paige said with an awkward shrug. "Besides, most jobs don't take long."

"Not for a pro like you."

"I don't think I'm the only pro at this table," Paige glanced around. "Besides, my priority is us."

"Does she know that though?" Jorge countered.

"She knows."

"But you're her best girl," Diego mocked. "Isn't that what she told you?"

"She did."

"I think it's because Paige," Jorge pointed toward his wife. "She can get in anywhere and no one suspects a thing."

"It's part of the job," Paige reminded them. "A big part."

"I think it's easier when you're a woman," Chase suggested.

"Not necessarily," Jorge replied and glanced toward Jolene, who was once again completely absorbed in Enrique. "But Paige, she used to disguise herself a lot."

"Oh really?" Marco piped up with wide eyes. "Like in the movies?"

"Not quite that extreme," Paige replied. "I tried to look inconspicuous. For example, there was a phase back in the day, I tried to resemble Paris Hilton."

"Oh yeah!" Marco replied. "No one would be suspicious of her."

"At least, not of killing someone," Jorge took a deep breath and glanced at the still tense Chase, who raised an eyebrow.

"It was the perfect cover," Paige said and paused. "She was the party girl, kind of sweet, nice, so when I dressed and acted like her, people automatically wrote me off as...."

"Dumb?" Diego nodded while scrunching up his lips.

"I don't know about that..."

"Who's Paris Hilton?" Chase asked. "Doesn't she do gossip columns or something?"

"That's *Perez*," Diego leaned forward. "And that's a man."

"Paris Hilton," Paige seemed to pick her words carefully. "She used to have a reality show..."

"She's one of those white girls that did a sex tape," Jorge cut in. "You know, back when these things kept getting *accidentally* leaked on the Internet?"

"Yeah, because that narrows it down, Hernandez," Diego shot back. "That's like *every* celebrity in those days."

"And now," Chase added. "I don't think that's changed."

"Anyway," Paige said and waved her hand in the air. "The point is I looked like an unlikely suspect, which is perfect. I walk in, do the job, walk out and no one noticed. There was this one time …"

"Yes?" Jorge raised an eyebrow.

"It doesn't matter," Paige said coyly. "Let's just say I was on the roof of a building and had to take care of a….situation. Anyway, when I left, no one suspected a thing. They thought I was an ignorant tourist, another young woman trying to look like a celebrity. One woman even rolled her eyes when I stupidly asked if the man laying on the ground bleeding was 'sick or something'…"

With a huge grin on his face, Marco appeared enthralled by the story while the others were giving a sideways glance toward Jolene and Enrique, who appeared more involved in their conversation. Jorge took a deep breath, glanced at the clock, looked back at Paige who gave a slight nod.

"Well, this here, it was fun," Jorge spoke loudly, with a certain sharpness to his voice. "But it is getting late and it was a long fucking week."

"I hear you!" Diego replied and Marco gave an enthused nod while exchanging looks with Chase. "And next week, it will be even longer."

"Do not say that already," Jorge cringed at the comment. "This here it does not encourage me."

Jolene and Enrique appeared to suddenly be out of their haze, pulled back into reality as if both had just woken from a long nap.

"I thank you for everything," Jolene gestured toward the table full of glasses and beer bottles. "It was nice."

"Well, we had to have a going-away party," Paige spoke evenly.

"Yes, to see you off," Jorge spoke curtly. "But Jolene, there is something you should know."

"Yes," She spoke with a warm smile. "What is that?"

"You," Jorge gestured toward her. "You are not coming back."

It was as if someone threw a bucket of ice of her.

"What? I do not..."

"Jolene," Diego shot back. "We know."

"Know what?"

"I went through your bookkeeping," Chase replied bluntly. "All the expenses you wrote off..."

"Lot of creative accounting," Jorge replied but instead of looking at her face, he studied Enrique. He knew nothing.

"I....it was just some lunches...."

"And other stuff," Jorge reminded her without getting into the details. "Not just lunches."

Silence.

"I...you know, you are always giving the others..."

"Jolene, there is a difference between me giving something and you taking it."

"But you give Marco a house!"

"I *gave* Marco a house," Jorge reaffirmed noting his IT specialist was shrinking in his chair. "I did *not* give you one."

Jolene looked nervous while Enrique appeared confused.

"Did you think that no one here would notice?" Jorge asked. "That you would go away and we would let it slide?"

"But you buy..."

"Jolene," Diego shot back. "Jorge bought Marco a house because of everything he's done for us...same with Makerson but you, you're just earning back your loyalty."

"It is because I'm a woman."

"It is because you were disloyal," Paige jumped in. "Don't use the woman card. It's not going to work. You betrayed us. It takes time to find your way back from that."

"And Jolene," Jorge sharply reminded her. "You were lucky to even get that chance..."

A chilling quietness filled the room. Tears filled Jolene's eyes and she bit her lip.

"You did not ask," Jorge reminded her. "You took. And from what we have found on the books, you took...and took...and took some more..."

Enrique moved away from Jolene, something Jorge noted and quickly addressed.

"And you," he turned toward Enrique. "I know you did not know. But I would suggest is that if this is who you want to be with, you take her by the hand, right now and you walk out of here while you still can."

Enrique opened his mouth and abruptly closed it again.

"You, my friend, you are still good with me," Jorge assured him. "But this one here, she is not."

Jolene started to cry.

"I will be taking over this house you bought…with the company money, Jolene," Jorge insisted. "So your home, it is now in Mexico and I suggest you keep out of my sight."

"But, I…" Jolene attempted to speak but couldn't as the tears ran down her cheek.

"Consider this a win, Jolene," Jorge insisted. "Most, they do not get one chance, let alone two….you're a very, *very* lucky woman."

CHAPTER 22

"Does this make me Miguel's Godmother *and* Godfather?" Diego asked as the two men sat alone in the VIP room after the others had left. The table before them was now empty and the room's silence, eclipsed by the sound of music and voices in the main bar. "Since Jolene is gone?"

"Diego, I do not think about such things," Jorge shook his head before finishing the beer he had nursed for the last hour. "But if you wish?"

"I do," Diego insisted and sat up a little straighter. "It's important that Miguel not be tied down with gender identity."

"Diego, it is late and I don't know what you're talking about," Jorge said with a yawn and paused for a moment before continuing. "But tell me something, how do you feel about this? What happened with Jolene? She is your sister."

"But you're my brother," Diego reminded him as his eyes widened. "That means something to me."

"I know this, Diego," Jorge attempted to reassure him. "But what I mean, is that your sister....she will never be welcomed back into our *familia*. I know that in the past, I have let things slide but the trust, it is broken."

"I know," Diego spoke with shame in his voice. "I am sorry for that."

"Diego, it is not you."

"I know, I know," He waved his hand in the air. "But she's my *sister*. I feel like she's kind of my responsibility."

"Jolene, she just decided to take," Jorge countered. "I do not know how much she has taken that we have not discovered but it is unsettling. I can honestly say, I'm surprised by what Chase found."

"Hey, maybe give him the house," Diego suggested with a spark in his voice. "You got it anyway, he's *always* been loyal and if he hadn't gone over the books…"

"This is true," Jorge nodded and felt a spark of energy with the suggestion. "That is a good point, Diego, perhaps I will talk to him about it tomorrow."

"Can I come?" Diego's eyes bulged out. "You know I love surprises."

"You can."

"But I gotta tell you," Diego continued as he shook his head. "I don't know what will happen with Enrique. Jolene, she don't have a great track record with men."

"Of course, it will go up in flames," Jorge predicted. "Already tonight, I could see that Enrique was concerned. He did not know about this."

"He only sees what Jolene wants him to see."

"And this could be problematic," Jorge insisted. "Because as much as I like to think we are through with Jolene, I cannot help but predict that she will show up at our door again."

Diego didn't reply but the two shared a silent look.

The following morning, Paige helped to bring some clarity to the situation over breakfast.

"Enrique will keep her wrapped up for a while," She assured him. "Even when the relationship goes down the drain, he'll feel obligated to keep her out of your sight because he'll fear that if she gets in your crosshairs, it'll also affect him."

"Maybe we should hold him to that," Jorge suggested. "It is always good to have leverage."

"But having said that," Paige added. "I don't think we've seen the last of her."

Jorge narrowed his eyes and the two shared a look.

"Diego," He changed the subject. "He has made an interesting suggestion. He would like to give her stolen house to Chase."

"The stolen house?" Paige quipped. "Well, you could sell it later and let Chase stay there meanwhile if he's not interested in keeping it."

"Why wouldn't he want a free house?"

"Well, he didn't exactly pick it out…"

"I do not think he will care," Jorge replied. "If he wants it, it is his but tell me, Paige, was Jolene right? Am I sexist?"

"You can be but I don't think that was the case here," She corrected him. "Jolene sunk pretty low with us at one time and although she'd made strides to find her way back, I'll give her that, I don't know that she was the same level as the others who's been consistent. Plus, they didn't just *take* a house. It was given to them like you pointed out. If this was a concern, she should've brought it up."

"This is true."

"That was her backpedaling when she was caught," Paige muttered as she stood up with a coffee cup in hand.

"Caught?" Maria piped up as she walked into the room. "I didn't *do* anything."

"You better not have done anything, Maria," Jorge gave her a warning look.

"*Papa,* I've been good as gold," She reminded him as she plunked down her backpack in the middle of the kitchen floor. "Other than hiding Cameron, I haven't got in shit at school or anything."

"Let's keep it that way."

Maria rolled her eyes as she met Paige on the way back from the coffee pot, causing her stepmom to smile.

"So who was caught?" Maria sang out as she poured herself a coffee causing Paige and Jorge to exchange looks.

"It is….a work thing, Maria," Jorge said and watched his wife shrug.

"Just tell her," Paige muttered as she sat down.

"Tell me what?" Maria asked as she mixed spoonfuls of sugar in her coffee.

"We a….we recently put Chase at the warehouse," Jorge started and watched his daughter rejoin them at the table. "This here, Maria, it is family business and you cannot repeat it."

"I know."

"Not to anyone including your *gay* boyfriend."

"I won't."

"Ok, well," Jorge glanced at Paige who gave him a small smile while Maria sat down with interest in her eyes. "Chase, he discovered that Jolene has stolen from the company."

"What??" Maria's eyes widened in exaggerated shock.

"Believe me, we were as surprised as you," Paige gently added.

Maria's face seemed to deflate as she shrunk in the chair.

"I could not believe...I did not think she would do that," Jorge spoke honestly. "But I guess sometimes, we just never know."

Maria mouthed the word 'wow' but she remained silent, still in shock.

"She stole a lot too," Paige added. "at first we thought it was just a dinner here or there..."

"Which would be fine," Jorge shrugged, "within reason."

"How much did she take?" Maria quietly asked.

"She bought a house and charged it to the company," Jorge replied.

"A house?" Maria asked as her head dropped back and her mouth fell open.

"Ok, that is enough drama," Jorge grinned. "It is a lot, I agree."

"How could she do that?"

"Maria, I do not know."

"She felt underappreciated," Paige replied. "But if that was the case then she should've discussed it with Jorge or me....or *someone*, she didn't have the right to take what she wanted."

"Wow!" Maria took a drink of her coffee. "That is *so* wrong."

"And Maria, you know how I feel about loyalty."

"You feel it's the most important thing, *Papa.*"

"This is true."

"And Chase found it?" She perked up.

"Yes, it was Chase."

"He's so smart."

"Yes, he is Maria.

"And loyal..."

"Yes."

"You should give him a raise."

"I am potentially working on something," Jorge nodded. "I have a meeting with him a little later this morning. We have to figure out some things now that Jolene is gone."

"So, isn't she leaving town with Enrique?" Maria asked skeptically.

"Yes, sometime today."

"Does Enrique know what she did?"

"Yes."

Maria wrinkled her nose.

Jorge reached for his phone. Glancing through his messages, he took a deep breath.

"I see that Athas is making another announcement later today about his new opiate law," Jorge moved his finger over the phone screen. "This here is good especially since the docuseries starts this weekend."

"So boring," Maria shrugged. "Why can't you like, make movies, or something?"

"Ah Maria, maybe one day," Jorge grinned at his daughter.

"Let's see how this series goes first," Paige pointed out.

"I could help pick out a script," Maria suggested as her stepmother stood up from the table. "I'm just saying…"

"I'll keep that in mind Maria," Jorge replied.

"I'm going to check Miguel," Paige said as she headed out of the room. "He's been a little too quiet. He might be destroying the entire upstairs."

"Ah! He's so bad lately," Maria complained as Jorge stood up.

"It is a stage."

"*Papa,*" Maria said before letting out a loud sigh. "I still can't believe Jolene did that to you."

"Maria, I wish I could explain but I can't."

"That's not cool."

He leaned over and kissed her on the top of her head.

"Kiss Miguel and Paige for me."

"I will."

Heading toward the door, he glanced at his phone again.

What time did you want to meet today?

This was from Chase.

Later, I am meeting with the series guys now. Also, we must wait until Paige is free to join us.

Satisfied, Jorge slid his phone in his pocket and swung open the door to find Jolene on the other side. She was crying.

CHAPTER 23

"Sorry I'm late," Jorge said as Tony led him to his living room where the series was being edited. Andrew was already there, watching the monitors on the large desk. "I had a little situation at home."

"Do I need to turn up the fires at the crematorium?" Andrew called out over his shoulder and Jorge attempted to hide his smile. The two men shared a look while Tony showed no reaction.

"You are fine, just where you are," Jorge commented with humor in his voice as he got closer to the working area.

"Have a seat," Tony pointed toward the mini office. "can I get you a coffee?"

"Nah, I'm good," Jorge replied as he sat beside Andrew, casually glancing at one of the monitors. "So, this here, are you editing some footage?"

"Yes, it takes so much time," Tony answered as the three men sat at the long desk which held a series of monitors, one lone laptop and clutter of papers, books and, stray notes scattered all over its surface. "That's why Andrew is helping out when he can."

"And your YouTube show," Jorge said as Andrew swung around in his chair. "That there, it is good. Especially since you interviewed Tony…"

"I know, right? The beauty of that is he shared the interview on his channel so we both picked up more subscribers plus we got them interested in the series."

Impressed, Jorge nodded.

Andrew pointed toward the monitor. A young woman's face was frozen on the screen.

"And what you're looking at here, is one of the first people I interviewed. Her name is Sarah and she's on the streets."

"Except, she didn't start that way," Tony jumped in enthusiastically. "She had a car accident, was prescribed all this massively strong shit and well, lost everything because she got addicted, lost her job...."

"It's fucking crazy how fast it can happen too," Andrew added. "Like seriously, we checked out her story too. You wouldn't believe us if we showed you her Facebook page...well, her former Facebook page. It's not so much a priority anymore."

Leaning ahead, Andrew started to tap on the keys. The familiar site popped up and within seconds, Jorge was looking at the profile of a young, white woman who displayed images of everything from the prom to her first day at a well-known Toronto company. She looked happy, healthy, and full of life.

"And this is her now,"

An image of the same woman now had a shocking effect on him. Jorge felt like someone had kicked him in the stomach. She looked like an old lady, someone who had a long, hard life. She was frail, her eyes were dead and she had scabs all over her face.

"She's 25," Andrew said as if to answer a question Jorge had asked. "She's like my age, man."

Jorge took a deep breath and nodded.

"These Big Pharma drugs," Tony shook his head as he worked on his computer. "They're probably worse in many ways because they're prescribed when people are in so much pain that they don't care, they'll take anything. It's not like they're going to the club and want something to get fucked up and *knowingly* look to buy them, you know?"

"True," Jorge finally found his voice and nodded. "Is this what you are hearing?"

"Like, almost every time," Tony turned toward him. "I don't have many people tell me that they sought out pills randomly. It's usually doctor prescribed and it got out of control. Sometimes, it's people who were already addicts that transition to pills cause, well, quite honestly, they're easier to get."

"Yeah, if you got the right doctor," Andrew jumped in. "You're fucking *golden.*"

"Some people even fake injuries or hurt themselves on purpose to get the drugs," Tony added. "I had this one chick that was so desperate she slammed her hand in the car door."

Andrew made a face.

"So, make sure," Jorge said. "All paths lead to Big Pharma. Avoid the street drug angle unless it is the user going from the pills to find something on the street."

"That's usually the case," Tony nodded. "They start with the pills, their prescription ends or isn't lasting so they look for something else."

"I have an idea," Jorge began. "What if, for the last episode, we decide to rally these people together, start a class action suit?"

Andrew raised his eyebrows, a grin formed on his lips as he nodded.

"Like a surprise ending…"

"Oh, I *like* that," Tony commented as he glanced at Andrew, who was nodding. "That would shake things up. If this show is a hit, it shouldn't be hard to find a lawyer to get involved."

"Plus, you got something to keep up anticipation for next season," Jorge reminded them. "People, they are going to want to see what happens behind the scenes."

"This will get us news coverage," Tony spoke thoughtfully. "You got a knack for the marketing, Jorge."

"I got a knack for a lot of things," He replied arrogantly than gestured toward the computer. "So you think dropping one show at a time will pay off?"

"Yup, I think this is the best way to do it," Tony commented. "If you drop the shows all at once, people will forget about you as soon as they watch them. We don't want that here."

"Oh for sure!" Andrew jumped in. "People are already talking. Plus, that fucking title, it's catchy."

"*Eat the rich before the rich eat you,*" Jorge grinned and nodded. "And when you think about it, that makes the class action suit an ideal ending. We are doing exactly what our title says."

Tony nodded enthusiastically.

"But we gotta find a lawyer without word getting out."

"I know someone," Tony spoke up. "I got a friend…if he can't help, he'll know who can."

"And they gotta keep their mouths shut too," Andrew threw in. "That whole, client, lawyer confidentiality thing, right?"

Jorge nodded.

"This here," He finally spoke. "It is going to be huge."

Later that morning, Jorge told Makerson more details on the series. The editor jotted down notes while the two men sat alone at the back of a coffee shop.

"So, of course, the lawyer thing, keep that to yourself," Jorge muttered and looked around. "It will be very explosive."

"Yes, and once you announce it," Makerson added. "You know a hell of a lot of other people will join in, from across the country."

"That's what I'm counting on."

"You guys are killing two birds with one stone."

"Best way to do it."

"So, the first show," Makerson said and looked up. "Did you see it yet?"

"It's fucking cool," Jorge nodded. "Very rock 'n roll in the beginning so it captures you. Then, we get into the real stories of how much these companies are making year after year and the tax breaks…"

"With Athas now ripping that away from them," Makerson said appearing amused. "You sure know how to line up your ducks."

"I do."

"So, he's coming down hard on them at the perfect time."

"And once this here is out," Jorge added. "It is possible he may have to come down harder again, if the people, they make it a controversy."

Makerson continued to look amused as he reached for his coffee.

"Wow, don't fuck with Jorge Hernandez."

"That is what I keep telling people," Jorge replied with a sinister look in his eyes. "And eventually, they listen."

"So have you seen any of the other footage?"

"Yes, I have seen some," Jorge confirmed. "It is quite disturbing. The people, their stories…"

"I can imagine. And you got doctors talking?"

"Yes, the ones who want this to stop."

"I saw Andrew's YouTube channel," Makerson said. "I'm keeping a close eye on it. It's roughly done yet, it's almost like he knows what he's doing but he makes it look that way on purpose. Like he's an amateur."

"Of course, this is part of the plan."

"I gotta hand it to you," Makerson shook his head. "You got this one."

It wasn't even noon yet and Jorge was back in his SUV and glancing at his phone. Before getting into traffic, he called Chase.

"Good morning," He answered his phone. "I heard you had an unexpected visitor earlier?"

"Oh, you were talking to Paige?" Jorge asked.

"Maria."

"Oh yes, of course," Jorge laughed. "She does enjoy the drama."

"How did that go? She said you pulled her in your office."

"I will tell you," Jorge said as he glanced around. "How about, we meet in the boardroom..you, me, Paige and Diego?"

"Sounds good."

"Maybe get some food."

"Pizza?"

"If you could."

"I'll order it in," Chase replied. "I'll call the troops together."

"Perfect," Jorge said. "Because we got a lot to talk about."

CHAPTER 24

"You know Big Pharma's gonna retaliate?" Chase asked as he reached for a slice of pizza while giving Jorge a glance across the boardroom table. "They're gonna be pissed and try to turn this around on you."

"Let them try," Jorge coolly replied as he took a drink of coffee before glancing at the pizza slices on his plate. "I can *take* them."

Beside him, Paige let out a giggle before taking a bite of her pizza as she raised her eyebrows.

"It will be a fucking bloodbath if they do," Diego shot out from the end of the table as he picked at his gluten-free pizza.

"Literally," Chase muttered.

"It doesn't matter because the public will see the truth," Paige calmly reminded them. "They'll have a difficult time trying to crawl back under their rock."

Just then, Marco entered the room with a bright smile on his face.

"The staff," He pointed toward the room down the hallway. "They're excited about the food."

"I realized when I ordered that we'd seem like dicks if we were here eating pizza and not giving them any," Chase spoke as he chewed.

"Hey, these here extra expenses, I do not mind," Jorge spoke calmly as he eyed the food on his plate. "It is the houses, the spying expenses.... you know, this kind, I do not like so much."

Marco let out a short laugh as he approached the table and peeked into the various boxes, choosing a vegetarian slice.

"Fuck, no joke!" Diego muttered.

"Sir, that was….very…bold," Marco seemed to search for the right word as he sat down. "But Chase, you have a new home because of it."

Chase didn't reply but merely blushed, looking down at the food. He had been overwhelmed by the kind gift.

"Benjamin is scouring the books to see if there was anything else," Diego referred to the companies leading accountant. "He thinks that's it."

"It better fucking be it," Jorge swallowed his food and took another large bite, the taste of sauce and cheese filling his mouth.

"So, she came to your place this morning," Chase asked as he reached for another slice. "Does she have a death wish?"

Jorge merely raised his eyebrows.

"She does have nerve, I'll give her that," Paige muttered as she reached for a napkin. "Even Maria was horrified when she saw her there."

"What the fuck did she say?" Diego narrowed his eyes, a piece of pizza tilted in his hand, almost as if it was about to fall on the plate.

"She just tells me that she was sorry," Jorge said with a shrug and glanced toward Paige. "She attempted to explain again, trying to justify what she has done. I finally say, 'Jolene, it is better to leave while you're ahead.' I did not wish to talk to her anymore."

No one spoke.

"She got a lot of nerve," Diego complained between bites.

"So she's gone?" Chase asked Jorge.

"Leaving today."

"*Adi-fucking-ous.*" Diego spoke dramatically swinging his arm in the air. "I can't handle this anymore."

"Well, no one blames you," Paige quickly reminded him. "This isn't your fault."

"Yeah, but she's my sister…"

"Diego, it is fine," Jorge shook his head. "We are not in Mexico. I am not going to react as violently toward her disloyalty as I would have at one time."

"Can we stop talking about Jolene?" Chase asked and shook his head. "I feel like she's created enough headaches for us in the last few years."

"That's what she does," Jorge agreed. "But we must move on. She is going to start a new life today and we have other things to worry about."

"So, I've been looking at some people to run the crematorium," Chase spoke up. "I got a few candidates."

"Can we trust them?"

"I think so," Chase shrugged. "I mean, it's just the office part. We have Andrew to manage his side."

"We need everything clean…"

"It will be once the bookkeeping issue is sorted out at the warehouse."

"And the bar? Warehouse?" Jorge asked. "We gotta get everything covered."

"Yeah, those I'm not sure about," Chase admitted. "I think maybe we have someone to look after the warehouse, a long-time, reliable employee and I'll go back to the bar?"

Jorge thought for a moment.

"It doesn't matter," Chase continued, glancing between Paige and Jorge. "Whatever you think."

"I wonder if you should oversee the three?" Paige asked. "But then if something comes up…."

"Yeah, that's what I'm a little worried about," Chase replied. "The 'if something comes up' part."

"Where are things more apt to happen?" Paige asked.

"The bar," Jorge answered. "It is occasionally the warehouse but…"

"If that's the case, we'll take care of it."

"We need someone who will keep their mouth shut," Jorge insisted.

"Make whoever sign a contract stating complete confidentiality," Paige suggested. "I'm thinking there's a way around it."

"There always is," Chase replied while Marco watched with interest, before speaking.

"Sir, if there is someone you want to manage anything," He spoke with wide eyes. "Let me look into this person first. I will see if they are trustworthy."

"Definitely," Paige agreed.

"Ok, so then, Chase," Jorge looked across the table. "What is it you want to do?"

"Honestly, I don't know," He replied. "I kind of like the bar but I also want to make sure everything else is running smoothly."

"Then maybe you should oversee the three as Paige said."

Chase considered the option.

"Pick a place for the office." Jorge said. "And keep an eye on everything."

"Do we even need the bar anymore?" Paige wondered. "We originally had it to…"

"Hmm….good point," Jorge thought. "But it is named after Maria, so she would be heartbroken if I sold it."

"Maybe she can one day run it," Marco suggested.

"I do like that," Jorge nodded.

"She'll turn it into a dance club," Chase started to laugh and Paige joined in.

"This here, it is probably true," Jorge grinned. "But hey, if we tell her this, maybe it will influence her to study hard, to have better goals than these silly 'being famous' dream she has now"

"It's not as bad but she's talking about it again lately," Paige added. "With Cameron…"

"Yes, he is not the influence she needs," Jorge decided. "But my Maria, she does not have many friends."

"Let her have it," Paige muttered.

"So," Diego jumped in and changed the topic. "This new series starts tonight?"

"It will be streaming tonight," Jorge confirmed.

"I see Makerson released a story about it," Chase threw in as he reached for his third slice of pizza. "Lots of comments."

"I bet," Jorge nodded.

"I saw that too," Paige replied. "Everything looks very positive so far."

"People, they must be educated on what these companies do," Jorge insisted. "They do not care about their health, they care about money."

"That title, sir, I love that title."

Jorge nodded toward Marco.

"I'm thinking of having the season end with us announcing that the people featured in the docuseries will participate in a class-action lawsuit," Jorge informed the group. "But this here, it does not leave this room."

"This sir, it has happened in the US already," Marco assured him. "The people, they won."

"And they will here too," Jorge spoke assuredly.

"That's fucking awesome," Diego jumped in. "We got 'em."

"But, as I said," Chase reminded him. "They're going to retaliate."

"We should consider how they'll do so," Paige spoke evenly.

"They'll say Jorge paid for this," Diego insisted. "Because he did."

"What? I can't have an interest in supporting independent artists?"

"It looks suspicious," Paige suggested.

"Let it," Jorge finished off his second slice of pizza. "This here is not a concern to me. I will remind the public that they're trying to distract them from the facts and the facts are that they are killing people."

"We don't want to rock the boat too hard," Paige suggested and they shared a look. "We don't want them digging too far."

"Like those fancy commercials say," Jorge pointed out. "If you plan to dig where you shouldn't be, make sure you know where the live wires are first because you might just get a shock."

CHAPTER 25

"You didn't exactly tell them the whole truth about Jolene yesterday," Paige spoke quietly the following morning as she glanced toward the stairs. Maria could be heard singing along to music upstairs as she got ready for school. "Do you think that's a good idea?"

"I would not have mentioned she was here if it hadn't been for Maria telling Chase," Jorge admitted as he leaned in close to his wife. "But, *mi amor,* sometimes it is best that we don't know everything. This here is one of those cases."

Paige nodded as Jorge turned on his phone followed by his laptop.

"She is gone and that is all they have to know."

Maria's music was suddenly turned off and her feet could be heard scurrying toward the stairs as the couple shared a look.

Jorge's phone beeped and he glanced through his messages.

"Ah! Beautiful!" He exclaimed as Maria walked into the room and dropped her backpack in the middle of the floor. "The ratings, they are looking wonderful."

"Is that for your show?" Maria sang out as she headed for the table. "I watched some of it but it was kinda boring once the doctors and other people started talking."

"Maria, they are talking about our corrupt world," Jorge informed her and continued to scan through his messages. "And it seems, many were watching because we have excelled our original expectations for the show."

"That's great!" Paige exclaimed as Jorge sat down the phone and began to tap on his computer. "Is there anything online?"

Of course, they knew there would be. Makerson had written a review about the Toronto-based documentary series, after scouring social media for reactions that would only enhance the series profile. It was a stellar reaction with comments like 'this fall's hottest docuseries tears the roof off to show the evil corporations we've blindly trusted with our health'. If it weren't for the Hernandez family of companies supporting the paper, this mightn't have been approved however, his money was as valuable as any other advertiser.

"Wow, *Papa*," Maria spoke gleefully as she glanced over his shoulder. "Look at the Twitter comments he added in the article. Your show is famous!"

"Maria, you know I have no interest in fame," Jorge shook his head. "Even when I was in politics, this here, it did not interest me."

"But that's so cool!" Maria spoke dreamily as she headed for the coffee pot. "I wish I was famous."

"'…this comes on the heels of the prime minister's announcement that he's about to increase taxes on pharmaceutical companies, insisting that money will be used to help those who are suffering from addiction after the prescribed use of their opiate-based medications…'"

"Yes, I see that," Jorge glanced at the passage that Paige was reading. "It *is* very interesting timing."

"Oh…they're not going to have a good morning when they see this," Paige pointed out a specific passage in the article that named a Toronto-based company.

"Their PR company will be spinning their usual nonsense," Jorge predicted with a sadistic grin on his face. "Let them spin."

"It says here," Paige pointed at another article on social media. 'That you've 'started a conversation that Canadians desperately need to have before this epidemic gets any further out of hand.'"

"Unfortunately, the previous government," Jorge said as he closed his laptop. "They did not wish to ruffle feathers but Athas, he has seen the problems first hand when he worked as a counselor. He knows what happens when people get addicted to these so-called *safe* medications."

"So, *Papa,*" Maria started as she returned to the table with a cup of coffee in one hand and a bowl of yogurt and berries in the other. She sat beside Jorge. "Why are they allowed to sell these pills if they're dangerous?"

"Because, Maria, they're rich, white men who think they can do whatever they want."

"Jorge!" Paige gave him a look from across the table.

"Paige, it is true," Jorge spoke sheepishly and shrugged. "Maria, she is a teenager now and it is time she knows the truth about the real world." He pointed toward the door. "We do not want to think certain people get ahead because they have money or because of the color of their skin but… unfortunately, this is the reality."

Paige tightened her lips but didn't say anything.

"I am not saying that all white people are bad," Jorge insisted and turned toward his daughter. "They take a lot of things for granted. This here is one of them."

"White privilege," Maria said as she reached for her coffee. "We were talking about it in school the other day. This huge argument broke out and it was weird cause it was mostly white kids arguing with other white kids."

"It is a rich school, so there would be."

"Jorge," Paige gave him a warning look. "I don't want Maria to think this is always the case. There's a lot of white people who don't necessarily have an advantage."

"Like poor people?" Maria asked as she dug into her yogurt.

Jorge suddenly wished he hadn't brought up the topic, recognizing that he didn't want to give his daughter the wrong impression.

"The point is," Jorge said as he put his hand up in the air, "is that rich, white men have run this country for a long time and they have done so to their advantage. They do not like it when someone like me comes along and shakes things up. And here I am."

"If there's a lesson here for you, Maria," Paige calmly added. "It's that he said rich, white *men*. Unfortunately, the world hasn't quite caught up to the fact that women are on equal ground."

"Like, I know what you mean," Maria sat up straight. "Because even my drama teacher last year said that a lot of leading women roles in

Hollywood is the wife or girlfriend to the 'real' star. Just a secondary character but that's kind of changing…"

"Maria, I have told you again and again that those Hollywood directors and producers are pigs," Jorge lectured and his daughter rolled her eyes and looked away. "If you do not believe me, watch the news sometime."

"I know, *Papa*, it's in my entertainment news too," Maria shook in her head. "They take advantage of women in the industry."

"And get away with it," Jorge added abruptly until he saw his daughter's face and immediately pushed his point. "Maria, this is why you always have to be strong, no matter what you do in the future. You cannot let anyone think that you are in a powerless position. I do not care if you are serving coffee in one of those shops or CEO of a company, you are powerful. Do not ever forget it."

Paige's eyes softened and she gave an approving nod.

"Which reminds me," Jorge thought back to the previous day. "your name came up in our meeting yesterday."

"Me?" Maria perked up. "What did you say?"

"We were talking about the businesses and who will run what…" Jorge began as he backed away from the table, then stopped. "I was not sure what to do about the *Princesa Maria* and considered selling it."

"Ah!" Maria's eyes grew sad.

"But I will not," Jorge continued and saw the relief on her face. "We were saying…perhaps one day, this is a business you would want to run?"

His daughter's eyes doubled in size as her mouth fell open.

"I take this to mean yes?"

"*Papa!!* I could do so many exciting things at the bar," Maria jumped up from her chair and her body began to vibrate. "I could have fancy parties, with celebrities and…I could have dance competitions and maybe tape a show there and…*Oh my God!* I can't wait to tell Cameron! He will be so pumped."

"Maria, please," Jorge pointed toward her chair. "Relax for a moment, please calm down. We are talking about the future, not tomorrow."

"I know," She continued to speak excitedly as she sat back down, dancing in her chair. "But that's so cool, *Papa!* I have so many ideas. Can I make changes to the bar?"

"Maria, it will be your bar to do as you wish," Jorge insisted. "But first, you must remember, it is not yet. I hope that you learn what you need to run a bar. It isn't just planning parties and the fun things, you have to know the financial side of things, marketing…there is so much."

"*Papa,* can I spend a day at the bar with Chase so he can teach me this stuff?" Maria asked with wide eyes and Jorge noted his wife attempted to hide her smile at the end of the table. "I mean, I know he can't have me do everything but you know, like learn the basics…"

"I think that could be arranged," Jorge nodded. "If he says he does not mind."

"Of course he won't mind!" Maria clapped her hands together. "Oh, this will be so awesome!"

"Now, Maria," Jorge continued. "Again, this will not be right away but it does give you time to think about what you need to know."

"And Chase can tell you the kind of courses you might want to focus on," Paige added. "So you can plan."

Maria nodded vigorously, her eyes full of light. It made Jorge smile.

"Perhaps," he continued. "Next summer, you can do a little job there. You will be 14, I think you can legally work…"

"If we sign off on it…" Paige quietly added.

"Of course, yes," Jorge nodded. "Maybe some little job while the bar is closed, of course, like decorate for events, maybe help clean up, put orders away…."

"I think that would be great," Paige nodded. "Learn everything about it."

Jorge turned to see his daughter's reaction. There were tears in her eyes.

"Maria, this here is good news," Jorge said as he turned in his chair and leaned in to hug her, giving her a quick kiss. "Do not cry."

"I know," Maria sniffed. "I'm just so excited. I can't believe you're giving me the club! That's so cool!"

"Of course, Maria," Jorge said before kissing her again. "You are a strong, powerful woman and you will make it a huge success."

On the other side of the table, Paige wiped a tear from her eye.

CHAPTER 26

"Beyond excited," Jorge admitted as he and Diego walked into the empty conference room, closing the door behind them. "I tell her about the club because I thought, you know, one day she might be interested in running it. Of course, I did not anticipate her reaction. I thought she actually might find the idea boring since it is not this celebrity world she is infatuated with."

"That's a phase," Diego waved a hand in the air as the two men sat in their usual spots. "Maria's smart. The older she gets, the more she will see it for what it is."

"Let us hope so," Jorge shook his head and took a deep breath. "I will admit, I do not like my daughter being in the spotlight. I fear that this will make her more vulnerable."

"Maybe you should tell her that," Diego suggested as he turned off his phone, and Jorge did the same. "Then she knows you aren't just being a hardass."

"I'm her father," Jorge reminded him. "It is my job to be a hardass."

"Well, at least she'd know why you're discouraging her."

"I mean, it isn't just for that reason," Jorge confessed. "I do think that it is fake and ridiculous too. The celebrities, with their 10 hours of makeup, fake tans, fake hair, fake tits, fake nails….I do not want my daughter to become a moronic Barbie doll."

"I don't think that's gonna happen," Diego reminded him. "But you know, this club thing will throw *that* off course."

"She is already planning it as if it is tomorrow," Jorge shook his head. "It is a big deal for me. I love seeing her excited over something that isn't acting or music…or whatever the fuck she's into lately."

"Plus she gets to work with Chase," Diego grinned. "You know that's a big part of it."

"And that is fine," Jorge shrugged. "Chase can tell her that she needs to work hard in school, what she needs to focus on. This here is the reason I suggested it to her. I want her to have a focus, to have goals and this will hopefully make her study harder. I pay a lot for her education and I hope that she takes advantage of it."

"The girl's gonna make it into a whole other thing," Diego said with a smirk.

"This here, it might be good."

A knock on the door interrupted their conversation. Makerson stood on the other side. Jorge waved for him to come in.

"Good morning," He said as he entered the room, his laptop bag swung over his shoulder. "You must be happy with the buzz about the series."

"I am thrilled," Jorge said but lacked the conviction in his words, causing Diego to grin, raising an eyebrow. "When Big Pharma squirms, an angel grows a set of wings."

"Is that how it works?" Makerson laughed as he sat across from Jorge.

"Yeah, we got a real angel right here," Diego mocked as he tilted his head toward Jorge.

"Ah, Diego, I certainly wasn't talking about me," Jorge said and leaned back in his chair. "I see that the vultures are hovering this morning."

"If you mean the media, then yes," Makerson replied as he opened his laptop bag and pulled out a tablet. "This series is creating a lot of push back especially with Athas making his announcements for Big Pharma. It's perfect timing because the public is behind his decision, which means there's a lot of PR people losing their shit trying to find a way to make themselves not look like pillaging assholes."

Jorge merely nodded as he leaned his head against his hand.

"Yes, well I'd like to see how they plan to do that," Diego piped up. "They come out looking like they'd whore out their mother for a fucking dime."

"Don't think they won't, Diego," Jorge muttered.

"Well, we do have a little pushback," Makerson tapped on his tablet and turned it around to show a statement made by one of his nemesis in the pharmaceutical industry. Jorge leaned in to watch the short clip.

"I want to remind you this is brought to you by the same people who believe in coffee enemas, anti-vaxxers, and potions made up of essential oils and spices from your cupboard. Do you really want to entrust these people to your health matters? We have science backing us up. Do they?"

"How does a series about how these scumbags killing people make us the voodoo witchdoctors," Diego ranted as he waved his hand toward the device. "They can't discredit us that easily."

"It was off the cuff and let's face it," Makerson turned the device back around "Makes them look like even bigger assholes."

"Yes, they are trying to say cannabis is one of these potions," Jorge said and rolled his eyes. "But we *do* have science backing us. And pot isn't killing people."

"They're grasping at straws," Makerson tapped on his device. "But you might want to keep your boy that's doing the documentary hidden away because these guys don't fuck around."

"*I* don't fuck around," Jorge spoke abruptly. "And this, they know about me."

"That's true," Diego nodded vigorously. "But maybe we should get him security or something?"

"Maybe," Jorge considered. "I will talk to Tony later."

"I also saw another article that targeted you specifically," Makerson continued. "A rival newspaper and guess who their main advertiser is?"

Jorge and Diego exchanged looks.

"The editorial talked about the series and how it 'unfairly made the pharmaceutical industry look like the bad guys' when in fact they're only out to *help* people." Makerson mocked.

All three men laughed.

"And she referred to this series as 'the Jorge Hernandez baby' and talked about how you have so much money tied up in it."

"Well, I do but perhaps I just have an interest in filmmaking."

"And even if he was pushing it because of his own company," Diego boldly added. "What difference? How is that any different from what these assholes do?"

"Because, Diego, they're rich, white men, and no one is supposed to ever come up against them," Jorge suggested. "That is how it works, is it not?"

"I don't know if they're all white," Makerson shrugged. "But they sure as hell are rich."

"Well, my hope is a little less rich after I'm done with them."

"And last but not least," Makerson continued to tap on his device. "I got this short clip where someone is asking Athas if he watched the series."

Turning the iPad around, Jorge watched as a reporter shouted out a question that was barely audible as Athas walked toward a door. He stopped, turned, as if in a hurry but taking a moment for the question.

"I'm not familiar with this series, no," Prime Minister Athas lied. "But I will check it out when time permits."

Another inaudible question could be heard, with only the words 'changes' and 'direct' could be heard, with Athas automatically shaking his head.

"Any decisions made by our government regarding pharmaceutical companies reflect stats that were brought to my attention and my own, personal experience working as a counselor for almost 20 years here in Toronto. I know about the drug addiction issues because I've worked with these people," Athas reminded them. "I know what happens when lives are taken over by addiction and these people need help."

"These companies," He continued. "They aren't stepping up to help with this dire situation, even though they were given a chance so our government decided to find a way to make them accountable. We're increasing their taxes to make up for the funds needed to ensure that those who suffer from addiction can get the help they need."

Another inaudible question was asked to which, Athas shook his head.

"It's not fair that the taxpayers are stuck with the bill," Alec Athas bluntly replied. "Our health care is already stretched. The pharmaceutical industry is worth *billions*. It's time they chip in and help us with a problem that studies *prove* are often started with prescribed opiate medications. Thank you for your questions."

With that Athas rushed away and the video ended.

"I think that went rather well," Makerson mused as he shut off his device.

"Exactly as planned," Jorge agreed. "It looked like he was bombarded. This here, it is what we want."

"Now, what Big Pharma will likely do is strike back with stats against pot," Makerson pointed out. "Or saying it's not a fair representation. They have the resources to try to pull us under."

"Let them try," Jorge said as his eyes narrowed. "Let the fuckers…"

A knock at the door interrupted Jorge. Marco could be seen on the other side, a bright smile on his face, if not with some hesitation.

"Sir," He stuck his head in the door. "Can I come in?"

"Of course."

"I need to know," He started as he crossed the floor and sat down. "Your devices, they are turned off?"

"Yes, all are," Jorge answered and glanced around the table to see Diego nod and Makerson turn off his tablet.

"This is good sir, because what I am about to tell you," Marco said and hesitated. "It cannot leave this room."

"Is this about…" Jorge began to ask but Marco was already nodding vigorously.

"It is one of the pharmaceutical companies you asked me to check," Marco hesitated. "And sir, it is quite disturbing."

All eyes fell on Jorge as he slowly raised an eyebrow and nodded.

CHAPTER 27

"Well, this here, it changes everything," Jorge leaned back in his chair with a pompous grin on his lips. "We might have a new ending for our series."

"I would wait on that," Makerson put up his hand defensively. "This doesn't sit right with me."

"What? You don't think they're soulless monsters?" Diego attempted to challenge him. "These assholes at Big Pharma?"

"No, that's not what I mean," Makerson shook his head but directed his answer toward Jorge. "It's just that I've heard this story before and dug into it. The problem is if Big Pharma creates a disease or a superbug like what Marco found this morning, then it takes time to create the antidote or a vaccine and meanwhile, it's already run its course and they lose money. That's unless it's a massive virus that affects the world and economy."

Everyone exchanged looks but no one replied.

"But that's not to say they aren't doing it for other reasons," Makerson continued. "We assume it's because they want to find the cure, be the heroes, and make a shit ton of money but what if they have other motives?"

Intrigued, Jorge raised an eyebrow, considering his words.

"For example," Makerson continued as he dug further into the hornet's nest. "What if someone wanted to have a disease created to say, take out an enemy? It would be completely off the books, of course, but it doesn't mean it can't be done. Who are they going to hire to do this? Who has the most knowledge in this area?"

Jorge didn't reply but shot everyone a devious smile.

"You're not fucking thinking of doing this, are you?" Diego muttered as if no one else could hear. "I mean…"

"Diego, no I am…thinking," Jorge corrected him and returned his attention to Makerson. "That is the most intriguing theory I have heard in a long time. And one that makes sense when I think of some places in the world that have been most susceptible to these viruses. It can certainly take a lot of attention away from other issues that governments may not want people to notice…"

"And sir," Marco jumped in. "It has been known to have a huge effect on the economy in certain countries where it happens. Do you remember the…"

"Oh yes!" Diego cut in, his eyes widened as he pointed at Marco, who nodded vigorously. "That one! They took a hit over there."

"Exactly!" Marco shared Diego's excitement. "So if it suited a, let's say, a company, a *government*…"

"The oligarchs of the world," Makerson cut in while Marco nodded vigorously. "Don't forget those people. They run the show."

"Yes!" Marco spoke excitedly and then as if it suddenly hit him, his face began to deflate as he turned to Jorge. "Oh my God, sir, this means that some of the most powerful people in the world could be purposely making people sick, causing death simply as a way to control people."

"And don't forget," Diego cut in. "Taking our eyes off the prize."

"That there, it is a big one," Jorge added as he twisted his face. "That is a bigger one than you might know. People are easily distracted these days. Our world has been designed that way."

"So now what?" Makerson replied sorrowfully. "What do we do with this information?"

"We gather more information," Jorge suggested, looking at Marco. "If this is the case, then we must expose them. This here, it could be the final nail in their coffin."

"If they find out…." Makerson began.

"We must be careful," Jorge replied calmly. "But we must also be looking for more proof."

"We can blackmail them," Diego suggested.

"Don't think I have not thought of that already," Jorge replied. "A million thoughts, they have already crossed my mind."

"We should stop them," Marco was insistent. "Sir, these viruses, they kill many innocent people."

"They're victims in a sick game," Makerson nodded. "I could be wrong but…"

"No," Jorge shook his head. "You are not wrong. I am sure of it."

"Have you seen anything else?" Diego asked Marco. "That might point you in the same direction."

"No," Marco shook his head. "I just saw that they had the formula for one of the well-known viruses…that, it was enough for me, I wanted to tell you before your meeting ended."

"Marco, you will do more research," Jorge suggested. "I am wondering if there is any way to hack into other country's government information?"

"This sir, we must be careful of," Marco warned.

"We mightn't need to go that far," Makerson reminded them. "If he's found this much already, here in Canada, then he can probably find more. If not with Big Pharma, then the Dark Web or maybe a former employee? Maybe we can learn who's behind this?"

"That person is probably too scared to talk…or dead," Jorge reminded him. "We will leave this to Marco to see what he can learn but we must also see what the word is on the street."

The four men ended the meeting shortly after, with each on a mission to see what they could learn while Jorge headed across town to see Tony, who was editing new material.

"Great feedback on the show!" Tony spoke excitedly as he pointed toward his desk in the living room. "I'm just making some final edits on the next episode."

Jorge nodded and glanced around his apartment. Although he was listening, his mind was off in another place.

"Tell me something," Jorge spoke bluntly. "With your other work, you stepped on some toes?"

"Oh yes!"

"Any threats?"

"Mostly just pissy people making comments but you still got to watch your back."

"But the GMO one, that didn't cause issues?"

"Nah," Tony said after a moment's thought. "But you know, they countered everything I said anyway as if I was wearing a tinfoil hat."

Jorge nodded and glanced toward the other rooms.

"You live alone? No girlfriend? Kids?"

"No, it's a....long story," Tony seemed hesitant to go on.

"Look, I got no interest in your personal life," Jorge automatically replied as they sat down. "I hear enough about Andrew's already but you, we are jumping into some pretty dirty water. We may need to figure out something security-wise for you."

Tony looked awestruck but didn't reply.

"I'm not saying there's gonna be an ax hanging over your front door," Jorge relaxed in the chair. "But you got to be careful especially with this."

Pointing at the computers and papers on the desk, he noted that Tony was nodding.

"We can't have you vulnerable," Jorge continued. "You don't know who's lurking around."

"Those cameras," Tony pointed around the apartment. "I got them when I started ruffling feathers, to make sure no one broke in."

"I'm not just worried about them breaking in." Jorge shook his head. "And they can be hacked."

Tony appeared vulnerable, like a child looking for support.

"I can find you a different place," Jorge suggested. "I can get you security, whatever you need."

"I never thought about me," Tony admitted. "I thought about securing the information, which I have ways of doing."

"Think about securing *you* as well," Jorge commented. "Because I'm about to tell you some information that might make us vulnerable. Big Pharma, they cannot know that we know but yet, we must find more proof to back it up."

"How big is this?" Tony tilted his head, intrigued. "Because I thought the Class Action lawsuit was massive."

"Let us say that Andrew brought something to my attention that I kind of thought about but let slide," Jorge replied. "Because he tends to get a little too eager at times."

Tony grinned and nodded.

"We were talking about the viruses that come out of nowhere…"

"Oh!" Tony's eyes grew big. "I know, he mentioned that to me too. But I did some research and the companies aren't interested in jumping in because they can't be assured that it's a home run so there doesn't seem to be a link."

"They aren't being paid to find the cure," Jorge suggested. "Maybe they are paid to create the disease."

The realization had a similar effect on Tony as it had with the others. He went through a stage of shock, followed by horror.

"That's fucking sick," He finally replied. "If that theory is right…"

"This is what we are trying to find out," Jorge replied. "I got all my soldiers on it. But we must be discrete. We must be careful. And already, without this, you are shaking a lot of trees and things are starting to fall out. And Big Pharma, they don't want anything hitting the ground. They have worked too hard making sure it was hidden in the leaves."

"Fuck!" Tony took a deep breath and seemed to relax. "Ok, well, ok. I guess we need to learn more before we decide."

"For now, carry on with the next show and keep your ear to the ground…carefully."

He left Tony with a lot to think about but Jorge knew he wasn't the only one. Turning his phone back on, he sent a text to Paige.

CHAPTER 28

"It is, what you say," Jorge said as he leaned back on the couch and closed his eyes for a moment before slowly opening them again, turning toward his wife. He watched her carefully. "The perfect way to create a diversion, to create panic, to gain power over enemies. There are so many things going through my mind, Paige, you do not know."

She didn't reply. Instead, she studied her husband. He was exhausted from the work he was doing on the docuseries, uncovering much more than he originally expected. It was empowering and draining at the same time. The information was often like a dagger that threatened an entire industry and it was difficult to ignore the blood that dripped off its sides. There was a human cost to the massive fortunes that these companies made.

"It is disturbing," Jorge continued to speak as he stared off into space. "People, they are nothing to them. And me? I know that I used to be involved in selling drugs, I get this, I understand. But for me, it was a choice. People, they could decide if they wanted to use cocaine. It was for recreational purposes."

Paige nodded but remained silent.

"True, people died," Jorge continued, showing no emotion in his eyes but remaining introspective. "But again, this here, it was a choice. They knew what they were getting into. These pills, the ones the doctors give out, it is not the same. People do not understand the risks."

"If they do," Paige added. "It's fluffed out as if it's a slight possibility."

"Yes," Jorge nodded and sat up straight before turning his body in her direction. "But what I learned today, it is much worse. If they are behind these viruses…they can cripple a whole country, a whole world."

"If you can create the antidote, you can create the disease," Paige quietly suggested. "It's like the people who start a computer virus then get a job working for a big, high-tech company because of their knowledge on how to fix the same virus."

"It does not seem like a stretch," Jorge replied and looked away while Paige felt her mind drifting off, to another time and place, another lifetime ago.

The memory had faded but was still there. It was a tiny back room of a strip club in Europe. She had coaxed a young dancer to invite a rich businessman into the secret room for a private dance. Intimidated by Paige, the young woman complied, understanding that she had little choice in the matter. She acted normal. A popular Britney Spears song played in the background while the woman moved to the music, grinding herself against the man's crotch. He blindly watched her, lost in a state of arousal, he was unaware someone else was in the room. Paige was watching, waiting for her opportunity, a weapon in hand.

As the song neared the end, an extra zest of excitement filled the room like a heavy, intoxicating power that suggested that the man wasn't about to allow the dancer to collect her money and go; he had something else in mind. Paige could see the fear in the woman's eyes, even though it was merely a quick flash, a sense that she had been down this road before and desperately wanted to escape to a place where she was safe, a time when her life had been much simpler.

It was just as the man was roughly grabbing the dancer's arm with one hand while the other reached for her throat that Paige came out of the shadows. Fortunately, his lust prevailed over other senses, as he pulled the frightened woman closer like she were merely an object for his pleasure.

And then it happened. It was the stripper who jumped, not the man. He hadn't had a chance. The needle drove into him so fast that he barely had time to realize what happened and he was already growing weak. His hands dropped to his side allowing the frightened stripper a chance to back away.

Paige ignored her frantic tears, instead finishing the injection that would take this monster's power away forever.

"Do you know that movie," Paige began to speak in her usual calm voice as the man slumped forward in the chair and she pulled the needle out of his neck. "Pulp Fiction?"

She watched the stripper nodding as she wiped tears from her face and backed away. She began to shake.

"You know the scene where the guy uses the needle to save that woman's life?"

The stripper stopped crying, touching her hair, which ironically was similar to that of the actress they were referencing.

"This," Paige pointed toward the man who was sliding off the chair as death took his body. "is the complete opposite."

The stripper appeared shocked, yet transfixed by what happened.

"Don't worry, you won't get in trouble," Paige continued to speak calmly. "Someone is waiting outside to pull him into the alleyway. And when they find him, it will look like he died of natural causes. It happens, right?"

The stripper nodded as her eyes filled with awe.

"You might want to check his wallet before that though," Paige suggested. "Just don't leave any fingerprints. And this here, it never happened."

The stripper shook her head as Paige pulled some large bills from her pocket and threw them on a nearby chair. Noting that the stripper was staring at her gloves, the two women made eye contact and after a moment's consideration, Paige reached in the man's pocket herself, pulled out his wallet, and found some cash. She added it to the collection.

"And if you ever tell anyone what happened," Paige said as she returned the wallet to the man's pocket and stood up. "You know... I don't think it's necessary I tell you what will happen."

"I assure you," Paige was suddenly back to the present moment as she leaned forward to run her fingers through Jorge's hair. "It's not a stretch. It happens. More than you might think."

"It is not a surprise," Jorge said, his eyes suddenly full of vulnerability. "We are getting into some dangerous territory, *mi amor*, we must be careful."

"Will Tony be safe?"

"That is what I am working on."

"Should we have someone with him?"

"This is possible," Jorge thought for a moment. "I want to get him to a safe house for the remainder of the recording, have someone with him when he goes out, this kind of thing. He may be in danger if the wrong people learn what we know."

"We have to make sure they don't."

"I was thinking," Jorge started slowly. "We could contact that lady you worked for...."

Paige immediately shook her head as her heart raced.

"But I thought, she might be able to help us."

"I would rather she forget that I'm in her contact list," Paige managed to stay calm. "If she does us a favor, then she might want one in return."

"Ah, yes," Jorge nodded, accepting her answer. "I still do not feel comfortable with her being in your life."

That made two of them but Paige merely hid her worry behind a smile.

"Are you sure we can trust her?"

"I'm too valuable to get on my bad side."

Although it was true, Paige still preferred to avoid this woman from her past. She had already caused enough grief.

"*Mi amor*, did you say something about Athas coming over for a meeting?" Jorge asked, suddenly reminding her of the time.

"Oh yes, sorry," Paige shook her head and glanced at a nearby clock. "This entire morning flew by. Miguel has screamed 'Ma' 75 times in a row then laughed when I checked in on him."

Jorge grinned while his eyes filled with pride.

"I know," Paige put her hand in the air. "Be careful what you wish for."

"Well, you did hope, not that long ago," Jorge once again reminded her, pausing to laugh. "That he say 'ma' or 'mommy' and now..."

"I know....now, that's all he says," Paige replied as she took a deep breath and glanced toward the ceiling. "Thank God Juliana took him for a walk. I think we needed some space."

Jorge slowly pushed himself to the edge of the couch.

"And he's always throwing things at me," Paige continued. "Is that normal?"

"Maria," Jorge shook his head. "She did that too at his age. I remember taking a nap on the couch one day and feeling something hitting me on the side of the head. I almost pulled out my gun. Here is my Maria, looking at me like I was the devil then started to cry."

"Well, fortunately, she isn't that dramatic now," Paige quipped and Jorge laughed as he stood up.

"Yes, we are fortunate that this stage has ended," Jorge continued with the joke as he slowly moved. "Paige, I will go to my office. I must make some calls before Athas arrives."

"Sure."

After he was gone, Paige stood up and headed for the kitchen. A bright, pink object on the floor caught her attention on her way. It was Maria's lipgloss. She picked it up and was about to take it upstairs when the doorbell rang. It was Alec.

"Come in," She said as soon as she opened the door, noting security waited outside. "I didn't think you could escape the insanity."

"I have ways of keeping things off the books now," Alec replied with new confidence, while the look they shared wasn't. "The longer I'm in, the more I find out."

"I bet," Paige closed the door behind him. "So you're learning the secret passageways and hidden corners?"

"You might say that."

"Jorge is waiting for you in his office."

"By the way," Alec lowered his tone and glanced around as if he expected Jorge to spring out of nowhere. "Your husband is fucking me from both sides."

Paige showed no expression and finally shrugged.

"He's very talented."

Alec gave her a look that should've made her laugh but it didn't.

"He's in the office," She spoke dismissively. "I'll meet you both in a minute."

Alec stalked off to the office while Paige ran upstairs. She had already replaced one of Maria's lost lip glosses earlier that week and she wasn't about to do it again. It seemed a bit pricey for something so basic. Teenage life was very different from what her own had been.

In Maria's room, Paige noted that everything was tidy and organized. Placing the lip gloss on her dresser, she was about to walk away when something caught her eye. She turned back for another look.

CHAPTER 29

"*Más sabe el diablo por viejo, que por diablo.*" Jorge spoke with arrogance in his voice as Paige walked into the office. "This is what I tell you."

"Knowing that I don't speak Spanish," Athas reminded him with a sense of frustration in his voice causing a sadistic grin to cross Jorge's face. "Could you possibly translate?"

"He said, 'The devil is wise because he's old, not because he's the devil.'" Paige replied as she shut the door and crossed the room to join them at the desk. "I think he's trying to tell you he's old."

"Very funny, *mi amor,*" Jorge replied and winked at her, ignoring the glare he received from Athas. "But what I mean is that it is not only evil that dictates our world but wisdom. If the two are comfortable traveling together, they make for an interesting combination."

"What you just told me about the viruses being created on purpose," Athas started but followed it up with a loud sigh before continuing. "That's beyond evil as far as I'm concerned. I don't even know how I'm supposed to deal with this."

"Well, for now, you cannot deal with it at all," Jorge reminded him as he leaned on his desk. "Because you do not know. And neither do we for certain. It is still being investigated."

"It is highly likely," Paige added her two cents. "If you're capable of creating solutions, then for a price, you can also create the problem. There's a reason."

Athas merely shook his head and although Jorge, himself had been briefly crippled with the news, he didn't tolerate this from the prime minister.

"Athas, you must get it together," Jorge instructed with frustration in his voice. "When we know something for sure then we will see from there. For now, you might want to back off for a time since you've already ruffled the feathers of Big Pharma. At least, you know, give them a few days to recover after you've fucked them up the ass."

"May I remind you that this was your idea?" Athas asked as his eyes widened.

"May I remind you that this here is making you popular in the polls?" Jorge spoke condescendingly. "Before this week, people thought you were doing nothing. That your government was sitting on the fence and laying an egg but now, they see that you are doing something. That you might have balls."

Athas opened his mouth to reply but Paige jumped in before he could.

"Ok, let's take it down a notch," She suggested and glanced between the two men. "The point is that extra taxes on Big Pharma, insisting on more training for doctors on the issue of addiction, making it difficult to give out opiates, and surprise audits is enough for now. These things keep them on high alert so, Alec, you're distracting them while we look into this some more."

"This here is good," Jorge nodded. "It reassures people you are looking after them. That you are taking on the evil corporations and making them accountable."

"They're saying that 'Big Brother is watching' as if we're spying on everyone," Athas reminded them. "That I'm using this as a way to gain information on people's personal lives, what they're doing, that I can hold it against them if they're on certain medications and it violates their privacy."

"You're the motherfucking government," Jorge laughed. "You already know too much about the people in this country. As if this law changes anything. You could've found that information if you wanted to anyway."

"But they think it will be held against them," Athas leaned forward. "Say, they apply for a federal government job and we see that they were taking opiates for the last year or had a problem with addiction..."

"So?" Jorge shrugged. "Like none of your boys in Ottawa aren't snorting coke off a hooker's ass every weekend? Give me a fucking break!"

"I mean that the people..."

"Ok," Paige cut in again and shook her head. "Why would you know or care about these things? You're looking at the big picture, not the small details."

"I know but people think that."

"They think that," Jorge cut in and pointed toward his bulletproof window. "Because Big Pharma has their minions out there trying to scare them. Be a man, Athas, have a fucking press conference and sternly let them know that you don't give a fuck about their lives. You're only doing this to help them and to make Big Pharma accountable. Why must I always do your job?"

"Because these ideas, are yours," Athas shot back.

"And may I remind you *again* that my ideas are making *your* government popular?" Jorge shot back. "You, *you* are doing what must be done."

Silence followed and Paige took a big breath.

"Ok, time out," She spoke sternly. "The bottom line is that it doesn't matter what these guys say. The laws are changed. Now, we have to focus on this series and learning about how these companies are creating diseases, then we'll get that information out and act accordingly. For now, we're on the right track. I don't think we can argue about that."

The two men hesitantly agreed.

"So....Tony, is it?" Athas started. "I think we need to protect him."

"I'm already on it," Jorge nodded in agreement. "I have Diego figuring things out."

"And his information?"

"He has ways of keeping it under lock and key," Jorge nodded. "This man, it is not his first rodeo."

The meeting ended shortly afterward and while Paige showed Athas out, Jorge checked his messages. One was from Chase.

We have to talk. It's about Maria.

Jorge automatically felt his heart race. He was already on the phone when Paige returned and stood in the doorway as if she wanted to say something. He waved her in.

"Hello."

"Chase, you got something for me?" Jorge asked as he watched Paige return to her seat with a look of apprehension on her face. "Wasn't Maria with you this afternoon, to talk about *her* bar."

"Yes, she came over after lunch. I guess the school said it was fine since it was an educational thing?"

"Yes, and thank you again," Jorge replied and noted his wife's expression, glancing at the closed door behind her. "Chase do you mind if I put you on speakerphone. Paige is here. If this has to do with Maria, I am sure she would like to know."

"Yeah, sure."

Hitting the button, Jorge sat the phone down.

"So, everything, it went well?" Jorge appeared hesitant as he exchanged looks with Paige.

"It did," Chase said in an echoed voice. "Ummm…she was interested in learning about how a bar is run, what she would need to know, she even had her iPad and was making notes. I think she has to do a project about it."

"That sounds good to me," Jorge nodded in approval. "So, Chase, is something wrong? Your message, it suggested such."

"That's the thing," Chase continued. "She mentioned something about having nightmares."

"Nightmares?" Paige repeated.

"Yeah, like a lot of them…"

"Did she say…." Jorge started.

"I don't want to alarm you both," Chase spoke slowly. "But it sounds like they are over her mother."

Jorge automatically felt his blood boil.

"That woman, I hope she is rotting in hell," Jorge spoke with venom in his voice. "After what she put my Maria through!"

"Calm down," Paige instructed as she raised her hand in the air and gave him a warning look.

He relaxed slightly but looked away.

"I think she's having them about…that night."

They had all been there when Maria's mother had held a gun to her own daughter's head, the vision still caused Jorge's heart to race in anxiety. He had never been so frightened in his life and would've done anything to save his daughter, even offering his own life in exchange for saving hers.

"I thought…" Jorge spoke with emotion in his voice. "I thought she was doing better. New school, starting over…"

"We all thought that," Paige replied with compassion in her voice. "She seemed back to herself."

"I thought so too," Chase chimed in. "But she admitted that the nightmares haven't stopped. "She didn't want everyone to worry."

Jorge exchanged looks with Paige, who reflected his concern.

"Look…I don't know what to tell you," Chase continued. "I don't want her to know that I shared this with you. I told her I wouldn't tell you but…"

"No, this here, it is fine," Jorge instantly replied. "We will figure out a way."

"I wanted to say," Paige jumped in. "I was in her room earlier and I saw something…"

"In her room?" Jorge asked.

"Yes," Paige nodded before slowly continuing. "It was a bottle of cream…to lighten her skin."

"What?" Jorge shot back. "What does this mean? Does she want to be white? I do not understand."

"A lot of girls do," Chase chimed in. "I'm no expert but I once dated this black girl who told me she used these funky creams trying to have lighter skin. I thought it was crazy but aren't those dangerous?"

"They aren't safe," Paige replied, shaking her head. "We'll have to talk to her about that and maybe when we do, this other stuff will come out."

"But I do not understand," Jorge was still confused. "Why would she want lighter skin? Is she ashamed to be Mexican?"

"It's because the media tells women they're always wrong," Paige said. "Too fat, too thin, too light, too dark. It doesn't seem to matter. She clearly feels like she needs to have lighter skin to fit in. I don't fully understand it myself."

"This here," Jorge spoke with sadness in his voice. "This here disappoints me."

"We'll talk to her," Paige said. "We'll find out."

Suddenly the problems of the day took a backseat.

CHAPTER 30

Jorge was squinting to read the fine print on the bottle of skin lightening cream when Maria bounced into the office. As soon as she spotted what he was holding, she immediately stopped in her tracks.

"I can explain," She blurted out with panic in her eyes. "*Papa*, I..."

"Maria shut the door," Jorge ordered and pointed toward the chair across from him. "And have a seat. Where's Paige?"

"She's with Miguel," Maria said as she followed his orders, closing the door and slowly crossing the room. "He's screaming again."

Jorge didn't reply but placed the container on his desk and waited for her to sit down.

"Maria, this here," He said while pointing at the bottle. "This here, it is very disappointing to me. I must admit, I don't understand."

"I thought...I don't know, *Papa*," She started as she shrunk down in the chair. "I thought maybe I was too dark and I would look better if I had lighter skin."

"Maria, you are Mexican," Jorge said with some humor in his voice. "You are not going to have lighter skin. This here, it is not natural."

"But I want to," She admitted with tears in her eyes. "Girls with lighter skin get treated differently."

"Maria," Jorge said and looked away. "Look at me, my skin is dark, do you think people treat me differently?"

"No, but it's different for you," Maria seemed to pick her words carefully. "You've been on tv and stuff. Plus you're a guy. It's not the same for girls."

"Why would it be different?" Jorge asked as he shook his head. "You must make me understand because I do not."

"It just is," Maria replied with a loud sigh. "All the darker girls at school use it and…"

"Just because these silly girls, they use this," Jorge shot back, pointing at the container. "It does not mean you should too."

Maria started to cry.

"Maria," Jorge said as he leaned forward on his desk. "Why would you want to change how you look? You're a beautiful young woman. Is this something your new friend…Cameron, is he suggesting you do this?"

"No," Maria automatically started to shake her head and their eyes met. "No, he told me not to."

"He is your friend, Maria," Jorge softened his tone. "Maybe you should listen to him?"

"*Papa,* the world treats white women differently," Maria insisted. "You should know, you *married* a white woman."

It perhaps was the worst time for Paige to walk in the room. Completely unaware, she closed the door behind her and headed for the desk.

"Is everything ok?" She asked in her usual soft voice. "Maria?"

With shame on her face, his daughter looked down when Paige touched her shoulder and sat down beside her.

"Maria is explaining to me how white women are treated differently than minorities," He spoke gruffly.

"Well, she's not wrong," Paige calmly replied. "There are people who *do* treat white women differently."

"When we went to the auditions last year," Maria piped up with tears in her eyes. "It was always the white girls who got the parts. One director told me I didn't look Mexican enough and another said I was 'too dark' for the role?"

"Oh really?" Jorge fumed. "And these director's names…"

"Let's pick our battles," Paige said with raised eyebrows before turning to Maria. "It's not right and it's not fair. I agree with you but these creams, Maria they are dangerous. They have chemicals that can make you sick."

"Yes, Maria and you should not be ashamed of who you are," Jorge added as he leaned back in his chair. "Anyone, whoever suggests that you should be, you tell them to go fuck themselves."

"Jorge, I.."

"Paige, she is 13," Jorge cut her off. "She's a very tiny person and sometimes, people, they are vultures with small, young women. I want Maria to stand up for herself and I do not care if it is polite. Neither is telling her she is 'too dark'. She is a beautiful young, Mexican woman and if people have a problem with that, I want her to tell them to go fuck themselves. And if anyone, her teachers, whatever has a problem with that, they can come to talk to me. And that's where that conversation ends."

Paige didn't reply but glanced toward Maria who watched Jorge with her big, brown eyes.

"Maria, we want you to be happy," Paige said and paused for a moment. "What you went through earlier this year with your mother…"

"She is *not* my mother," Maria automatically had a lion's roar, completely changing in her demeanor, causing Paige to lean back in surprise. "She is *nothing* to me but an evil woman."

Satisfied, Jorge nodded and exchanged looks with Paige, who appeared unsettled.

"It is true," He agreed. "Your….Verónic, she was evil. When I think what she did to you, Maria, it makes my blood boil. Even today. Even now. It does not matter that time passes, these feelings, they do not go away."

Deflating slightly, Maria's eyes filled with tears again and she nodded. Paige put her arm around her and Jorge felt powerless as his daughter started to sob uncontrollably.

"Maria," he spoke in a gentle voice and moved ahead to reach across his desk, indicating that he wanted to hold her hand. "Please, you must know we are here for you."

She nodded and slowly, her small, delicate hand met with his as Paige continued to comfort her.

"You can tell us anything," Jorge continued. "It may upset me to hear about your pain but it upsets me more to *not* hear about it."

"*Papa,*" She finally managed between sobs. "I keep seeing her, with the gun. I keep feeling like she is going to come back…"

"Maria, I assure you," Jorge glanced at his wife. "She is *not* coming back. I was there. Paige was there. That woman, she is dead."

"I know but…I have dreams and then I wake and I swear she's there," Maria sniffed. "She wanted to kill me."

"Maria," Jorge said as he let go of her hand and walked around the desk to the empty chair on the other side of her and quickly swooped her up in his arms. "It was me, not you, she wanted to hurt."

"What she did was wrong," Paige added as she moved back but continued to touch Maria's shoulder. "So very wrong, Maria."

"Your…Verónic, she was troubled," Jorge attempted to explain. "But it is no excuse. We can never understand why people do what they do."

"She was desperate and not thinking," Paige added.

"Maria, I know it is hard but you must try to move on," Jorge continued as he kissed the top of her head. "We will help you."

"I was doing better," Maria muttered and sniffed. "But lately, I started having those nightmares again."

"You must tell us when you do," Jorge insisted. "This here is important."

"Maria, remember when I showed you how to meditate?" Paige gently added. "We need to get you back into that."

"It did help," Maria slowly pulled away from her father. "I guess I thought I was better and stopped."

"It takes time," Paige reminded her. "There's no shame in feeling this way. It was traumatic and we hate that you had to go through it."

"Maria, we will work through this," Jorge insisted. "Please listen to Paige, she will help you."

"I know," Maria said as she moved away and glanced at the cream on the desk. "I'll be ok."

Slowly rising from the chair, she pointed toward the bottle on the desk.

"You can throw it out," She spoke quietly. "It didn't work anyway."

With that, she headed toward the door. Jorge exchanged looks with Paige but waited to speak until she left the room.

"I hope that we can help her."

"We can't put her in counseling because what's going to happen if she tells someone what happened?"

"It was not like the police were involved," Jorge said as he reached for his phone and turned it back on. "Not that counselors are always useful anyway."

"Some are..." Paige insisted.

"Did you ever get over..."

"No," She automatically answered, knowing he was asking about her past. "But she needs to feel safe, empowered, and loved."

"We can do this," Jorge assured her as he turned and glanced at his phone. "I hope she is ok."

"She will be," Paige replied as she stood up. "I'm going to go upstairs. Talk to her some more."

"Thank you, *mi amor.*"

Glancing at his phone, he saw a text from Diego.

Everything is taken care of.

That meant Tony was safe.

Perfecto. Gracias, Diego.

Sitting his phone down, Jorge thought about everything that had happened with his daughter. He decided to message Chase.

We talked to her. Everything came out. This is good. Thank you.

Chase responded right away.

Let me know if there's anything you need me to do.

Sitting his phone down again, Jorge thought about his daughter. He worried about her. She was so frail, so sensitive, he feared for what the world would do to her.

His phone rang, interrupting his thoughts. It was Marco.

"*Hola.*"

"Hello, sir, I have some....documents we should go over when you have time."

"I got all the time in the world."

"Want to meet me here or at the bar?"

Jorge thought for a moment.

"I'll meet you there."

CHAPTER 31

"I cannot picture you with a dog," Jorge automatically replied after hearing Diego insistence that he needed a pet. Although it wasn't part of the meeting agenda, Diego boldly walked into the boardroom before Marco could even speak. "You? Walking a dog? I cannot see."

"It's for protection," Diego spoke with widened eyes, swinging his arms around dramatically. "If anyone fucks with me, I got my dog. They can be trained to do anything. I just say the right word and he will fucking eat that person alive."

"Don't you have a gun?" Marco asked curiously. "I mean, I am thinking…"

"No, a *gun,* it can't wake you up in the middle of the night if there's an emergency," Diego shook his head. "A dog will warn its owners if someone breaks in, if there's a fire…"

"Diego, you live next to me," Jorge cut him off with a smooth grin on his face. "There better not be any fires."

"No, but you know what I mean," Diego said as his hands waved back and forth as if to shoo away Jorge's comment. "The point is that dogs can be an extra layer of protection. You should get one too, Jorge."

"With two kids in the house?" He shook his head. "Not with a baby who might torture it and get bit. No, this here, would not work."

"I knew a family back in the Philippines," Marco spoke up, his eyes widened. "They had a dog and he bit the baby in the cheek."

Diego made a face.

"Yes, so no dogs for me," Jorge insisted. "Now a tiger…"

"Ah yes!" Diego laughed and clapped his hands together. "Remember that guy in Mexico?"

"Oh yes, you did not want to be the man introduced to his tiger," Jorge said and turned toward Marco. "Those fuckers eat a lot of meat and they do not care if that piece of meat, it's still alive and screaming either."

"Really?" Marco said as he leaned in. "So they fed…"

"Let us just say you did not piss off this particular man," Jorge nodded. "He was a powerful one and disloyalty, lying, losing money…"

"He'd fucking feed you to the tiger," Diego jumped in, cutting him off. "Alive and if you were a friend of buddy, this guy would make sure you saw so you knew what was coming to you if you didn't stay in line."

"You stayed in line," Jorge assured him. "People often do when they know the consequences."

"Oh wow," Marco shook his head. "Sir, that is a lot."

"So Marco," Jorge decided to change the subject. "You got something for me? I know you were trying to talk before Diego crashed the meeting."

"Hey, I'm acting CEO, I crash things," Diego insisted with a sinister grin on his face as he leaned back in his chair.

"Sir, it is fine, I was going to talk to you about what I found," Marco insisted as he turned on his iPad and tapped on the screen. "I was looking at the pharmaceutical company and I found this."

Turning the iPad around, Jorge squinted as he looked at the screen.

"You got those old eyes, Jorge," Diego said without missing a beat. "Want me to get my glasses?"

"I am fine, Diego," Jorge replied as he continued to squint. "Oh, ok, so this here is…"

"Sir," Marco said as he leaned ahead on the table. "It is not *quite* what I originally thought. Yes, this company is behind this particular virus but they were careful to not have it created in *their* lab. I think perhaps, there was a fear that it would contaminate other, lucrative products if it ever got out."

Jorge nodded.

"So, this document, it shows that it was created elsewhere but *for* this company," Marco continued to explain as Jorge scanned over the screen. "It was made for a major client and as you see, this client was willing to pay a lot of money to have it."

"That's a lot of zeros behind that number," Jorge said with a raised eyebrow. "It does not say who?"

"No, this I cannot find," Marco continued. "They are referred to as 'the client' throughout these documents. What you are reading was encrypted when I found it."

"You managed to hack it," Jorge asked with surprise on his face, glancing toward Marco. "I thought that was hard to do."

"It is tricky, sir," Marco shook his head, "but certainly not impossible."

"So where were they creating this super virus or bug or whatever?" Diego asked with interest. "Here in Canada?"

"It is another building owned by this company," Marco replied. "But separate for obvious reasons."

"And the people creating it?"

"Sir, this is the thing," Marco said with some hesitation. "I am still looking, however, it is almost as if they fell off the face of the earth."

"Missing?"

"One is dead," Marco replied. "from the virus they made."

"And the others were killed because they knew too much," Diego guessed.

"*She* went missing," Marco corrected him. "Not even her family know what happened. I did some extra research in case they did but it does not seem so. If others worked on it, I cannot find their names."

Jorge exchanged looks with both Marco and Diego.

"But we have this proof they made it," Jorge said and thought for a moment. "This here is very valuable."

"There is something else," Marco continued as he turned off his iPad. "The building where it was created, coincidentally caught on fire shortly after the virus was completed and changed hands. Also, the virus killed thousands of people worldwide and had devastating effects on the economy in Asia."

"They had to get rid of their ties to it," Diego said and scratched his head, narrowing his eyes on Jorge. "So now what?"

"This here, I am not sure," Jorge replied. "We could use it in the series but all we got is this document."

"And if we use it," Marco added. "They might know they were hacked."

"What if Tony gets it anonymously?" Diego suggested.

"That could happen," Jorge said and felt his mind drift away, his attention diverted toward the door. He was surprised to see Makerson on the other side. He signaled for him to come in.

"Did we have a meeting?" Jorge attempted to remember.

"No, but I have something for you," Makerson replied as he entered the room. "When I got your voice mail I figured your phone was turned off. I called Paige and she said you were here."

"Is this so?" Jorge asked as he pointed toward the seat beside Marco, across from him. Makerson sat down.

"I heard something," Makerson said and shook his head as if he seemed confused. "I'm not sure if it's true or if it's going to make any sense but I had my ear to the ground…"

"Let me be the judge of this," Jorge suggested as he leaned forward on the table. "What is it you hear?"

"The opposition has this whole propaganda thing going against Athas," Makerson started, his face somewhat flushed. "Trying to say he hasn't fulfilled any of his election promises."

"Has he?" Diego piped up and innocently shrugged.

"Do any of them?" Jorge countered then returned his attention to Makerson. "This here, it is not new."

"Yes, that is true," Makerson nodded. "But there's more. They're also saying..or implying, that Athas is behind the docuseries to justify why he's changing the laws for Big Pharma."

Jorge merely shrugged. It wasn't completely untrue.

"And that you're behind it."

This also didn't cause a reaction with Jorge. He didn't care what *they* said anyway.

"And the cartel is behind you."

"The cartel?" Jorge said and raised an eyebrow. "So, who is saying this?"

"It's coming out of Big Pharma," Makerson replied and took a breath. "They have an agreement with a major news channel to 'break' this story in the upcoming days. A reporter named Charlie Redalson is working on it and he's a vulture."

"Well, unfortunately for Charlie Redalson," Jorge perked up. "So am I."

"He is going to release a buried article from Mexico that suggests you're backed by the Mexican cartel," Makerson continued with some hesitation. "And that you're trying to make Canada as corrupt as Mexico."

"Well, first of all," Jorge replied with no reaction to the news. "People may be surprised to learn that most countries, if you look under the hood, have some corruption and this country is not immune to such things."

"True," Makerson agreed. "But this other stuff…"

"Tell me more about this Charlie Redalson," Jorge suggested as he glanced at Diego. "I must know my enemies."

"He's a senior reporter," Makerson said as he pulled out his tablet and turned it on. "Old as fuck, been around for years. I met him once when I was starting and he's an arrogant asshole."

"Sir," Marco immediately spoke up as he glanced over Makerson's shoulder as he tapped on the tablet. "I can look into this man if you wish?"

"Marco, this here would be perfect," Jorge replied with ease. "I will need to know everything you can find."

"I will do it," He rose from his chair and headed toward the door. "Right away."

Turning the tablet around, Makerson showed him a picture of an older man with a handsome face and a pretentious smile. His bio indicated he had worked as a journalist for many years, starting at a young age.

"This man, he has done this for a long time?" Jorge asked as Diego leaned ahead and squinted his eyes, making a face.

"When I said old as fuck, I wasn't exaggerating," Makerson replied. "And he tends to run on a more…conservative side of things. He also tends to simplify things, to appeal to the low hanging fruit."

"I've seen this guy," Diego jumped in.

"Yeah, he's on tv all the time," Makerson nodded.

"Nah, not on tv, who the fuck watches tv anymore?" Diego said and made a face, shaking his head, turning his attention to Jorge. "I mean, I saw him in person. When you were running for politics, I saw him at some of the events. I think for Athas too."

"Yeah, he kind of smeared you both," Makerson confirmed as he retrieved his tablet and tapped on a few buttons. Turning it around, there was a list of articles that attacked both Jorge and Alec Athas. "Again, as I say, his audience is low hanging fruit."

"Well, Diego," Jorge said with a dark grin on his face. "I guess we will have to check in and see how hungry the tigers are today."

CHAPTER 32

"He is a pretentious, old fuck," Jorge said to his wife as they sat together in the back corner of a small, downtown restaurant later that day. "He works closely with the opposition but attempts to say that he is an unbiased journalist. People, they trust him because he's been around since the dinosaurs."

"Well, I don't know if that's necessarily true," Paige shook her head. "I remember my parents watching Charlie Redalson as a kid but…I think he never gained steam with our generation or the ones after us."

"It does not matter, *mi amor,*" Jorge was quick to remind her as the waitress made her way to the table. "Because he ain't gonna be around much longer."

After the older lady took their order and left, the couple sat in silence and communicated with their eyes.

"So, I guess the real question is when?" Paige said as she leaned in. "And how?"

"I have a few ideas."

"So do I."

"This here, I can take care of."

"So can I."

"Oh, *mi amor,* this I know."

"I think we should both….take care of this problem."

Jorge didn't answer but instead watched her carefully.

"Did Marco learn anything else in his research?"

"You know, the basic things," Jorge replied as he glanced at the waitress coming back with their coffee. Thanking her, he waited until she left to continue. "He's got a lot of money, got a lot of rich, powerful friends, and has a thing for 20-year-old Asian girls."

"Interesting."

"Also, he lives alone, divorced."

Paige nodded with a smirk on her face.

"In a big house."

"Of course."

"Actually, not far from us, *mi amor*."

"You don't say?"

The food was delivered shortly after, halting the conversation. It was while he took a huge bite of his BLT that his wife tilted her head, thoughtfully staring at her food.

"Was there anything we should know about?" She wondered. "Food allergies? Late-night visitors? Fetishes? Drinking problems? Anything?"

"Marco, he has tapped into everything…phone, computer, doctor records, banking…he lives a quiet life."

"Hmmmm…yeah, you know something is going on there."

"Exactly what I was thinking too."

"Or maybe, he's just boring."

"Either way," Jorge said as he reached for his coffee. "He made a bad enemy."

"And we know he's ready to release this story?"

"He is still working on it," Jorge confirmed. "Attempting to do some snooping in Mexico."

"Mexicans don't like people who snoop."

"Mexicans, we appreciate those who mind their own fucking business," Jorge spoke quietly, gently as if using words of seduction. "And in Mexico, this type of reporter, he would have a short life span."

Paige nodded and glanced at someone as they walked by, waiting to continue.

"I think we should do it soon."

"I agree."

"Marco, he.."

"He has hacked his system, cameras in his house, even his Alexa will go dead."

"Seems appropriate."

"We just gotta get in the house."

"I find waking someone in the middle of the night is best," Paige spoke with innocence in her voice. "You aren't fully awake, yet you're not completely asleep so it's hard to get out of that groggy period."

"I want to have a little talk with him about honesty and journalism," Jorge suggested. "It will not be a long conversation but he must know what he did wrong. Also, it is important that those around him who think they may pick up this story, have second thoughts."

"They won't take on this story when he's gone," Paige calmly predicted. "They won't even touch it."

It was because of the simplicity of a man like Charlie Redalson that the couple was able to move fast to take care of the situation. It was only a few days later when they paid the reporter a late-night visit. Unfortunately for him, he was asleep when they did.

His house was as large as their own yet it lacked character, Jorge noted. The kitchen was dull, his living room barely had any furniture but an older style typewriter prominently sat on display on the coffee table. Exchanging looks, Paige pointed toward the stairs to indicate the victim's bedroom.

They crept upstairs, each with a gun in hand. The journalist had no guns registered under his name but then again, neither did they.

They found Charlie Redalson asleep in his room. His vulnerability made Jorge grin. Glancing down at his gloved hand, Jorge suddenly brought it down hard on a nearby dresser. The man jumped and sat up in his bed just as Paige turned on the light. Fumbling for his glasses, Charlie looked white as a ghost when he saw who was standing in his bedroom.

"Wha…what are you…how did you…what…"

"You know my English, it is still not great, but that there," Jorge pointed toward the man as he proceeded to sit down in a nearby chair while pointing a gun toward Redalson. "That does not make sense. Maybe you are having a stroke."

"What are you doing in my house?" Charlie said as if suddenly alert. "I have an alarm and…"

"It's disabled and so are the cameras," Paige spoke in a smooth voice while also pointing a gun in his direction. "No one knows we're here."

"No alarms but let's face it, *amigo,*" Jorge shrugged. "Would it matter? The police, they are useless, *si?*"

"What do you want from me?" Charlie managed to pull the covers over him as if they gave an extra layer of protection. "I don't..."

"Hey hey," Jorge pointed at him accusingly. "Don't you be moving too fast because if you move too fast, my wife, she tends to get nervous and reacts."

"It's true," Paige calmly replied as she tilted the gun slightly. "Sometimes, I shoot and think later."

"This is about...." He paused as if second-guessing what he was about to say. "What is this about?"

"You *know* what it's about motherfucker," Jorge corrected him. "Do not play dumb. This here, it is not a good look for you."

"I don't know if you are aware of this," Paige quietly added. "But in Mexico, there's an understanding that sometimes it's better to not shake up a hornet's nest."

"And this time," Jorge agreed. "You not only shook it up, but you sat on it and thought no one would notice. Unfortunately for you, I see everything."

"They call you *el diablo* in Mexico," Charlie Redalson suddenly said as he nervously pulled the sheets closer. "The devil. That's how people know you. How did you think no one in Canada would find out?"

"Oh, *amigo,* they have found out," Jorge corrected him. "They just knew better than to talk."

"Like Tom Makerson?"

"Makerson works for me."

"And Athas?"

"You do not have to worry about such things," Jorge was quick to cut him off. "Right now, this here is the least of your worries."

"I can drop the story."

"There's no *can* about it," Jorge spoke abruptly. "But this is the problem. I do not trust you and *amigo,* I trust my instincts. And my instincts, they say that your ego, it may be bigger than your brain."

"I can drop the story," Charlie Redalson nervously repeated. "It's not worth it."

"You know, in Mexico," Jorge ignored his remark. "We cut out the tongues of people who talk too much. I've personally done it."

"Please, I.."

"See, in Mexico, we believe in sending a message," Jorge continued. "It is important that enemies, they know about consequences."

"Please, I have…"

"And you, I know what you had on me," Jorge continued. "I saw the first draft of your story. Not that anyone else will because I had someone erase it from everything…your computer, your hard drive, there will be no trace that it ever existed."

"I was asked…"

"I know you were asked and by who," Jorge replied. "I also know what you have said about me. I believe the article was called, *A Devil Named Hernandez* and it tells how I own politicians, the media, how I manipulate everything to gain power and you know, it is true."

The reporter looked shocked by his candor.

"These things, they are true," Jorge spoke evenly as if the two were in a casual conversation. "But the thing is, no one else can know."

The man's face paled.

"See, this story, it has not come out before for a reason," Jorge insisted. "And it won't."

"Look, please," Charlie Redalson spoke breathlessly, fear overcoming his presence. "I can bury the story. I can…"

"Ah, Canadians!" Jorge spoke with a smooth grin on his lips. "Always so accommodating!"

"Whatever…whatever…I can…"

"Except, of course, this is not true," Jorge reminded him. "Was there not a story before that you broke? I think it was something about a lady? She was trying to get her kids back and you *promised* her that you would remove some damaging information from a story so that it could not be held against her?"

"Despicable," Paige spoke gently. "And completely unnecessary. He joked about it with colleagues later."

"Ah yes! And the woman," Jorge continued. "She didn't get her kids back. She couldn't even see them. After much struggle, she ended up committing suicide. So, I do not believe you when you say you will bury my story either. The only person you buried back then, was that lady."

"Please….please…."

"The only person who has to worry about being buried this time, *amigo,* it is you."

CHAPTER 33

"Journalism," Jorge said with a sense of disappointment in his voice. "This must be a very stressful job, *mi amor*. I see another journalist who has committed suicide. Charlie Redalson?"

Paige took a sip of her coffee, tilted her head slightly, showing no emotions. On the other side of the table, Maria looked up from her tablet with a vague interest but her eyes quickly returned to what she was reading.

"There must be enormous pressures to produce stories..." Jorge said as he looked back at his laptop with a grin on his face.

"It's...tragic," Paige agreed but showed disinterest.

"So, *mi amor,* what are your plans for today?" Jorge closed his laptop and slid it aside. "Are you going to the office?"

"Yes, I have a meeting with Marco to tie up some loose ends," Paige said as she sat her coffee down. "Check in on a few things, the usual."

"And you, *señorita* Maria, how does your day look?"

"School....blah...."

"I thought you were more interested in school now that you want to learn how to run the bar?" Paige asked with a humored expression on her face. "Not so exciting anymore?"

"It is but....that's like a million years away and there's so much to learn," Maria appeared discouraged. "Plus, now I have to write a report on it. I asked if I could do a video project but they said no, it has to be a typed document."

"Well, Maria," Jorge jumped in. "Part of running a business is sometimes doing things you don't like."

"Part of any job," Paige corrected.

"Yeah, I know," Maria said with a yawn. "I guess."

"Did you sleep well last night?" Paige asked with concern in her face.

"Kinda."

"What does kinda mean?" Jorge asked.

"I had some bad dreams and stuff."

Jorge exchanged looks with Paige.

"It's not a big deal," Maria quickly added. "Everyone has bad dreams."

"Yes, but Maria," Jorge shook his head. "If this is effecting your sleep..."

"I'm fine," She insisted. "I promise."

Jorge wasn't convinced. Something told him that much more was going on than she was saying and he intended to find out what. He shared a quick look with Paige before rising from his chair, announcing that he had a meeting with Tony and Andrew.

Once in the SUV, he texted Paige.

See if she will tell you more.

After a moment, his wife replied.

I will.

Driving to Tony's new secret hideaway, Jorge was lost in thought when his phone rang. It was Diego.

"I found a dog!"

"You did?"

"Yup, I'm going to bring her to your house later."

"Her?" Jorge grinned. "Why does it not surprise me that you got a female dog?"

"Cutest dog in the place," Diego jumped in as if he wasn't even listening, "and vicious too."

"Diego, where did you get a dog at this hour?"

"I got her last night but I didn't want to scare her so I didn't invite you over," Diego paused. "You know, cause you got an evil presence."

"*I* have an evil presence?"

"Yeah, so you guys can meet her later," Diego continued. "I'm staying home today to help her adjust to everything. Also, she pees on the floor sometimes."

"This is why I don't have a pet," Jorge insisted. "Kids, they are enough."

"Your kids are gonna love this dog."

"Great, they can go to your house and see her," Jorge replied as he turned down the street leading to Tony's temporary home. "I don't need no dog or cat pissing on my floors."

"Hey, did you see…" Diego started but was quickly cut off by Jorge.

"Yes," He replied abruptly as he drove up to Tony's new home. "Saw it online."

"So things are?"

"Resolved," Jorge confirmed. "Paige is going to the office to make sure this morning."

"Paige is going to the office?" Diego asked excitedly.

"Yes, Diego, does this here make you want to go to work?" Jorge quipped as he parked the SUV. "To see Paige. You do know we are still neighbors, do you not?"

"I might drop by the office," Diego said. "You know, maybe bring the dog."

"I gotta go."

Ending the call, Jorge took a deep breath. Even though he should've been encouraged by everything positive around him, his heart weighed heavy for Maria. He felt certain she was going through something that he couldn't resolve with the same ease as he had dealt with Charlie Redalson. If only he could find a way to make his children's lives perfect, he would do it. He feared Maria would always have problems. She already had suffered from bullying at school and so much death in her family, perhaps this was the one area where he was powerless.

With great apathy, he got out of the SUV and headed toward Tony's door. Glancing around, he couldn't see anything unusual in the neighborhood that alerted him as he rang the doorbell. Things were heating up with the docuseries and Andrew's YouTube channel. He wanted to put out any fires before they had time to start.

Andrew answered the door and appeared surprised to see Jorge on the other side.

"What did I tell you both about checking before you answered" Jorge automatically began to lecture as he walked inside, "What did I say?"

Andrew seemed oddly quiet even for that early in the morning and merely stepped aside, put his head down, and didn't reply. It wasn't until Jorge looked up that he understood his behavior. Tony was slumped over in the next room with a look of shock on his face.

Closing the door behind him, Andrew ushered him into the kitchen.

"What the fuck is going on here?" Jorge automatically asked in a low tone. "What happened to him?"

"His mother was killed," Andrew whispered. "I didn't know either, I just got here and he told me. She was shot."

Jorge's brain automatically went into overdrive. They couldn't get to Tony, so they got to his mother instead.

"They don't seem to know much so far," Andrew continued. "From what he's told me, it sounds like she was going to the mall last night and was killed in the parking lot. He keeps saying 'for money' but I'm thinking…"

"I know what you were thinking," Jorge quickly nodded. "You take care of him and I will take care of this."

"Ok."

"And his stuff, his footage, everything…"

"It's all there."

"Give it to me," Jorge insisted as he reached for his phone and texted Chase. "It's going to my house until we sort this out."

"Ok," Andrew shook his head nervously. "So, you want me to…"

"Find out his info, passwords, everything because while he's taking off time, you're taking care of it."

"And the crematorium?"

"Anyone else can work when you're tied up with this?"

"Yeah…I mean, he's new…."

"Then you will find a way to do the two."

"Yes," Andrew nodded abruptly. "I can. I mean, I will, I'll figure it out."

"And then, after you drop him off and get everything we need to work on this show," Jorge continued. "You pack up your shit and come to my house because no one's gonna fuck with you at my place."

Andrew paled while his eyes grew in size.

"Look, last night's show," Jorge started and then abruptly stopped when he heard crying in the other room. "We both knew that it was going to shake things up."

"That lady who spoke, she revealed a lot," Andrew nodded. "She worked for Big Pharma and she's talking…"

"Well, rich oligarch types, they don't like their secrets getting out," Jorge insisted. "This, it was their warning to Tony to back off."

"Things are getting sticky."

"They're only gonna get stickier," Jorge reminded him. "We barely started."

"Did you see online, *Toronto AM* said…"

"I know," Jorge nodded as he glanced toward the next room. "This series, it is shaking things up and there couldn't be a worse time for this industry. But now, *amigo,* you have to help that man. He has suffered a huge loss."

Andrew nodded but appeared uncomfortable. He followed Jorge when he returned to the room where Tony was working. Hunched over in the chair, Tony cried uncontrollably, in a way that was beyond heart-wrenching and, unfortunately, Jorge was hardly the person to comfort anyone. Glancing at Andrew, he could see he was about to tear up too. Taking a deep breath, he stepped forward.

"Tony, I am deeply sorry for your loss," Jorge spoke evenly and watched the man slowly looking up. "I cannot…. I cannot even begin to say how tragic this is but Andrew, he will take over things from here until you feel….ready to return and until that time, if you need anything, please do not hesitate to contact me. Money? Help to find…..anything…"

Jorge was shocked when the large man stood up and pulled him into a strong embrace. He was expecting anger, perhaps blaming him for the death of his mother, apathy, anything but certainly not a hug. Unsure of what else to do or say, Jorge, hugged him back.

CHAPTER 34

"So what's the big emergency?" Diego arrived at the door holding a pink blanket in his arms. Suddenly, a chihuahua popped his head out and automatically began to shake. "I have a new baby to look after."

"Diego," Jorge shook his head and moved aside to let his friend in the house. "What the fuck is that?"

"It's my new dog," Diego sharply replied. "I told you I got a new dog. Remember? Or is old age creeping in?"

Jorge grimaced just as Paige walked up from the garage. She automatically turned her attention to the dog.

"That....that's your new dog?" She looked amused, exchanging looks with Jorge.

"Hey, listen," Diego spoke defensively then suddenly stopped and turned his attention back to the shaking dog in his arms. "Does Jorge's evil presence scare you?"

"Diego, maybe you," Jorge pointed toward the dog as Paige made her way over and petted the shaking animal. "Maybe it is you that scares him?"

"It's a *her*," Diego replied gently as if Jorge's words were offensive to the animal. "And her name is Priscilla."

Jorge rolled his eyes.

"She's cute," Paige spoke warmly as she stepped back. "I guess, we thought you wanted a guard dog and Priscilla…"

"The first time someone breaks in your house," Jorge spoke sharply. "That dog there will piss on the floor and hide under the bed."

Priscilla gave a sharp bark causing Diego to pull her close and kiss the top of her head.

Jorge made a face and glanced out his window.

"Chase is here," he said as he walked toward the door.

"I know she don't look ferocious," Diego spoke slowly as if to bring a point home. "*But* I dare the person who pisses her off. She might be small but she's mighty."

"Yes, Diego and when someone, they break in your house," Jorge said as he opened the door for Chase. "They will step on her and she'll be..."

"Hey!" Diego said as he made a face and pulled the dog closer. "Don't talk that way around my baby!"

Chase glanced at the dog as he walked in the door, a smile slowly crossed his face.

"He looks just like you," He teased causing everyone but Diego to laugh.

"*She,*" Diego quickly corrected as he narrowed his eyes on Chase. "Does the pink blanket not tell you people anything?"

"Ok, this here, enough," Jorge quickly jumped in. "Let us not talk about the dog all day. She *is* cute Diego but hardly a guard dog."

Priscilla let out another yip.

"I don't think she agrees with you," Diego said as he continued to snuggle with the dog.

"Marco's here," Chase said as he glanced out the window. "Are the film guys coming too?"

"Ah, no but that is what we need to discuss," Jorge said with some hesitation. "Something came up."

A few minutes later, the five of them were sitting in the office with the door closed. Miguel could be heard crying upstairs while Paige appeared exhausted as soon as he started.

"Do not worry, *mi amor,*" Jorge reassured her. "Juliana is here, she can take care of him."

"He's always crying for me though."

"He must learn you cannot always be there," Jorge gently reminded her. "This is fine. He will be fine."

Paige appeared uncertain but remained seated.

"So this morning, I had an unexpected situation to deal with," Jorge said as he pointed toward cameras, lights, computers, and other equipment sitting in the corner. "Regarding the docuseries."

"Did your guy quit?" Chase asked.

"No," Jorge said and thought back to the broken man he had witnessed earlier that morning. "I arrived at the house for our meeting and I learn that Tony, my producer, director, everything, the brains behind all of this, his mother was murdered last night."

"Shit!" Chase spoke up. "Because of the series?"

"Well, perhaps it is a coincidence," Jorge hesitated for a moment. "But I do not think so."

"And he quit," Diego guessed, nodding his head while snuggling the dog. "We're fucked."

"Calm down, Diego," Jorge said as he put his hand up in the air. "That is not what I say. He is...temporarily unavailable."

"But isn't it a bunch of people who do these shows?" Chase asked. "Like a whole crew?"

"This man, it was only him and Andrew," Jorge said and shook his head. "He wanted full control and to keep it quiet, this was the best way to do both. But he recorded the interviews, edited them, did voice-overs, whatever else is involved but he was pretty insistent on keeping things small."

"Sounds like he worked like a dog," Diego said as he kissed the top of Priscilla's head.

"Sounds like," Chase spoke firmly. "*They* knew this and wanted to take out your key player before the series grabs more steam."

"It might backfire though," Paige suggested.

"It *will* backfire," Jorge said as he leaned forward on his desk. "In the fucking face of the person who did this."

"Sir," Marco spoke up for the first time. "I can research this and see what I find. Maybe I can hack into the police files..."

"You can do that?" Chase asked with interest.

"I can do anything," Marco spoke with assurance. "I have before."

"Where did it happen?" Paige jumped in. "Was it at her home? Does she have cameras or anything?"

"It was at the mall."

Marco stopped what he was doing and looked up. His face was pensive, as if in thought.

"So, she was shot at the mall?" Chase jumped in, not noticing Marco's expression. "Like, *in* the mall?"

"Oh, I heard that on the news earlier," Paige cut in. "It was outside the mall, in the parking lot, right? I think she worked at the mall."

"Yes," Jorge confirmed and watched Marco sit up straighter. "Last evening, I believe."

"Oh, sir," Marco began to speak nervously. "I think I made a grave error."

"You?" Jorge was surprised. "Marco, it is not like you to make errors."

"But this time, I didn't know," He spoke sheepishly. "When I hacked that company's site, I saw an email but at the time, I did not think it meant anything."

"About this?" Paige calmly asked.

"Yes," Marco replied to her then returned his attention to Jorge. "It was cryptic but there was something about the lady at the mall. I thought they were referring to a complaint mentioned earlier in the same message."

"What exactly did it say?" Jorge asked.

"I will have to look again," Marco shook his head. "But something about dealing with the lady at the mall so things didn't escalate. I thought they meant a complaint about a product that they wished to smooth over."

"But that doesn't necessarily mean they were talking about this situation," Paige reminded him.

"I...I felt like it sounded strange," Marco said as he stared into space, lost in thought. "And I read that news this morning as well. It was the same mall and....there was something odd about the email. I must look back but it got my attention but then I thought, no...this is nothing."

"Regardless, it sounds like it would've been easy to miss," Paige insisted.

"Yeah, not everyone thinks like a psychopath," Diego pointed out. "For all you knew, it could've been anything..."

"It does not matter now," Jorge attempted to get their attention back. "It is too late."

"But sir, if his mother was killed and I could've..."

"Marco, please, do not do this," Jorge insisted. "This will not help out anyone."

"It ain't like you can do anything," Diego insisted as he looked down at his dog and kissed her again while Chase turned away, a horrified expression on his face.

Marco continued to look upset.

"Unless there were details," Paige jumped in. "which I doubt. It still would've been a long shot to put this together."

"It is over now," Jorge repeated. "Now, we must find out who did this and take care of them. Lights fucking out."

"Meanwhile?" Chase asked.

"Meanwhile," Jorge said and paused for a moment. "Andrew...we need to protect him because he will be taking this on."

"So the safe house?" Paige asked.

"We need him closer," Jorge insisted. "Here...or maybe Diego's house, somewhere where we can keep an eye on him."

"Is that necessary?" Chase asked.

"I'm afraid yes because we have no way of knowing what they might do next to stop us," Jorge replied. "What do you think, Paige?"

"There's lots of room here," She replied. "But there are children in the house so..."

"He can stay at my place," Diego spoke up. "As long as he doesn't upset Priscilla."

Jorge rolled his eyes.

"That seems fair," Paige went along with it. "But can he do the work on his own?"

"He can," Jorge assured them. "But I may have to get more involved."

"So, last night was the interview with the lady who worked at Big Pharma," Chase started. "Good thing her face was hidden."

"And she made them look bad, sir," Marco jumped in. "I was watching with my family. It is scary how they only care about money, not people's safety."

"So what's the next one about?" Chase asked.

Jorge didn't answer but darkness fell over his face and a grin spread over his lips.

CHAPTER 35

"*It's the Big Pharma rabbit hole,*" The man's words filled the room while Jorge and Andrew watched the footage for the upcoming episode of the docuseries in Diego's secret room. "*They give you one drug, which leads to another drug, which leads to something else. What people don't realize is that many conditions can be cured without pills because pills aren't always the answer.*"

His words offered the viewer a sense of comfort, filled with compassion which represented the polar opposite of how people viewed pharmaceutical companies. Jorge watched with interest, observing everything from the interviewee's words to the look in his eye, and the tone in his voice because Jorge knew that these details mattered. It was the big picture, the small psychological triggers would have an impact. The viewer would be left to draw their own conclusion but in the end, there was only one that could be drawn.

"And check this out," Andrew said as he leaned forward and hit a key on the laptop while Jorge glanced around the stark room. "This part is gold!"

Jorge returned his attention to the laptop to hear the same man's voice while images of various, popular ads from throughout the years flashed on the screen. All were colorful, interesting, and captured the eye.

"The greatest marketing tool in Big Pharma's toolbox is fear. Fear of getting fat. Fear of having a sexual dysfunction. Fear of losing your sex appeal. Fear of getting sick. Fear that your child is abnormal. Fear that you're abnormal."

"This here is true," Jorge replied as Andrew leaned forward and paused the video. "This is what they do best. Scare the shit out of people and work on their insecurities but then again, isn't that all advertising campaigns?"

"Yeah, but we don't need to talk about them," Andrew reminded him. "The key is to skip through these facts quickly so that people don't have time to think about them and we're moving on to the next."

With that, Andrew clicked the button to continue.

"This is first level marketing used by Big Pharma. This is what's going to get you in the door because once they can get you in the door, then they can also pull you down that rabbit hole."

Andrew once again stopped the video.

"This here, it is good," Jorge nodded in approval. "This is exactly what I want."

"It makes people feel like they're stupid," Andrew pointed out with maturity that was vastly different from the kid Jorge had met a couple of years earlier. "And no one wants to feel stupid."

"Or gullible," Jorge added. "This here, it is perfect."

"Yeah," Andrew fell silent for a moment. "I still can't believe…you know, with Tony's mom."

"I know," Jorge replied and observed the young man's reaction. "But these people, they are powerful and you do not mess with a man and his power."

Andrew nodded without replying.

"But we will find out who is responsible," Jorge assured him. "And then, we will destroy them."

Andrew nodded but still had sadness in his eyes. It was because Jorge's own life was often centered on death and destruction that he sometimes forgot that to other people, this wasn't normal. It didn't create the same level of shock and trauma for him because, in his world, it was the price of doing business.

"Tony said you were gonna pay the funeral expenses," Andrew spoke with a softness in his voice. "I think that's pretty cool, man. You don't even know the guy."

"To me, Andrew, he is an associate," Jorge spoke bluntly. "And I believe in loyalty above all. He has shown me that his loyalty to me is strong and for that, I will do the same for him."

"It's a lot of money."

"It is just money, *amigo*," Jorge replied and swung his hand in the air. "This here, all of it, it is never about money for me. It is about power. Money, it means nothing if you have no power."

"I thought money gave you power."

"That is simply not true," Jorge said as he shook his head. "Money gives you options and sometimes those options, they lead to power but you must have the lion inside of you or nothing will ever give you power."

"I don't have a lion in me," Andrew said with a grin. "Maybe a pussycat."

To this, Jorge laughed heartily while Andrew hesitantly joined in.

"It could be worse," Jorge insisted as he gestured toward the next room. "You could be Diego's dog."

Their meeting ended shortly afterward, with Jorge cautiously leaving Diego's house, his eyes scanning the neighborhood for anything that stood out. Nothing seemed out of place but Jorge knew that this meant nothing. The last time someone was watching him in his neighborhood, they did so from behind closed doors not from a car on the street as insinuated on television and in the movies.

Jumping in his SUV, he tore out of the driveway and headed toward the office. Noticing a message on his voicemail, he played it back. It was Tony.

Look, we should meet sometimes today if you're free. I want to discuss something with you.

Biting his lip, Jorge considered what this could mean. Although he reassured the others that Tony would be returning to the project, it was just as possible that he wanted to bail on it. In the beginning, Jorge assumed if anyone was the target of Big Pharma's wrath, it would be Tony himself, since he had no family of his own. His mother's death was unexpected.

Arriving at the bar, Jorge sent a quick message to Tony before going inside. He found Chase at his desk while Marco was on the other side, staring at his laptop.

"Any luck with the fucker that killed Tony's mother?" He spoke abruptly as he entered the room.

"We got a face," Chase replied as he leaned back in his chair. "But we don't know who he is."

"The police, have they seen?" Jorge asked curiously.

"Nope," Marco answered. "Sir, the mall's cameras weren't operational at the time."

"Ah, of course!" Jorge nodded with amusement as he sat beside Marco. "This here, it must be going over well in the media."

"They're hiding it," Chase replied. "Making sure it don't get out so people won't be scared to shop there."

"But the police, sir, they did not check other cameras in the area," Marco said as he looked up from his laptop. "One woman, she contacted them to see if they wanted to see the footage from her nearby business before it was taped over but the police, they didn't get back to her. Luckily, when I learn this, I hacked her cameras and got it."

"Well, of course," Jorge said with a shrug. "Marco, you are certainly more ambitious than the police. The police, they will do as little as possible, like they always do."

"For our sake," Chase said as he raised an eyebrow. "That might be a good thing."

Jorge shrugged and glanced over Marco's shoulder. He was scanning through something so quickly he wasn't even able to read, so he turned away.

"I was looking at the upcoming episode of our series," Jorge informed them. "It is quite good. That reminds me, Tony, he is coming here to meet me."

"Do you think he's gonna quit?" Chase asked with concern.

"He will not quit," Jorge insisted. "Regardless of what ideas are in his head when he walks through that door, I will make sure he does not quit. I will take care of this problem where the police have done nothing."

"Sir, I would rather have you on my side," Marco spoke with sincerity in his voice. "Because I know you always find those responsible."

"It's because I try," Jorge suggested. "And of course, I have a better staff than the police department."

"We stop at nothing, sir," Marco added and took a deep breath. "Here is the picture of the killer."

"Ah, great work!" Jorge moved closer.

"This man, this is the man who shot her." Marco pointed at the frozen frame on his MacBook.

"And you have the video?"

"We watched it," Chase nodded. "May I remind you that the police didn't even make an effort to check this footage?"

"Was it erased from their cameras?"

"Sir, would you like me to erase it?"

Jorge thought for a moment.

"Yes, Marco, could you?" Jorge turned his attention to Chase. "If we have the footage, we will take care of this. We do not need the police getting in our way."

"No problem, sir."

"So this man," Jorge moved closer as Marco turned the laptop to show him the blurry image. "Is there a way to find out who he is?"

"I am not sure," Marco spoke skeptically.

"Isn't there face technology?" Chase asked.

"It is complicated," Marco offered. "But I will figure it out."

Jorge's phone buzzed and he glanced at it.

"He's here," Jorge said as he rose from the chair, noting the doubtful expression on both men's faces. With some hesitance, he headed for the main door, checking the security camera before opening it.

"Thank you for meeting with me," Tony said as he walked into the bar, showing the signs of a broken man. "Again, I appreciate everything you've done."

"It is not a problem," Jorge said and paused for a moment as a thought crossed his mind. "There is an image we have found. We think it is of the shooter but I understand if…"

"I want to see," Tony said as he stood taller. "I want to see the man who killed my mother."

"But you know," Jorge said as he put his hand out. "I do not know if this here is a good idea…"

"No, I want to see," Tony insisted and glanced toward the office. "In there?"

Jorge merely nodded and watched Tony walk toward the small room behind the bar. A small smile crossed his lips. In a time of vengeance, you simply had to make a man crave the taste of blood to ensure his loyalty. Where the police investigation had its limitations, Jorge Hernandez did not.

CHAPTER 36

"They've been clear that they intend to fight me every step of the way," Athas stated with frustration, the usual lackluster in his dark eyes. It was plain to see that politics was slowly sucking away his soul. "I told them if they do, I will come up with even tougher legislation, more red tape, and essentially, I was going to make their lives hell."

To this, Jorge threw his head back in laughter. Clapping his hands together, he glanced toward the desk and shook his head.

"I take it you approve?" Athas said with a smirk slowly starting but quickly ending, on his lips. "This is a Jorge Hernandez type move?"

"It would be," Jorge thought for a moment and shrugged. "One move I would consider."

"I can't do your other moves," Athas said, this time with a smile stretching across his lips even though, his eyes showed otherwise.

Jorge once again threw his head back in laughter before quickly recovering, pushing his chair forward.

"It is coming together," Jorge finally said and raised his eyebrows. "The docuseries, its ratings are very high, it is being talked about online, on social media, this is what we want. Your new laws, they are coming out at the perfect time because people see them as a benefit and not heavy-handed."

"Not *all* people," Athas corrected him. "There are people who are pissed because they can't get their drugs with the same ease they used to. They claim that I'm holding them hostage in the middle of a battle with Big Pharma."

"Well, we did know that there would be unhappy people," Jorge reminded him. "But this here, even though they do not see it, might be to their benefit."

"And yours," Athas reminded him as he started to stand up. "Don't tell me this isn't affecting your sales."

"Well, as of now, I do not see a huge difference, no," Jorge said as he stood up. "But that will change because one of the upcoming shows in the series will be talking about the benefits of marijuana as an alternative to many medications, specifically those for pain."

"I have to admit," Athas replied as the two men headed for the door. "This time, I think our goals are actually aligned."

"Are you suggesting," Jorge smirked as he opened his office door. "That they usually are not?"

Athas didn't reply but gave him a cold look before slipping out of the office.

"So, Athas," Jorge started as they headed toward the front door. "Where are you supposed to be this morning?"

"According to my itinerary," Athas replied as he glanced out the window at his security who was carefully concealed near the house. "I'm supposed to be on the other end of town talking to a young mother about the benefits of various social programs to improve current policies."

"Is that right?" Jorge asked with interest. "So is she sitting somewhere feeling rejected and alone?"

Athas gave him a wry look before he opened the door and walked out.

Amused, Jorge headed back toward his office just as Paige walked downstairs.

"Was that Alec?" She pointed toward the large window in the living room, tilting her head. "Did you have a meeting this morning?"

"Yes, *mi amor*, remember I told you yesterday?" Jorge said as he met her at the end of the stairs.

"You know, between Miguel's temper tantrums and Maria's complaining," She muttered as they headed toward the office. "I don't even know which end is up anymore."

"Oh, I can tell you which end *should* be up," Jorge spoke flirtatiously as he slapped his wife's ass, causing her to jump. "Step into my office, we will discuss this topic further..."

"Jorge, I'm so not in the mood," Paige said and shook her head as they walked through the door. "This morning has been hell. Miguel's turned into the devil's child."

"Well, *mi amor,* some people, they would say he is," Jorge suggested as he closed the door behind them. "And you don't want to talk about which end should be up? Ah, don't tell me that the magic is gone?"

She answered by grabbing him and kissing him with such intensity that he was about to slide his hand under her top when she backed away and started to cry.

"Paige! What is wrong?" He automatically moved forward to instead give her a loving embrace. "I was teasing you..."

"I know," She sniffed. "Miguel just threw one of his toys at me and started screaming. I think he hates me."

"*Mi amor,* he does not hate you," Jorge started to laugh but quickly grew serious. "He is going through a crazy stage. It will end soon. You will see."

"I don't know about that," She replied and moved away, wiping her eyes. "I feel like I'm a terrible mother."

"You are *not* a terrible mother," Jorge corrected her. "I told you before, it is just children, they can be difficult sometimes."

"Not like this," She appeared defeated. "I feel like I never bonded with Miguel."

"Paige, come on..."

"I feel like he looks at me like I'm a stranger."

"Paige, you know this is not true," Jorge insisted. "You worry too much. You're his mother, he loves you."

"And then Maria," She ignored his remark, shaking her head as they walked toward the desk. "*She's* mad at me because she wants to dye her hair blonde and I said no."

"Blonde?" Jorge stopped in his tracks. "What the fuck?"

"I know," Paige turned around to face him. "I told her it wouldn't suit her, she's too dark and that it would damage her hair because they'd have to bleach it too much and she got mad, said that celebrities do it all the time..."

"Oh, fucking celebrities!" Jorge fumed as he walked behind his desk. "Does she not see these celebrities, they are not real people?"

"Well, they are real people," Paige argued as she sat in her usual seat. "But they don't exactly live realistically sometimes. I explained that some of them, it might not even be their real hair but it didn't matter, we argued and she got mad...I can't take it."

"I know, this here, it is hard," Jorge shook his head. "Deranged and psychopathic people, I can handle. Children are a different kind of monster."

Paige started to laugh.

"See, *mi amor*, I make you laugh," Jorge spoke flirtatiously. "I didn't even have to fuck you and yet, I can put a smile on your face. Although, if it will help..."

"I don't want to seem...how did you put it earlier?" Paige spoke evenly. "Like the magic is gone but today, I feel zero magic about anything."

"Well, for today," Jorge said and took a deep breath. "I can cancel my day? We can go somewhere that has no children? No screaming children, at least."

"Don't you have meetings today?"

"Well, *mi amor*, I am hoping Marco can find the identity of who shot Tony's mother so I can take care of that person," Jorge said as he leaned back in his chair.

"I can't believe he's back to work already."

"He is a man on a mission," Jorge said and took a deep breath. "I believe his exact words were 'they killed my mother so I'm taking them down'. The man, he has a new passion driving this project."

"But do we know for sure it was Big Pharma behind the murder?"

"The man, in the recording, he is a professional," Jorge confirmed. "He showed the signs of a man who had no reluctance also, he stole no money, just shot her and left. That was definitely a hit."

"It does sound like a professional hit," Paige agreed.

"Maybe you," Jorge leaned on his desk. "Would know this man, if I show you the picture?"

"I know I lived the life," Paige replied. "But, I didn't know other people in it."

"But your boss lady, the one with no name, she would know."

Paige made a face.

"I know, you do not want to talk to her but, we must find this man."

"I don't want to talk to her because I'm afraid if I ask her for a favor, she'll want something from me."

Jorge didn't reply but nodded.

"And she's not going to give up the name of one of her people," Paige continued. "So you can kill him. After all, I already killed one of her people. I don't know if she'll appreciate if I take another."

"But is it possible," Jorge considered. "That it is not one of her people but she might know who it is?"

Paige thought for a moment. "I…I don't know…"

"We must find the man's identity."

"But even if it is a hitman," Paige reminded him. "We have to find out who hired him, then go after that person. I know Tony probably wants him killed but honestly, he's just doing a job for someone else."

"Yes, this is true," Jorge considered. "Maybe we can skip the middle man and go right to the top."

"When I did professional killings," Paige thought for a moment. "They used to write me off as an advisor expense in their books. That's how they got away with it. They made up fake charges that looked legit on paper. At least, at one company I did work for."

"Interesting," Jorge thought for a moment. "*Mi amor,* we must swing by the office and enlighten Marco on such things. I believe he might be able to pinpoint it in the books if not find the man himself."

"I can tell him what he might be looking for," Paige suddenly seemed to brighten up. "And then we need to know who sent the order."

"This here," Jorge said as he started to stand. "This would be perfect."

CHAPTER 37

"Is that Jolene?" Paige suddenly asked out of nowhere as they drove through downtown Toronto. She turned in her seat, twisting her neck around and swung back. "I'm sure I saw her."

"*Mi amor,* although I expect almost anything from Jolene," Jorge replied with a casual shrug. "I do not see her returning to Toronto anytime soon, if ever, after my last conversation with her."

Paige didn't reply but simply nodded.

"However, if she does," Jorge continued. "I think I was pretty clear on the potential…consequences."

"But when has Jolene ever listened?" Paige muttered and sighed loudly.

"Paige, right now, I am more worried about you," Jorge insisted, brushing off her concerns over Jolene. "This here, it is not you. Maybe you need some time on your meditation pillow?"

"I think I need a month on my meditation pillow," Paige admitted as they moved through traffic. "It seems like between the kids and my former…boss, for lack of better words, with her showing up and the extra responsibilities…"

"Which you can drop at any time," Jorge quickly cut her off. "me, I can take on everything and anything. You worry about the kids, yourself, do not worry about this other stuff."

"But that's not realistic," Paige insisted. "Life isn't about cutting things out when it's inconvenient. You're busy too. You have a lot on your plate. I can't seem to handle anything. Maybe something is wrong with me."

"*Mi amor,* there is nothing wrong with you," Jorge assured her as he reached over to touch her hand then looked back at the road. "This here, it is life. Things, they will get better."

"Jorge, I'm not telling you everything," She suddenly burst in tears. "I was afraid you'd get upset."

"Paige," Jorge felt his heart race as he crept closer to the office building. Pulling into the underground parking lot, he quickly swung into the first spot he saw and shifted the SUV into park. Unbuckling his seatbelt, he reached out for his wife who now covered her face with both hands. "Paige, please, you are scaring me. What is going on? Are you sick?"

"No, I'm fine but everything… is going wrong," She finally managed the words. Stopping, Paige turned and looked in his eyes. "The woman, the one who hires me to assassinate…"

"What? What does she want?" Jorge automatically grew defensive. "I will fucking shoot that bitch if she…"

"No, just no," Paige shook her head. "She…when she was at the house, the day you came home, I didn't tell you everything."

"I do not understand," Jorge attempted to move closer as his hand gently touched her back. "What does she want? For you to kill someone?"

"Yes," Paige answered and swallowed, slowly turning around in her seat. "you."

"What?" Jorge started to laugh and quickly stop. "Paige, I…I do not understand."

"She didn't know we're married," Paige continued to sob. "I thought she was lying at first but it was clear she was shocked when I told her we had been together since the night I broke into the wrong room."

Jorge was stunned. He couldn't speak. He thought back to when he met Paige, as she prepared to kill him until she realizing that she had the wrong man. He had finally turned around to see the face of an angel.

"After everything came out," Paige spoke slowly. "I begged her to tell me who wanted you dead. That's when you came home. The only promise she made me that day was she would stall everything. Since then, I've been secretly trying to find out on my own."

"*Mi amor,* this here, it is a lot," Jorge gently caressed her shoulder with his hand. "I wish…I wish you had told me sooner."

"I couldn't," Paige said as she looked into his eyes. "I thought I could do this myself. But now I'm scared. She's not getting back to me. I still don't have my answers. I'm not sleeping at night, scared someone will break in the house. I'm worried about everything with the kids. I wanted to take care of this myself.…"

"Paige, we are married," Jorge cut her off. "You do not have to take care of this yourself. I do appreciate you doing this for me however, it is not the first time someone wanted me dead. It does not mean they will or should be successful. We must take care of this now. Find out who is behind it. And your boss lady? This here, it is going to be resolved. We are cutting the cord on her."

"But what if we can't?" Paige cut in. "She's very dangerous."

"She may be," Jorge replied. "But so am I. And for that matter, so are you. And she knows this."

"So what do we do?" Paige said as she shook her head.

"You say, she is not getting back to you?"

"No."

"Let her know you would like to have a meeting," Jorge said as he pointed toward the phone. "You tell her you want to discuss killing me."

"Jorge!" Paige snapped. "I am *not* saying that."

"Well, then," Jorge said with a shrug. "You tell her that you are demanding a meeting. That we need resolution here."

Paige didn't reply.

"First, we find out who is behind this," Jorge insisted. "Then second, we find a way to negotiate for her to no longer be in your life. This ends now."

"I'm scared she won't listen."

"We will make her listen. Tell her I know."

Paige looked troubled but didn't speak.

"Send her a message now," Jorge insisted. "Make arrangements for us to meet as soon as possible. I will find who wants me dead and take care of them. And if she will not cooperate, then *she* might be my next victim."

Paige nodded but still appeared hesitant.

"*Mi amor,*" He tilted his head. "Is there anything else you aren't telling me?"

"What?" Paige shook her head as if confused. "Isn't *this* enough?"

"Paige, I know that you are upset but as I said, this is not the first threat I have experienced," Jorge reminded her. "And I am not afraid. We will take care of her. One way or the other."

Paige tapped on her phone before sitting it down, staring into space.

"I'm so afraid she won't answer," She finally spoke in barely a whisper. "I..I never wanted to...this life..."

"Paige, if she knows I know, she will," Jorge insisted and took a deep breath. "We will take care of this problem and from there, we can see. Maybe we need to move out of the line of fire as we have always said. I do not know but we cannot figure this out until we know all the facts."

Paige's phone dinged. She glanced at it with a look of surprise on her face.

"She said we can meet tomorrow."

"Ok."

"At the house," Paige took a deep breath. "I don't want to meet her at the house. The kids..."

"Maria, she will be in school," Jorge reminded her. "And Miguel, he will be with Juliana. That way he is safe."

Paige nodded as tears slid down her face.

"This here, it will be ok," Jorge nodded. "Tell her you will meet with her tomorrow."

Paige tapped on her phone and stopped.

"I feel like I'm going to be sick," She finally whispered.

"Paige, tomorrow, we will be prepared," Jorge reminded her. "We will see what she has to say, find out who is behind this and we will take charge."

"She's not going to reveal the names that easily."

"She will if we can promise her something in return."

"But what?"

"That is a good question."

"Ok," She appeared hesitant.

"And Paige, we must remain calm," Jorge reminded her. "You must talk to Marco and find the identity of the killer at the mall. If I had to guess, it is the same people who also wish me dead."

"It would make sense," Paige nodded. "She wouldn't say but she did visit around the same time that you embarked on this film project."

"There are no such things as coincidences, *mi amor*," Jorge said and reached out to touch a strand of her blonde hair. "And this here timing, it is not a coincidence. We both know this."

"I know," She said in a quiet voice. "I wanted to protect you. I wanted to believe I could do this on my own."

"You can," Jorge assured her. "But why should you? You got me."

He stared at her for a long moment before he reached forward and gave her a gentle kiss.

"Now," He moved away. "You must go to the office and talk to Marco. If we can find where the money is coming from, we can also learn who is responsible for Tony's mother's death. Once we know that, we might also learn who would like to see me dead too."

Paige nodded before silently, almost mechanically, getting out the SUV and heading for the elevator. It was only after she was gone that Jorge called Diego.

"Hey, what's up?"

"Paige is on her way upstairs," Jorge spoke quickly. "But you, you gotta try to avoid her and come down here. We need to talk."

"Ok," Diego grew serious on the other end of the line. "What's wrong?"

"We got a problem," Jorge insisted. "A big fucking problem."

CHAPTER 38

Her heart raced in anticipation of the meeting. She dreaded it but at the same time, wanted to look the Argentina woman in the eye, knowing she no longer had any power over her. The secret was out. Jorge knew that someone wanted him dead. Although Paige had made every effort to protect him, to take matters into her own hands, she regretfully had been unsuccessful.

There comes a point where you have to put your cards on the table. It was something Paige still struggled with, even though she had technically left the assassin life a few years earlier. Her old life required a lot of secrecy and there were times when she had to make a conscious effort to not fall into her old ways. It's so difficult to change your habits, the same ones that had once kept you alive. Although she had come a long way, something was different this time. Perhaps it was the suggestion that she kill her husband.

Paige couldn't tell Jorge the whole truth. If he knew that her former boss specifically requested Paige murder her husband, that there was no confusion that the two were married, he would've flown in a rage. That, in itself, could've been a trap that he'd walk into when his emotions were bubbling at the surface and perhaps not be as vigilant. Paige knew her husband. She knew how he acted in any given situation and for that reason, she had to plan carefully. She had hoped to resolve this behind the scenes while he was busy with the docuseries but all she found were roadblocks.

"She's not going to tell us anything," Paige assured him that morning, knowing that the likelihood that he'd have any success shaking her down was slim. This woman had grown rich by keeping her mouth shut despite what was waved in her face, whether it be threats or money. She had a reputation to consider.

"Paige," Jorge shook his head as he glanced out the window, expecting her to arrive. "I have dealt with this kind of woman before."

"But she's probably not going to be alone," She reminded him. "And if we..."

"She was alone last time, Paige," Jorge reminded her. "And *mi amor*, she does not fear us so why wouldn't she?"

Paige wasn't so sure.

"Trust me, the message you sent her, it was not threatening," Jorge insisted. "She thinks she is here to negotiate. She may not even want me dead at all. It is a way to persuade you to do a bigger job, as a way to protect me. She thinks this here, it will be a negotiation session."

Jorge stated his theory as a fact and for a moment, she admired his overly confident manner however, she feared that he was barking up the wrong tree. The woman they were dealing with was very manipulative and devious. It was never that simple.

She arrived shortly afterward and as Jorge guessed, she was alone. Wearing a beautiful, white designer suit, she strolled in with confidence, her dark eyes staring through Jorge while he gave her a polite smile.

"Please, we must go to the office," He pointed in the general direction, throwing on his usual charm. "Would you like something to drink? Coffee? Tea? Anything?"

"No, this is fine," Her reply was formal, giving nothing in return.

"Then please, this way," Jorge said and the three of them headed toward the office. The Argentinian turned her attention on Paige as they did.

"You, you are the quiet one this morning."

"I'm always quiet," Paige answered evenly.

"You look pale," She said as she studied Paige's face with a cold stare. "Maybe, maybe you are pregnant again. Another baby, perhaps?"

Jorge laughed heartily just as they reached the office.

"Oh, that there, she will not like to hear," Jorge spoke lightly, turning, he winked at his wife. "Isn't that right, *mi amor,* no more screaming babies?"

"One is enough," Paige said, allowing a hint of a smile on her face as she followed them both into the office and closed the door behind them. "Thanks just the same."

"Children, they are a handful," Their guest spoke abruptly as the three of them took their seats around the desk. "I could never have any, myself."

"This is unfortunate," Jorge said with compassion in his eyes. "They are a handful but they are beautiful, at the same time."

The Argentinian merely nodded.

Paige bit her lower lip and took a deep breath. She felt her heart race. Something was unsettling about having her past and present in the same room. While Jorge was her whole life now, at one time, the woman sitting beside her was not only her boss but her mentor, the person who discovered and made Paige into the woman she was today. It was as if she was responsible for bringing these two worlds together.

"So, we are here to discuss what Paige has told you, *si?*" She took over automatically. It was a power-play however, Jorge had his version of the same game.

"Yes," He answered graciously as if he didn't want to murder her with his bare hands. "I thought, we need to put everything out in the open."

Paige nodded but remained silent. Observing the mood in the room, the tiny hairs on the back of her neck were rising, she knew it was better to step back.

"I believe so too."

"You told my wife that someone wants me killed," Jorge spoke with no judgment, no anger, it was almost as if they were casually discussing something that had no meaning. "I am here to ask who."

"And not why?" She appeared amused.

Jorge shook his head.

"*Senorita,* do you *really* think I do not know *why* people want me dead?"

With that, she threw her head back in laughter, causing Paige to jump. Her reaction was so bizarre, that of a crazy woman. Jorge smirked, his dark eyes appearing amused. Paige felt a chill run through her body.

"You find this humorous?" He finally asked with an amused expression on his face.

"I do appreciate a man who recognizes....where he fits into the world," She spoke pointedly.

"Well, if you have been in my world for long enough," Jorge said as he leaned back in his chair. "This here is to be expected. I do tend to rile up the animals regularly."

"This is what I hear."

"So, you must tell me, who have I riled up at this time?"

"You do not know?"

"My guess?" Jorge said and shrugged. "Big Pharma? They are, after all, my nemesis."

"Perhaps."

"Someone from my past?"

"This is possible too."

Jorge continued to look at ease if not somewhat irritated.

"Lady, I think we need to talk about who it is for sure," Jorge spoke a little more sternly this time.

"I do not reveal my clients."

"Well, sign me up as your client," Jorge spoke flippantly. "I will pay more."

"It is not about money but loyalty...trust."

"I know all about loyalty and trust," Jorge replied and leaned forward on his desk. "This here is what my life centers on so I respect what you say. However, I must know who wants me dead so I can resolve this situation."

"This, I cannot tell you," She replied. "However, I know how to alleviate this situation."

"What do you mean?"

"If Paige is willing to potentially consider another victim," The Argentinian turned toward her. "My client says that he will let you go."

"Let me go?" Jorge was humored. "So, he will let me live? This is interesting. Who is it that compares to me so much that this person, they feel that we are an equal trade?"

"And how do we know this is true?" Paige found her voice. "Who's to say that takes my husband out of danger?"

"It is my word, Paige," She spoke abruptly, her dark eyes narrowing. "I do not give you my word unless I mean it and you know this is true."

Paige didn't reply.

"It is a man that is as powerful as you," She returned her attention to Jorge. "Someone who also has caused a great deal of misery to my client. And it is someone Paige has access to."

Before she said it, Paige knew. She felt her blood turn cold and heaviness in the pit of her stomach. A quiet fury started to simmer in her heart, slowly moving through her veins. She felt something light up inside of her, a spark that seemed to ignite a power that sent a force of rage through every inch of her body.

"He is," The Argentinian continued. "Alec Athas, your prime minister."

Paige shared a look with Jorge.

"I can't do that," Paige answered with a little more emotion in her voice than she intended.

"Well, you have no choice," The Argentinian insisted. "It is your former lover....or your husband. There is no third option."

Jorge appeared concerned as he looked into her face.

"Perhaps, this is, a much more difficult decision than I originally thought," She continued. "I believed it would be an easy choice. Maybe I underestimated the strength of your relationship."

The last remark was directed at Jorge who remained calm, glancing at his wife who took a deep breath.

"But that is the options," She rose from her chair and glanced at Paige, then Jorge. "You kill your husband or you kill Alec Athas. And if you refused to do this, then I will have someone else take care of it. And I cannot guarantee that my client, he won't grow anxious and simply insist on killing them both."

Paige turned toward her, making sure to show no emotion.

"Imagine, losing your former...it is, *former* lover, isn't it Paige? Or your husband," She spoke flippantly and glanced at Jorge. "Of course, if there is still something going on with you and Athas, I am guessing that I will not have to worry about *you* killing him."

With this, she let out another hearty laugh.

Paige felt the anger burning through her veins like a bullet as she jumped out of the chair. Without giving it a second thought, she lurched toward the Argentinean woman, locking both her hands around her neck. The woman attempted to struggle but her grip was so tight that she had little strength to fight back. The only thing that stopped her from killing the woman was Jorge yelling in the background.

"We must find out who hired her!"

Paige stopped, stared into the frightened eyes of her victim, and with one sudden movement, she backhanded her with such power that the older woman fell to the floor. It was there that Paige stood over her, she pulled out her gun.

"We're playing by my rules now, bitch."

CHAPTER 39

"Lady, I got no use for you," Jorge remarked after he pulled out his gun and demanded that the older, Argentinian woman get back on the chair. Her original shield of power had dimmed slightly but not as much as he had hoped. "So, there are now two new options on the table."

He glanced at Paige who was also pointing a gun at her former boss.

"Option one, you tell me who wants me and Athas dead," Jorge said as he glared into the woman's eyes. "And you can go home and live happily ever after. The second option is you don't talk and we kill you."

"I cannot reveal the identity of the client."

"Oh yeah, you willing to take this to the grave?" Jorge asked with interest.

"I've had a gun pointed at me before."

"So, why shouldn't I kill you?" He countered.

"Because this will not stop the man who wants you dead," She insisted. "This is not the magical solution you have hoped for."

"Just tell us!" Paige snapped.

"I agree, enough with these games," Jorge shouted. "We do not like games here. You knew very well that Paige was not going to kill either of us. So what do you really want?"

"You haven't had me on a wild goose chase for nothing," Paige added. "He's right, there's more to all this."

"Well, to put it simply," The Argentinian shrugged. "The options I gave you were what was asked of me."

Jorge saw his wife's face turn pink in response.

"But I knew you. I knew how you would act," She continued. "I knew you would not tell him, that you would get upset and try to figure it out and not be able to and out of frustration and desperation, you would come back to me and that is when I would suggest that you take the other option and kill Alec Athas."

Paige didn't respond. Jorge watched her reaction closely but also kept his eyes on the Argentinian.

"It is him that they really want," She continued. "At least, for now."

"Why didn't you tell me that from the beginning?"

"I had to make you desperate. Only then, I could make you do something that even you, did not want to do," She spoke coldly. "Paige, you have no soul. This, you have proven again and again. You were trained by a navy seal. They turn off their emotions when they kill. I knew that you could do the same. Not with your husband, of course, but Athas? I figured this was a fair trade-off."

Before Jorge could stop her, Paige abruptly jumped ahead and once again backhanded the Argentinian with such force, he thought she was going to fall off the chair. Stepping back, she pointed the gun at her head this time while the older woman attempted to blink back the tears.

"Tell me!" She yelled. "Tell me now or I will blow your fucking head off."

"Ah, but *mi amor,*" Jorge attempted to calm the situation. "But this here, it will leave a mess in my office. You know, blood, brains, it is hard to clean up. I do not want this *puta's* brains on my lampshade if you know what I mean."

Paige didn't respond but continued to hold the gun close to the woman's head.

"But you know, I do have another idea," He continued. "I am thinking of contacting Andrew."

Paige exchanged looks with him.

"You see, Andrew," Jorge continued. "He can heat the ovens and although this woman is on her way to the burning flames of hell, she perhaps was hoping to meet them *after* she was dead."

"What is this you are talking about?" She shot back as she regained her composure from Paige's attack.

"Well, you see," Jorge stated with some arrogance in his voice. "I recently had the foresight to purchase a crematorium."

He saw it. She tried to hide it but there was an obvious shift in her reaction.

"And the beautiful thing about owning such a business is that you have the option of burning a body," Jorge continued. "It is the perfect way to get rid of it. I cannot believe I never thought of it before."

The woman kept a stiff upper lip but her defenses were fading.

"And to send someone in, fully awake and conscious and seeing the fire," Jorge continued as he tilted his head down. "Smelling it. Feeling the heat. Knowing the pain as the flames burn through your body."

"I've burnt people alive before," Paige spoke calmly as she raised an eyebrow, sharing looks with Jorge. "The screams, there are no screams like the ones of someone about to catch on fire. It's like an animal being slaughter."

"It is not much different, *mi amor,*" Jorge insisted.

"You bluff," The Argentinian insisted.

"I do not bluff," Jorge replied as he reached for his phone while continuing to point a gun at her with the other hand. Turning it on, he exchanged looks with Paige. "Andrew, he is next door. Maybe we can make a little road trip."

"You bluff," She repeated from the chair.

"Oh yeah," Jorge said as he found the number and hit it. "I'll put him on speakerphone."

"Hey," Andrew's voice could be heard.

"Andrew, we have you on speaker," Jorge spoke loudly. "I have someone here who does not believe me when I say, that I own a crematorium."

"Really?" Andrew laughed. "Someone who obviously doesn't know Jorge Hernandez well. Yeah, he fucking owns it."

"And Andrew, tell me something," Jorge continued. "What are the chances, do you think that we could sneak someone in this morning?"

"Pretty good," He replied. "I'm going in later today but I can go sooner."

"And Andrew, tell me something else," Jorge continued. "How surprised would you be if I suggest to you that I might want to roast a live chicken? Would you say on a scale of 1 to 10, how likely I would do this."

Andrew laughed.

"Ah, with 10 meaning you would most likely do it?"

"Yes."

"Oh, then like, definitely 21 or something."

With that, both he and Andrew burst into laughter while the Argentinian looked less humored.

"This here, it does sound right," Jorge agreed.

"Whoever you got there," Andrew spoke up. "If they know you, they *know* you got no conscious. You'll do it. And you'll laugh."

A grin appeared on Paige's face.

"Thank you, Andrew," Jorge replied. "That's all I need to know."

"Do you want me to set it up?" He replied.

"Hmmm....it depends," Jorge replied and glanced at the Argentinian. "You ready to talk lady, or what?"

"I do not believe this little act." She replied.

"I say, go get the home fires burning," Jorge instructed. "We will meet you soon."

"OK, will do."

They ended the call and Jorge challenged the Argentinian with his eyes.

"So, you got a change of heart yet or what?"

"You do not scare me," She replied. "I know this is not true."

"I guess you'll soon find out," Jorge suggested.

"But if you kill me," She reminded him. "You do not have your information. So it is pointless."

"Something tells me that when you're face to face with your torturous death," Jorge insisted. "You will feel very differently. It is easy to say now when you could simply be shot, die automatically. That is too easy. But in Mexico, as you probably know, we believe that sometimes people, they have a change of heart when you turn up the flames."

She didn't respond.

"Although, we usually mean this figuratively," Jorge continued. "In this case, it is, in fact, quite literally."

"Do you want me to call Diego?" Paige asked.

"Yes, he is waiting for our instructions."

Paige moved away and reached for her phone while Jorge continued to study his victim. Leaving the room, his wife nodded at him on her way out.

"I do not understand why you are protecting this person so much," Jorge continued "It is just business."

"But in my business, silence is golden."

"Is it worth more than your life?"

"You will not kill me because I have the answers."

"You wanna bet on that, lady?"

"But then, how will you know who wants Athas dead?"

"Why do you think I care so much if he lives?"

"You don't but your wife, she feels differently."

"She'll get over it."

"You will take a chance on this man dying? The man you control?"

"I'll control the next prime minister too."

"You really think it's easy."

"Lady, I've run the show here since moving to Canada," Jorge insisted. "I can have whatever I want. If Athas dies, he dies."

"Paige she will not be happy to learn this."

"As I said, she will get over it."

They glared at one another.

He was winning. There was doubt in her eyes.

He always won.

And he always would.

CHAPTER 40

"So this is the one here," Diego asked while nodding his head toward the Argentinian woman, tied up, lying on the crematorium floor. Nearby, Chase stood beside Paige, while watching Andrew check the temperature on the cremation oven. "Is this the pig we're about to roast?"

"This is her, the lady with no name," Jorge spoke with satisfaction, making eye contact with the older woman as she struggled to sit up on the floor. "Hey, lady, you may as well keep lying down cause Andrew's gonna put you in a box anyway, so you know…"

"It doesn't matter," Andrew quickly jumped in, calmly, as if what they were about to do wasn't out of the ordinary. "Even if she tries to sit up when the conveyor belt moves, she'll have no option other than lie down or she might have her face scrapped off."

"Ah! But does that matter at this point?" Jorge spoke with pleasure in his voice. "She will be dead soon anyway."

"If you kill me," She spoke up in a hoarse voice. "You will never know who wants Athas dead."

"I am sure that, we can figure it out," Jorge insisted. "And regardless, we will make sure he has added security so, this here, it does not worry me."

"If they do not get him, they will get you," She threatened, however, this was met by laughter.

"Oh, lady, you do not know me that well," Jorge said as he approached her. "Otherwise, you would know that me, I do not scare easily. This here, it will not work."

"But you," Jorge continued as he walked away. "*You*, on the other hand, I am not so sure about. You see, this here oven, it gets up to, what is it, Andrew? Is it 1000 degrees celsius?"

"About 800 is nice but I can go higher," Andrew answered as he picked up a large, coffin-shaped cardboard box and walked to the center of the room. "And it takes about 3 hours to burn the body, approximately."

"See, this here is good news," Jorge spoke joyfully. "We can all go out, enjoy a nice meal while she cooks. We never *do* get enough time together."

Chase made a face while Andrew nodded.

"Oh yeah, you got lots of time."

"I don't know if I want to eat after hearing about any of this," Chase looked ill. "The idea of her body burning here and going out to have lunch…"

"Ah! The boy has become a man but yet, he has a way to go," Jorge commented with humor in his voice. "One day, Chase, one day, you will think nothing of this."

"Yeah, you just don't want to stick around while we're cooking the body," Andrew piped up. "It's a fucking stench you can't unsmell if you know what I mean."

"Sometimes," Jorge said with an evil grin on his face. "You sniff the flowers and you cannot get the scent out for days."

Chase looked like he was going to vomit.

"Chase, I think you might want to go get some fresh air," Jorge commented. "You are not looking well."

"Yeah, um…I'll be in the office…"

They watched as the group's youngest member left the room, closing the door behind him.

"I guess, Chase, he did not wish to witness your death," Jorge commented in a calm voice. "But me, I do not have a queasy stomach. I am looking *forward* to it."

For the first time, he could see something change in her eyes. Perhaps it was the flames coming from the oven nearby, as Andrew checked it once again before returning to the center of the floor where he proceeded to tape the cardboard coffin together.

"Well, Jorge," Paige started in her usual, even tone. "It's not for everyone. It's a pretty graphic way to murder someone."

"It *is* a very horrendous way to die, *mi amor,*" Jorge agreed with her as he approached his wife, putting his arm around her. "But it is, you might say, justifiable. After all, she wanted you to kill your husband and of course, our prime minister. Such disrespect!"

"And she knew I wouldn't," Paige said as she nodded. "So if she really wanted either of these things done, she would've had someone else do it."

"You have access to both," The Argentinian attempted to argue from the floor. "That is why I picked you."

"But you *knew* I wouldn't do it," Paige reminded her again. "So what did you really want?"

"Maybe it's a loyalty thing," Diego suggested. "You know, maybe in exchange for their lives, you come back to work for her…this would be an advantage to her."

"Come on," Jorge said and shook his head. "She must know that Paige, she would never do that. She is not going to leave her whole family behind for that kind of life once again. No one in her right mind would think this."

"*Right* mind," Diego repeated.

"Well, this here, is a good point."

"I thought she would kill Athas," The woman attempted to repeat her same story. "That is all I wanted. If she does this, I will leave her alone. I will leave you alone. I will not return to your life again."

"The way I see it, lady," Diego pointed toward the oven before glancing down at Andrew, as he completed taping the coffin-shaped box. "You won't be anyway."

Jorge let out a hearty laugh and squeezed Paige's shoulder before moving away from her and closer to his victim.

"This here, it is true, Diego. So very true."

"You will not kill me," She insisted. "You wish to learn who wanted you and Athas dead, do you not?"

"Yes, but if you will not tell me, then what difference does it make?" Jorge spoke logically. "I am no further ahead but at least, I get the satisfaction of knowing that you can no longer return to Paige's life."

"I know you are trying to frighten me."

Jorge ignored her remark and turned toward Andrew. "You ready?"

"We just got to put her body up there," Andrew said as he stood up and pointed toward the conveyor belt. "Then start moving her in."

"The cover?" Jorge pointed toward the cardboard that was to be placed over the body. "We do not need. I want her to see everything."

"Good point," Andrew nodded.

"Then, let us do this," Jorge commented as he pointed toward the woman on the floor, her eyes now full of doubt. "She looks small, but she might fight so let us all put her in the box.

The three men approached her and despite her best attempts to wiggle away, they had no issue fitting her into the cardboard box, while Paige watched from the distance. Hoisting her body up, they sat her on the conveyor belt while, Jorge could see the terror in her black eyes, indicating that she finally recognized that he wasn't bluffing. He had every intention of burning her alive.

"Paige, there is a digital camera somewhere," Jorge turned toward his wife. "Maybe, we should take pictures. That way, if anyone thinks that this woman's life is of any value and wants to retaliate, we can show them what we do to people who try to fuck with us."

"Yeah, don't put that shit on your phone," Diego jumped in. "Big Brother is always watching."

"Well, they aren't always Diego," Jorge corrected him. "They are probably too busy watching unaware, teenage girls undress in front of their phone but yes, sometimes, they do watch. And let us not give them anything to work with."

"Camera's over there," Andrew pointed toward a desk in the corner.

Paige followed instructions while Andrew walked closer to the oven, studying some buttons. The flames seemed to grow as heat filled the room, something that made Jorge smile, his dark eyes turning toward the woman.

"You know, I do not even know if I care who wanted us dead," He spoke quietly, so only she could hear. "I think it would give me great pleasure to see you burn to death in front of my eyes. You have put my wife through torture this last few weeks, Now, it is time for you to see how *I* do torture."

"But you want to know…"

"I keep hearing this song and dance but lady," Jorge shook his head. "You are like a virgin who keeps saying she wants to fuck but yet, I don't see you taking off your clothes. So you better start talking…"

When the door suddenly flew open, Jorge expected Chase to walk in but instead was stunned to see Jolene Silva prance in the room, dressed professionally, her heels clicking loudly on the floor. Evaluating the situation, she grimaced.

"Jolene, what the hell are you doing here?" Diego spoke for them all. "Aren't you supposed to be with your *lover* in Mexico? You're *out* Jolene, accept it."

"Do I look *out, Diego?*" She snapped back as she approached the woman on the conveyor belt. Glancing at the Argentinian, then back at Jorge, she waved her hand in the air. "What are you waiting for? Why do you always talk to your victims? This one here, just kill her!"

Before Jorge could respond, he watched in disbelief as she approached the oven and was about to press the button when the woman on the belt let out a blood-curdling scream, stopping them all in their tracks.

"For fuck sakes, Jolene," Diego snapped as he rushed behind her. "Jorge got a way to do things, you need to back off and let him."

"No, you know," Jorge considered the idea for a moment, glancing at the Argentinian. "I got things to do today, she ain't gonna talk so let us get this over with, so I can talk to Jolene and find out why the fuck she's back here."

"*Perfecto!*" Jolene spoke hastily and reached for the button. "I have to talk to you too, Jorge. It is important."

Paige exchanged looks with her husband just as Jolene casually pressed the button as if she was waiting for an elevator to arrive on her floor. The conveyor belt started to move much more quickly than Jorge anticipated while the Argentinian began to scream again.

"Lady, do not bother, the walls, they are soundproof," Jorge insisted as he gave her a dark glare.

"Stop! Please! I talk!"

Rolling her eyes, Jolene reached out and hit the button that halted the production.

"I got other bodies to do today," Andrew reminded Jorge. "I got to do this soon."

"I'll talk!" The woman continued to scream as tears ran down her cheeks. A glance down her body revealed she had urinated in the cardboard box. "Please, I talk!!"

"I'm listening, lady," Jorge spoke gruffly. "But you give me the wrong name, you give me the wrong information, this here is merely postponed *not* canceled."

"I will give you the name," She cried. "Please, do not do this, please, I beg you."

"For fuck sakes, are you going to tell us or what?" Diego snapped while the others around her showed no compassion. "Give us a name!"

"She lie!" Jolene insisted as she returned her finger to the button. "Let us kill now."

"Melvin Gates!" She screamed. "That's the man, he wants you both dead."

"Who the fuck is that?" Jorge asked as he gestured for Jolene to step back from the button.

"He is an investor," The Argentinian replied. "He has made millions off Big Pharma and now, he is losing and it is because of you. Your cannabis, your series, law changes. He wants you both dead but he said he would settle for one."

"Tell us where we can find him," Paige instructed.

"Will you let me live?"

"Tell us what you know," Jorge replied with a sharp tone. "And I'll fucking think about it."

CHAPTER 41

"I'm going to see Marco," Diego spoke in a low tone as the two men stood on the other side of the room. Jorge listened to his friend while simultaneously watching the Argentinian woman sitting in a chair while Andrew prepared for his first official cremation of the day. Jolene and Paige were having a quiet discussion nearby. "I'll get him to do some research. I'll be back."

"This is good," Jorge nodded as his attention returned to his *hermano*. "I do thank you."

"Find out what the fuck is going on with Jolene," Diego's eyes narrowed on his sister. "I thought she was gone."

"Do not worry my friend," Jorge insisted as his face darkened. "I do plan to find out. With Jolene, we never can guess."

Diego followed his gaze and made a face.

"I'll be back," He repeated as he headed toward the door, just as Andrew turned his attention back to Jorge.

"We gotta get her out of here,' He said, gesturing toward the Argentinian woman. "As much as I'd love to show her what we were about to do to her, I got another guy coming in soon and she can't be here."

"We could lock her in the upstairs office," Paige suggested before turning her attention toward Andrew. "Or is there a better place?"

"I got a place for her," He quickly replied. "But we gotta take her now."

Paige agreed as they gestured for the Argentinian to get off the chair. She did so awkwardly since her hands were still tied. The urine stain was prominent through her white outfit. Jorge looked away quickly but glanced at Paige as they helped her along.

"Do not forget to cover her mouth and tie her legs again," Jorge spoke abruptly, ignoring the pained look on the woman's face. "We don't need her kicking and screaming."

"I got duct tape," Andrew replied as him and Paige walked past with the Argentinian moving awkwardly along. "Don't worry, she's not going anywhere."

"No, she can sit and…think about everything," Paige gently suggested. "Perhaps that is punishment enough."

Jorge shared a look with his wife. He knew exactly what she was thinking.

"Perhaps, *mi amor,* perhaps."

Left alone with Jolene, Jorge automatically turned to her with a dark glare.

"What the fuck are you doing back?" He snapped at her. "Are you stupid, Jolene? I thought I was clear with you in our last conversation."

"Some things, they changed," She replied sheepishly causing Jorge to grow angry. "I need to talk."

"How the fuck did you know we were here?"

"I call, you did not answer," Jolene replied as her eyes widened. "I call Diego, no answer. I knew something was up. I call the office and no one was there. I call the bar, no one was there. So, I…"

"Ok, Jolene," Jorge put his hand up to signal for her to stop. "Let us go somewhere to talk before the other employee arrives."

"My office?"

"It is no longer your office."

"You know what I mean."

Jorge shook his head before pointing her toward the door. Sighing loudly, he followed her upstairs and down the hallway to the office where he found Chase sitting behind the desk. He looked shocked when he saw Jolene. He opened his mouth to say something but Jorge shook his head.

"Don't ask."

"Ok," Chase stood up and headed toward the door. "I'll leave you guys…"

"Thank you, Chase," Jorge replied. "Can you go to check on the others? They are taking our friend to a secret room of some kind."

"I think I know the one," Chase nodded before giving Jolene a skeptical glance then leaving, closing the door behind him.

"This better be good, Jolene," Jorge snapped as he walked behind the desk. "I am not in the mood for some big story."

"Enrique and me, we did not work out."

"This already sounds like the kind of story I do not care about," Jorge commented as he sat down while she found a chair on the other side. "You know, I do not like the soap operas..."

"It is not a *telenovela*," Jolene insisted with a fierce assertion. "This is my *life*."

Jorge didn't reply.

"His wife, she come back," Jolene spoke with tears in her eyes. "I found them, in *our* bed."

"Jolene, what did I just tell you?"

"I know but this is the story," She spoke weakly. "Just imagine how you would feel if that were Paige and she..."

"I will not imagine that!" Jorge snapped. "Jolene, you broke up their marriage. Are you really in the position to get angry now."

"But what if Paige, she was with someone when you met?" Jolene challenged. "You would not pursue?"

Jorge looked away.

"The point is," Jolene continued. "I found them and I was in shock! I did not know what to do but my first instinct was to kill both."

"Is this what you did?" Jorge was suddenly intrigued. "Did you kill them both?"

"No, almost, but no," She replied sheepishly.

Jorge lost interest again. He looked away.

"I say....what would Jorge Hernandez do in this situation?" She started and tears once again formed in her eyes. "I wonder, what if you found..."

"Jolene, do *not* go there," Jorge snapped at her. "Do I have to remind you that I told you *never* to come back or what *I* would do to *you*? If I were you, I would realize that getting on my last nerve, it is not a good idea right now."

She sat back in her chair and looked away.

"What do you want, Jolene?"

"I want back."

"It is not happening," Jorge stood up. "You had your chance and in fact, you have had a few chances so this here, it will not work."

"But I need back, you are my only family," She cried as she jumped up from her chair. "You cannot turn me away."

"Jolene, you had every chance," Jorge barked at her. "I am *done* with you. This here is over. I do not wish to continue this conversation. You already knew the consequences of your actions. And yet, you steal from me. I do not care to hear you justify your actions."

"But please, I need my family now," She continued to cry. "You cannot leave me alone."

"I can and I will."

"But I am your son's godmother!" She cried. "Does that mean anything?"

"Not anymore," Jorge spoke coldly as he rushed toward the door. "Jolene, this here, is not my problem."

"But I need…"

"I do not care what you need," Jorge snapped as he opened the door. "This meeting, it is over. You can stay in Toronto but you do not come back and the key, the one you used to get in today, give it back."

Her face was full of shock as she began to shake, digging in her purse, she pulled out a set of keys that included those to the office, the warehouse, and crematorium. Tears fell from her chin as she passed them to Jorge who showed no emotion.

"But I can…."

"No, Jolene," Jorge shook his head as he snatched the keys. "No, you cannot."

Walking away from her, he ignored the broken women behind him, feeling nothing for his former associate. She made her choice.

Finding Paige and the others down the hallway, he noted that the Argentinian was tied to a chair, her mouth covered and an emotionless Paige approached him as soon as he entered the room.

"Chase is going to stay with her till we find out more," She spoke in a quiet voice. "Andrew is downstairs working with the other guy. Hopefully, Diego has some information soon."

Jorge nodded but didn't say anything. He exchanged looks with Chase before leading Paige out of the room and closing the door.

"So what happened with Jolene?" She asked in a hushed tone. "Why is she back?"

"Her romance is dead," Jorge replied and shook his head. "Enrique, he was a weak man. Weak men, they never stick around strong women. It may attract them but it don't keep them. She wants back but that day, it is over. I told her this."

Paige didn't reply but nodded.

"Do you think this was right?"

"I don't know if we can ever trust her again."

"Unfortunately, I do not think this is the last we see of her."

"She's going to keep coming back unless…"

"I know, *mi amor,* I know this."

"We can deal with her later but for now…"

"Now we must take care of this man, this Melvin Gates."

"Marco won't be long," Paige reminded him. "This should be easy. I was looking at my phone and he's in the Toronto area."

"Anything else?"

"The usual," Paige shook her head and moved closer to look into his eyes. "His history in business, how wealthy he is…he's pretty fierce when it comes to making money. There's even one article where he challenged his daughter in a situation a few years ago. It made her come out looking bad but it didn't seem to matter to him."

"How old is he?"

"Well, he's not young," Paige grinned. "He's close to 90."

"Ah! It might be an easier day than I thought."

"But he's also a gun enthusiast."

"Ah! But *mi amor,*" Jorge quipped as he pulled her close and kissed her on the top of the head. "So am I!"

"From what I read, he enjoys shooting animals."

Jorge laughed out loud, his head falling back as if the comment gave him pleasure.

"And *so do I.*"

CHAPTER 42

"Sir, this man, he's a complicated one," Marco said as he walked through the door of the conference room to join Jorge and Paige. Holding his iPad, he halted for a moment to turn around and wait for Diego who came barreling in right behind him.

"Crazy as fuck is what he means," Diego automatically took over the conversation as his eyes bulged out. "White supremacy, racist asshole…"

"Wait, what?" Jorge shook his head as he leaned back in the chair. "What does this have to do with investing in Big Pharma? I thought that was his issue with me and Athas, that we are causing him to lose money."

"Yeah, well, I'm sure that's what he's gonna tell the *Argentinian* lady to get the deed done for him," Diego insisted as he found his place at the head of the table while Marco sheepishly sat across from Jorge and Paige. "He can say it's investing but we know that's not the only reason. Back in the 90s, he started a group to keep immigrants out. He said that we needed to protect the Canadian culture by preserving its *white* roots."

"He did not say *white* exactly," Marco attempted to cut in but was automatically waved away by Diego.

"He didn't *have* to," Diego insisted. "It was obvious."

"Ok, so this here," Jorge shook his head. "You are trying to tell me it has nothing to do with my company or Big Pharma?

"It might have *something* to do with it," Diego agreed with some reluctance. "But come on….if you saw the emails."

"This is the thing, Diego," Jorge cut him off. "I have not had a chance to see anything because you just flew in here and took over. Marco, could you possibly give us a little more *clear* answer?"

"Yes, well," Marco said with a grin on his face. "There is some racist stuff in here but I think it is more about losing money."

"He called you a wetback in his email exchange with some rich fuck," Diego complained. "What the fuck else would you call him"

"He *does* have an anti-immigration background but that was many years ago," Marco spoke evenly. "I do not know if that is part of his agenda now but what Diego says, this is true too. He did call you….he did say some racist things in an email."

"Right," Jorge shrugged. "This here is not my first time hearing such things."

"I know but don't it say it all?" Diego asked while dramatically swinging his arms in the air. "He can *say* whatever he wants. It's pretty clear what's going on here."

Jorge took a deep breath and exchanged looks with his wife.

"I think we need to step back and calm down," She replied with her focus on Diego. "Now, other than that, can we focus on the facts. Does he even have a hit on Jorge and Alec or both? Is that true and if so, do we know for *sure* why and even more importantly, what kind of lifestyle he leads so we can find him?"

"Ok, so," Marco started to tap on some buttons. "To answer your first question, he complains in emails about the government changing rules and how he is already losing money. He specifically says that Jorge is 'in bed' with the federal government and that they will do whatever he says but he does not talk openly in emails about wanting either dead."

"He wouldn't anyway," Paige said. "What about the emails for…"

"That lady who arranges everything?" Marco asked.

"The lady with no name?" Diego smirked. "Why, exactly, are we not allowed to know her name?"

"It's her thing," Paige attempted to explain. "She feels that it's better…"

"This here, no concern to me," Jorge cut in and shook his head. "Her name could be Queen of the Universe for all I care. Either way, she has gotten on my last nerve."

"I think we can agree on that," Paige muttered and leaned closer to her husband.

"This here lady," Marco said with a raised eyebrow. "I will get to her in a moment. But about Melvin Gates, as I said he had an issue with Jorge and Alec, complaining about them but nothing in *his* inbox, other than some reference to a meeting with someone who would 'assist' with the problem. This, I assumed was regarding this situation because it was mentioned in the same email."

Jorge nodded.

"Now, he lost a lot of money since cannabis became legal," Marco continued. "But especially in the last few weeks, something that, it almost seems he took personally. He is a big believer in the party that opposes Mr. Athas. He feels they should've won and he put a lot of money into their campaign during the last election."

Jorge raised an eyebrow.

"Also, I see that he spends a lot of time in a couple of places," Marco continued. "He has an expensive home where he has a lot of staff looking after him. Some of which, I think are not legal and sir, he spends time golfing."

"Interesting," Paige spoke up. "I think it's a little late in the season to find him there?"

"No, he still does according to his messages today," Marco said and tapped on his iPad, turning it around to show Paige. "He has a tee time at 4 p.m. this afternoon."

Jorge and Paige exchanged looks.

"Now, regarding this woman….the Argentinian lady," Marco continued. "She *did* have their meeting in her notes. Her phone wasn't easy to hack but I got in."

"You are the king, Marco," Jorge commented while Diego seemed to lean in.

"Thank you, Sir," Marco blushed and grew serious. "So, this here, shows that she had planned to meet with Paige as well but had no set time. Her meeting with Melvin Gates was earlier today."

"So, before ours?" Jorge asked.

"Yes, he was going to give her some money," Marco continued. "I did a little more research and I learned that it was not only this Gates man who had an issue with both you and Athas but another man, who I learned was his son-in-law, a prominent man who works for...."

"Big Pharma," Diego jumped in scrunched his lips up as he nodded. "That's his connection and they both want to take you and Athas down."

"This man, more so, sir," Marco continued to tap on the buttons of his iPad. "When I checked his email, sir, he wasn't as smart as the older man. He talked openly about finding a way to get Athas out of the picture so he could get his own person in as prime minister."

"Now him, he's been talking to that Argentinian bitch for months," Diego continued. "Him and the old man, they are willing to pay any price to have one or both of you killed."

"So, she was telling the truth?" Paige said.

"They want Athas dead," Diego continued even though Marco was also attempting to speak. "You have access to him and they knew you could do it. They wanted to send a message to Ottawa."

"But why would I agree to kill Alec?" Paige was confused. "Even if we didn't have a history..."

Jorge cringed at that last comment but jumped in.

"Because *mi amor,* under normal circumstances you would not," He turned toward her. "But if you thought it would save me, you would."

"I wouldn't."

"See, this here is where she ran into problems," Jorge continued. "That is why she made it seems like she was doing you a favor by allowing you to kill Athas and not having someone else come along and kill us both. It was, as you say, the lesser of two evils."

"It was not only that, sir," Marco spoke with some reluctance, his face turning red. "I have more."

With that, he tapped on the iPad while Diego appeared more infuriated at the end of the table.

"Sir, they...they weren't sure if Paige would do it," He appeared hesitant to continue and took a deep breath before he continued. "They were going...they were going to threaten your children, sir."

Jorge felt his blood turn cold but it was automatically followed by intense fury.

"What did you say?" He spoke calmly even though he felt a storm racing through his body. "Did you just say what I think, Marco?"

"Sir, I have the proof..."

"I saw it," Diego jumped in with matching anger. "That *puta* whore you have back at the crematorium suggested that Paige would do it if her kids were threatened. She would listen. They wanted to take them hostage."

"They are *all* fucking dead," Jorge said as he turned toward his wife. "Your boss, that lady, she will be burned alive today and those two men, Gates and his son-in-law, I will fucking kill them with my bare hands for threatening my children. Nobody ever fucking threatens my kids and gets away with it."

"It was the lady," Marco attempted to explain. "It was her idea."

"But they agreed?" Jorge challenged him and Marco reluctantly nodded.

"Tell me where and when to find them," Jorge replied as Paige reached out to touch his arm to calm him. "Because they are *dead*."

"They are golfing this afternoon," Marco reminded him. "The tee time, it is at 4. I have the address."

"Are there cameras...." Paige started but Marco was already nodding.

"I will take care of them."

"Anything else?" Jorge asked while his heart raced.

"No, sir," Marco shook his head with compassion in his eyes. "They are golfing alone."

"Perfect targets."

"The old man, he likes to hunt," Paige calmly suggested. "Maybe this will be karma for him."

"Diego," Jorge responded. "Can you talk to Andrew. Tell him to meet us at the crematorium later tonight? Tell him to let Chase know."

"Do you need my help at the golf course?"

"No," Paige answered. "We got this."

CHAPTER 43

"I know you're upset," Paige attempted to reason with Jorge as they arrived at the golf course after stopping home briefly to change into more casual attire. "I am too but we have to be careful…"

"They think they are going to use my children as a way to manipulate you into killing Athas? When was she going to bring up that tidbit of information?" Jorge ranted before she could even finish her sentence. "And they call me *el diablo*? I do not think so, *mi amor,* these people, they are monsters."

"They are," Paige attempted to calmly reason with him. "Believe me, I feel the same way. We must be careful. This is broad daylight and there could be people around."

Jorge didn't respond as he parked the SUV.

"So then, what shall we do?" He finally asked as his defenses drop. "You know me, Paige, when it comes to family, especially my children, no one who makes a threat gets out alive."

"And these men, they won't either," Paige assured him. "You have to trust me on that."

"I do, of course, *mi amor* but what can we…."

Paige's phone rang and Jorge fell silent as she answered. Although she spoke as if having a regular conversation about the weather, it turned out there was much more that was being said and he was about to learn the details.

"We can't get them on the course, too many people around," Paige quickly commented after ending the call. "It's too risky."

"Then what?"

"We find a way to get them *off* the course and into the woods nearby," Paige explained. "Once we're hidden in the trees, they're ours to take."

"Me, I think we should shoot them right on the course and go…"

"Too risky," Paige countered. "No, we need to get them out of sight because no one will see a thing. Your way, there are too many chances of getting caught."

Jorge didn't reply. With anger seething through him at the thought of someone threatening his children, he was unable to focus, to think straight. Fortunately, Paige worked better under pressure than he ever did.

"Ok, so this here, it makes sense," Jorge nodded in agreement. "But that is the thing, how do we do this?"

"We need to find a way to lure them."

"A golden golf ball or what?" Jorge joked. "I naked woman? I am not sure what else would take them away from their game."

"I'm thinking something a little more simple," Paige replied as she tapped on her phone. "I wish I had more time to study these men, I could find out what makes them tick."

"They're men," Jorge insisted with a shrug. "We are not complicated. We thrive on food, sex, and power. What more do you need to know, *mi amor?*"

"Trust me, things are sometimes much more complicated under the hood," Paige insisted but Jorge was already shaking his head.

"*Mi amor,* I assure you, these men, they are not complicated," Jorge laughed. "They are very simple. We must find one of those things and we can lure them anyway."

"You know who would be good for this?" Paige asked with a sad smile. "Jolene. She could lure a man anywhere."

"Oh please," Jorge shook his head. "This here is the last person I wish to deal with."

"I'm just saying…"

"We cannot let her back in, she cannot be trusted."

"I didn't say anything about letting her back in," Paige spoke sternly.

A small smile crossed Jorge's lips as he slowly began to nod.

"I think she wants to prove herself," Paige suggested. "Let her do it this time."

Jorge glanced at his phone. They had 45 minutes until tee time.

"You know she will do anything for those kids," Paige continued. "She'll do this."

"You are right...but..."

"We tell her there's no guarantee. A baby step in the right direction."

Thirty minutes later, Jolene was pulling up close to them in a rental car. She stepped out wearing a revealing dress and high heels. Jorge nodded in approval while Paige cringed.

"You don't come to a golf course dressed liked that," She murmured as Jolene approached the SUV.

"You do if you have no intention of golfing," Jorge reminded her. "Maybe she is here with a boyfriend that left her behind? Maybe..."

Jolene jumped in the backseat.

"I am so glad you call!" She exclaimed. "I do whatever you need. Just tell me."

"What we need," Paige turned around in her seat, looking at Jolene. "Is a distraction and you're it."

Paige quickly filled her in on what was going on and what her role would be in the situation. The two women hatched out a plan that sounded reasonable to Jorge, who merely listened to them conspire. Although he resented Jolene for a lot of reasons, he couldn't deny she was someone they could count on when it came to dicey situations.

"I cannot believe!" Jolene complained. "They threaten to hurt the kids! It would give me pleasure to kill them."

"Ah, no!" Jorge insisted. "That there, I plan to do."

"I wanted to actually..." Paige started.

"No, you are both too close to this situation, let me do it," Jolene insisted. "Plus, me, I need to prove myself to you both. This is how."

"No, Jolene you, you shoot and ask questions later," Jorge complained. "I want to learn what this is about."

"*She* shoots and asks questions later?" Paige sounded slightly humored. "I think that's one delicate glass house you're throwing rocks from."

"What does this mean?" Jolene appeared confused by the expression.

"She means that she thinks I'm the same way," Jorge said with a shrug. "And sometimes, this is true, but this time, I must learn what is going on for them to do this. Everything, it is not adding up. Me, I wonder if there are others."

"Maybe this man," Jolene started. "Maybe he was representing others. Maybe he just is the one who talks to the lady…the boss, you had, what was her name, Paige?"

"She won't reveal it," Paige replied flatly. "It's possible but if they end up dead, do you really think anyone else will take the risk?"

"True," Jolene nodded. "So, I will go in and ask to look around because I might buy a membership for my boyfriend?"

"Try to just wander around and avoid being asked anything."

"And I will instead find these men? The ones in the picture."

"We know exactly where they will be," Jorge replied. "You will not have to look hard."

"I get them in the woods."

"Yes," Paige replied. "Just come along and say, 'I am looking for….'"

"Your dog," Jorge added. "Cat, you can be looking for whatever, Jolene just show some T&A and get them out of sight. I do not care how."

"I wouldn't quite put it that way," Paige said as she cringed. "But you get the idea."

"I show anything," Jolene insisted as she unbuttoned the top button of her dress. "You know, this here, it does not bother me."

Jorge didn't reply. He still found it frustrating that they were even using her in this plan. He briefly considered killing her along with the two golfers but decided against it. Regardless of any bad blood, she *was* Diego's sister which complicated the situation. She was taking a risk even trusting him at this point, something he took into account

"So, I go now," Jolene reached for the door. "My phone, It is off but I will find you."

"I have a virtual shot of the course they're on," Paige said as she pointed at her phone. "Just find some way to get them into the woods and we'll find you."

"Will do."

She got out of the SUV and Jorge exchanged looks with Paige.

"I don't think this is a good idea," He said. "I do not trust Jolene and I am having second thoughts about this place."

"Trust me," Paige said with a calming expression on her face. "I got this one. It will be easy."

She wasn't exaggerating. The two wandered around without questions or even being noticed. Everyone was so involved in their games and conversations, that they could've easily been invisible. Jorge had noticed that people in Canada were somewhat less vigilant than Mexico. Then again, you had to be more vigilant in Mexico.

They wandered into the trees as if merely city dwellers looking to escape in nature, discovering a course they might consider joining, not appearing out of place. It was as they got closer to the edge of the trees that Jolene's voice could be heard.

"I know, I cannot bring my dog here but they tell me it was ok," Jolene was speaking loudly. "My boyfriend, he left me, then my dog...he go missing...."

Jorge noted that the younger man of the two was following Jolene into the trees. Even from a distance, he could sense the lust behind his interest in helping the Colombian while left standing on the course was Melvin Gates, who appeared uninterested in Jolene or her antics.

He's old as fuck. What's he going to do with a woman like Jolene?

She continued to ramble like a moron until they were deeper in the trees and that's when she pulled out a gun. The son-in-law backed up with fear in his eyes.

"If you want money..."

"I do not want your money!" Jolene snapped back.

"You might want to reconsider that," Jorge insisted as he wandered out of the trees to make eye contact with the terrified man, especially when he came face to face with Jorge Hernandez. "You got that house you stole from me, remember?"

"I give back!" Jolene snapped. "I will make it up."

Noting that Paige wasn't behind him, he glanced toward the course.

"Please, leave my father-in-law alone," The man spoke up. "He's old. He doesn't have much time left."

"You're fucking right he don't," Jorge snapped back. "You do not threaten my children and live. This here, it is my rule."

"But, I…"

A shot rang out and the man collapsed to the ground with blood splattered everywhere; the trees, shrubbery, and even some fell on Jolene's shoe, which she promptly attempted to wipe off on a nearby leaf.

"For fuck sakes, Jolene, could you not wait?" Jorge snapped as he monitored the situation. "We might have learned something."

"He talk too much already," She complained as she waved her free hand around. "Enough already!"

Paige returned with Melvin Gates walking slowly, a gun pointed toward his back while holding a golf club in her other hand.

"I see Jolene was trigger happy," Paige commented as the old man discovered his son-in-law on the ground. "Some things never change."

"You killed…"

"Old man, the only words I want to hear from you," Jorge pointed his gun at Melvin Gates. "Is why you thought killing me and Athas would be a good idea? Why you thought using my children as a bargaining chip would somehow give you good results? You know, there are some people you cannot play this card with and I am one of them."

The old men's eyes squinted and his face grew more wrinkled as he frowned.

"Fuck you, Hernandez," Melvin Gates spoke gruffly. "And fuck your half-breed kids."

Abruptly putting his gun away, Jorge rushed forward, grabbing the golf club out of Paige's hand, he used all his force to hit the old man in the knees, knocking him to the ground. While the two women jumped back, Jorge saw red as he furiously hit the old man repeatedly with the club, first in the head followed by the rest of his body. Locked in such rage, it took Paige's voice to pull him out and step back. Still shaking in anger, he was able to see the bloody mess that was once a life. A soulless corpse only steps away from his son-in-law. Jorge stepped back as his heart continued to race. Although he calmed, his mind raced.

Were his children still in danger?

CHAPTER 44

"One of the hardest lessons for me in this life," Jorge spoke loudly, his voice echoing through the crematorium. The frazzled Argentinian lady sat on the floor, still tied up, her mouth taped shut while Andrew, Paige, Diego, and Jolene stood nearby. "Is that not all *chicas* are made of sugar and spice."

The woman on the floor looked up at him with pleading eyes, something that Jorge had no conscience about as he quickly looked away, towards Diego.

"It was a hard lesson for me, you know," Jorge continued as if he were sharing a powerful realization. He took a deep breath and continued. "I remember her, this young woman when I was a man of 16. She was beautiful, such a beautiful girl but yet, I should've known that something was wrong. I guess I did but I chose to ignore it."

"You see," He turned back toward the woman on the floor, now with tears in her eyes. "I thought she was my true love. I thought we would be together forever. She was older, you see, much older than me and I was naïve when it came to matters of the heart. I thought that I was in love with her but as it turned out, she was a dirty *puta* who had been with every man in the neighborhood but again, I was young. I did not know that such women existed."

"Of course, we learn lessons the hard way," Jorge continued as he rubbed his hands together. "The most powerful of lessons, we learn in the most painful of ways. I learned that day when I caught her sucking off my friend, that she was, indeed, not a good woman. That women, in general, you could not necessarily trust even though they may bat their eyelashes, act sweet and like you, *señora,* even with tears in their eyes, it means nothing. Women know how to use emotions and their body to manipulate men."

"Jolene, she does it," Jorge pointed toward the Colombian who showed no expression. "She did it today. She was capable of doing something that I, as a man, could not. I recognize that. I appreciate that. Women, you have special gifts that men, we do not. I see that now. I did not see that as a young man with my broken heart. Because in those days, all I see is my future going up in flames."

Jorge began to laugh and shook his head.

"Oh, but we all have that naïvety in our lives," He began to nod and walked closer to the woman on the floor. "We believe, what we want to believe. We see the world as we wish not always how it is. Paige, she used to see you as an idol. As a woman who empowered her but at the end of the day, you were not made of sugar and spice. You are a soulless woman and for me, Jorge Hernandez to call *you* soulless, well, I would say that this here is a pretty low place to be, *senora.*"

Diego laughed and soon the others joined as Jorge turned and stepped back, glancing toward his wife.

"You know, after my heart was broken, as a young man," Jorge continued. "I never thought I would ever feel that way again. And I must admit, I went out of my way to avoid it. I had no plans, no intentions to ever fall in love, to marry, none of this here was an idea in my head. But then it happens. You have this child and everything, it suddenly looks very different. All the evil women of the world, maybe they are not so evil. After all, how could this little girl, you hold in your arms on the day she is born…how could she be evil?"

"And then, you meet someone," Jorge turned toward his wife. "Who breaks those ideas into pieces. Shatters what you once thought was reality. It makes you see that some things you thought didn't exist, just wasn't for you yet. It wasn't the right time or place. Life is not always so black and white. That moment, when you look into that person's eyes and you know, something is very, *very* different this time."

Turning away from Paige, Jorge paused and thought for a moment.

"It is a shame though," He looked toward the woman on the floor. "That you perhaps never had such things. And I know this because you have no heart. And I know you have no heart because you were willing to threaten my children. And you know what else, it also means you have no brain because anyone who did, anyone who knows me, knows that threatening my *familia,* it is signing their death certificate."

He could hear a whimper from the woman on the floor. She suddenly seemed so small, so helpless, not the same woman who eased into his house earlier that day, as if she had owned a piece of his world. How quickly things had changed.

"Me?" Jorge continued and made a face. "I have no conscience either. Many, they would also say, I have no heart. And you know what? Most of the time, this is true. But throughout my entire career as a criminal, as a narco, as whatever it is you want to call me, I have not *ever* hurt children. Early in my career, I have threatened but the man I work for, he scolded me. He said, 'Jorge, you must never threaten a man's family because if you do, you will unleash a monster, a *lion* that will tear you into pieces'. This lesson, it was powerful and he was right. I did not see that as a young, stupid man but now, I am older and I have a family. I do understand. I would rip anyone apart, with no conscience who threatened to hurt my family, my children. The last person who threatened my child is dead."

He turned around to look at his wife again.

"It was not even me who did it but Paige," He shared a look with her. "Because if it had been me, I would've tortured her."

The woman on the floor let out a cry as tears poured from her eyes.

"I would've tortured her until she begged to die," Jorge spoke in a lower voice this time and paused. "I would've made her suffer and it would have given me great pleasure to see this. I would have made her wish she had never been born. She would've regretted every single terrible thing she had ever done in those last moments of her life. She would've seen what an *animal* I can be when someone, *anyone* threatens my family. Because there is a reason why they called me *el diablo* when I lived in Mexico. It is because I *am* the devil and today, you, lady, you are about to meet your hellfire."

The woman continued to struggle, attempting to get free from the rope that bound her arms and legs together but she wasn't successful.

Jorge stared at her feeling nothing for the fear that was so apparent in this helpless animal. She would die in the most excruciating way possible.

"Do you want us to put her up?" Andrew pointed toward the cremation oven.

"In a moment," Jorge replied. "I have one more thing to say."

Andrew nodded.

"Lady," Jorge looked down at the struggling woman and stepped forward. "You did help us get the men who wanted me and Athas dead, I give you that credit. But it was when I found out you were planning to use my children to threaten my wife that I suddenly didn't give a fuck if you lived or died. Paige, she was, as you have said, one of your 'best girls', and yet, you wanted to threaten her children?"

"Hey, you know how it is now," Diego spoke up with an exaggerated tone. "We're all just a number."

Jorge couldn't help but grin and shared a look with his wife.

"This is true, Diego," Jorge nodded. "Loyalty to employees, it is not there anymore. It is only about money. If companies must sacrifice a few sheep along the way, this is fine."

"Paige is no sheep," Diego pointed out.

"No, she is not," Jorge agreed as he looked down at the woman on the floor. "She was loyal. She did a lot of work for you. She was exceptional, you have said that yourself, did you not? This here, is how you treat her? First chance to make a little more money and you throw her to the wolves? If this is what you do to your 'best girl', an employee who has made you a lot of money over time, it makes me wonder, what you do to your worst employee? Or is it the same for you?"

"But, me, I guess I am biased," Jorge said with a grin and glanced back at Paige. "She is, after all, my wife. She was originally going to take care of this matter on her own to protect me. I wish she had not but I do understand. That is who she is. And if it were the other way around, I would do the same for her."

"You *did* do the same for her," Diego reminded him. "Remember, that man who threatened her…"

"Ah, yes!" Jorge clapped his hands together. "That man, we took care of him good, didn't we Diego?"

"A million little pieces."

"Indeed, he was in about a million little pieces after we cut him up with a chainsaw," Jorge commented casually, glancing at the woman on the floor who looked even more frightened. "Ah, such memories, Diego. That was a *good* day. I felt, how you say, validated?"

Andrew raised an eyebrow.

"So yes, Diego," Jorge glanced at his friend. "You are right, I have done the same for Paige. She did not know until after the fact. And for this, she tried to do the same because as you know…." He stopped to look back at his wife. "They will one day say that I was the devil and she was my angel."

Paige smiled and they shared a look for a moment before he turned back to the woman on the floor.

"And lady, you're going to need all the angels in heaven," He spoke abruptly, coldly, showing no emotion. "Because you are about to suffer in the same way you had hoped my family would suffer. Except, of course, no one is going to miss you when you're gone. No one even cares you are alive and they will care less when you are dead…if they even notice."

He ignored her tears as he gestured for Andrew and Diego to lift her body and placed it on the conveyor belt. He wasn't concerned with her struggle, with her pleading eyes because none of that mattered. Jorge stood back and watched everything. He noted that neither Andrew or Diego showed any emotion toward the woman, their expressions hardened, with no second thoughts or regrets floating through the room. Looking over his shoulder, he could see Jolene cared nothing for this woman, her eyes were cold, dark as she watched the conveyor belt start to move. However, he was surprised to see Paige's expression. Unlike the others, she appeared upset and had to look away.

Instinctively, he walked toward her and pulled her into a hug.

"*Mi amor,*" He spoke softly, making sure to block her view. "This was the right thing to do."

"I know," She quietly replied. "But…she was once my hero, my idol. I thought she was so powerful, so strong…"

"Our idols, they often disappoint us," Jorge said as he hugged her tightly. "Did you wish to stop…"

"No," Paige automatically answered and pulled away to look in his eyes. "This is the only way."

CHAPTER 45

"Oh, *mi amor*," Jorge commented as they drove home that night. "I am so glad that this day is over but you know how it is…these things, they bring out my most primal instincts."

They shared a quick look as a smooth grin crossed his lips.

"I know all about it," She replied in a soft, silky voice.

"I cannot help it, Paige," Jorge continued as they drove through the traffic. "Murder, it makes me hungry, and horny every time and as I always say, not necessarily in that order."

"You are one sick puppy," She teased.

"I know, *mi amor*," Jorge laughed with her. "I am beyond a 'sick puppy' but I accept this about myself. It's instinctual."

"Unfortunately, when we get home," Paige spoke evenly. "We'll be welcomed by a crying baby and a cranky teenager."

"There's always a way," He replied seductively. "I do believe that we can find a way."

"We usually do," Paige reminded him just as her phone beeped.

"Who is that?" Jorge asked. "Maria, wondering where we are?"

"She's a teenager," Paige shook her head. "She doesn't care where we are."

"Then, who?"

"Marco," She replied. "He said he has some 'documents' to go over with me tomorrow or at my earliest convenience."

"Perhaps he has located some answers for us," Jorge suggested as they turned down their street.

"Maybe I should call him to make sure…"

"It is fine," Jorge shook his head feeling his desires grow as they got closer to home. "I am sure it is maybe a small clue otherwise, he would've stressed the importance in his text."

"I'm surprised he texted me and not you."

"He knows you are also involved in this," Jorge reminded her. "Maybe he thought I had my hands full since the next episode in the docuseries is about to drop. I have to meet with Andrew and Tony tomorrow to see what's next."

"The numbers continue to grow?" Paige asked innocently but for some reason this caused his desires to build.

"They are not the only thing growing, *mi amor*," Jorge teased her and she smirked.

"We'll be home soon."

"Not soon enough," Jorge insisted as they headed toward their house.

"Your phone just beeped…"

"Can you check it for me?" Jorge asked as he focused on his driving.

"It's from Alec," Paige commented. "He said he has to talk to you tomorrow."

"Yes, well, I did send him a message earlier today," Jorge replied. "Regarding what we learned and in turn, took care of…"

"Do you think there are any other threats to him or you?" Paige suddenly sounded vulnerable. "I mean, I know we got this but…"

"Paige, we cannot play the 'what if' game."

"I know but I worry…"

"We can have Marco do some more research if you wish," He suggested. "Maybe he can look into any of your…former bosses contacts to see what he can find. See if she discussed this with anyone else."

There was a pause.

"Yes? No?" Jorge asked.

"Yeah, I think so," She agreed after some hesitation. "But I think we might have to go beyond. Maybe he can check the dark web."

"We will ask Marco to cover all the bases," Jorge insisted as they pulled into their driveway. "It will be fine, *mi amor*, you will see. You need not worry so much."

"It's…too risky," Paige admitted with a nervous expression. "I thought we wanted to get away from all this but sometimes, it seems like we keep getting a little too close to the fire."

"I know," Jorge replied as he parked the SUV. "I understand but I guess…it just happens."

"It doesn't just happen," She calmly reminded him. "You started this series and it's ruffling feathers."

"Yes, this is true," Jorge admitted. "I love power a little too much, *mi amor*. It is my weakness."

"The point is that we have to eventually decide what is more important," She turned toward him. "Power or peace. How do we want to spend the rest of our lives?"

"But Paige, we would not be *us* if we did not do these things," Jorge reminded her.

"But the children…"

"You are right," Jorge nodded. "Maybe we need more security for the children."

"I don't know," Paige shook her head. "I just want them to have normal lives."

"They can," Jorge said as he leaned in and kissed her on the forehead. "It will be a different kind of normal."

With that, the couple got out of the SUV and headed into the house. Their mood was slightly solemn but Jorge was still determined to get his wife alone. Everything was silent, causing him to think this was possible until Maria pranced in the room with Cameron in tow.

"*Papa*, can we order pizza? *We're* starving," She gestured toward her friend who looked curiously at Jorge. "We've been practicing our dance moves for like, hours and there's nothing in this house to eat."

"There's lots of food in the kitchen," Paige pointed out as she headed toward the stairs.

"Yeah, but we don't want to cook stuff…I don't know how."

"Well, maybe it's time you learn," Jorge shot her a dirty look which she dismissed. "Cameron, nice to see you again."

"Thanks."

"You make it sound like he's never here," Maria rolled her eyes. "He's here all the time."

"I have not seen him in a long time," Jorge attempted to explain, glancing toward the stairs, hoping Paige was about to join him in the office as his hormones went into overdrive.

"That's because you're never home," Maria spoke slowly as if he didn't understand. "He's here like, *every* day."

Jorge gave her a look. She challenged it.

"Order some pizza Maria," Jorge finally relented. "Make sure there's lots for everyone."

Maria clapped her hands together and Jorge reached for his wallet, pulling out some bills.

"This should cover it."

"Wow, for sure!" Cameron's eyes widened as Maria grabbed her phone and began to tap on it.

"I have to go to my office," Jorge commented but noticed they weren't listening as he walked away. He texted his wife.

Why don't you join me downstairs? We have some things we should discuss.

Grinning to himself, he ignored Maria and Cameron arguing about what pizza place to order from and walked into his sanctuary. Heading to his desk, he took a deep breath and collapsed in his chair. It had been a long day.

His phone beeped. Assuming it was Paige, he felt a grin form on his lips while his desires continued to churn.

It wasn't Paige. It was Tony.

I know what I want to do for the next episode. Ratings are high but this will make them go through the roof.

Jorge thought for a moment.

We will meet in the morning.

Thank you.

Sitting his phone down, he took a deep breath and picked it up again.

Mi amor, where are you? Food is being ordered in so in the meanwhile…

Smiling to himself he set the phone down again.

It beeped.

It was Diego.

Know that song 'we live in dangerous times'? I think that's what it's called.

Jorge knew this was Diego's way of letting him know that something noteworthy was on the news. Switching to a news app, he quickly saw the story he had in mind. The headlines told of a wealthy businessman and investor found dead at a popular golf course. A relative was with him but details were currently unavailable. Since their money was missing, it was believed that it was a robbery gone wrong. Police were investigating. This made Jorge laugh out loud.

"Do I even want to know what you're laughing at?" Paige asked as she walked in, closing the door behind her.

"Oh, *mi amor,* now that you are here, this is the least of my worries." He insisted while pushing his phone aside.

"I was checking in on Miguel," She said while walking toward the desk. "Juliana somehow worked her magic and got him to sleep."

"Now it is time for *you* to work your magic on me," Jorge suggested. "We have some time before the food arrives, don't we?"

"We certainly do."

CHAPTER 46

"You got to be fucking kidding me," Jorge spoke breathlessly as he reached for the phone. It had been pushed aside when he feverishly lifted his wife onto the desk after removing her blouse. "Why can I not have this one beautiful thing after such a day?"

"What?" Paige asked breathlessly while attempting to pull him closer. "Just ignore your phone and concentrate on me."

Her lips met with the side of his neck, her tongue softly teased him as it slowly moved toward his ear. Her hand slid toward the front of his pants but her attempt to distract him was unsuccessful.

"He is here," Jorge complained and let out a loud sigh, breaking the trance that Paige was in. Moving back he grabbed the phone and grimaced.

"What?" She was confused. "Can't it wait? Who's here?"

"Athas," Jorge grumbled. "Leave it to that fucker to ruin my sex."

"He's here?" Paige continued to show confusion. "*Now?*"

"Apparently so, *mi amor,*" Jorge moved away, attempting to calm himself. "This here is not how I had hoped to end my day."

"That makes two of us," Paige muttered as she slid off the desk, fixing her skirt. "I can't believe he just showed up here…at this time of day."

"I bet when you dated him years ago," Jorge shook his head. "You never thought he would haunt you for the rest of your fucking life but yet, here we are. Athas, the original cock block."

Paige made a face and reached for her blouse.

"At least," She attempted to reason. "He won't be here for long."

"He better *not* be here for fucking long," Jorge complained.

"It's not like the day is completely over," Paige reminded him.

"I know, but the mood, *mi amor*," Jorge said and shook his head. "You know my passion, it is at its highest level after a kill. This is very disappointing."

"We'll get it back," Paige insisted before leaning forward to kiss him. "Later tonight, in bed, I promise."

Jorge attempted to hide his disappointment but it only changed to anger when he headed out of the office.

"*Papa,*" Maria sang out when he returned to the living room to find his nemesis waiting for him. "I know I'm not allowed to answer the door, like *ever*, but I assumed that the prime minister probably was safe."

"Maria," Jorge replied while noting the look of disbelief on Cameron's face. "You assumed correctly. Athas, come to my office."

As the two men walked away, he could hear Cameron whispering.

"You just, like, have the prime minister drop in from time to time."

"It's a secret," Maria insisted. "So, you can't tell, *right?*"

Jorge took a deep breath and suddenly felt exhausted. It had been a long day and despite its success, he was growing tired and cranky.

"So this here," Jorge started as he ushered Athas into the office, where Paige was already sitting in her usual chair. "This is how we roll now. You show up anytime you want."

"I remembered I was going to be tied up tomorrow," Athas replied as he nodded at Paige. "I'm sorry, I didn't mean to just show up but…"

"But you did," Jorge reminded him as he walked behind the desk. "So, I will tell you now. Someone wanted you dead but we took care of that today."

"Someone wanted *me* dead?" Athas started with some hesitations, sitting beside Paige. "I don't…"

"The murder victims at the golf course earlier today," Jorge abruptly cut him off. "Had a hit on you but we took care of them."

"But…why?"

"Major investors with Big Pharma and your laws were already sinking their ship," Jorge replied bluntly. "I sunk their ships before he found a way to sink *you*."

"When I heard about it," Athas slowly began. "I had a feeling… but… they wanted to kill *me* because I was going to cause them to lose money? That seems so…extreme."

"Welcome to the real world," Jorge said while waving his arms in the air. "This here is how it works with the powerful elites. You do not see this where you come from because it is *not* where you come from but me, I know this whole world better than you. To this man, your changes would cause him to lose a lot of money. He figured taking you out would relieve this problem and of course, send a message to your party that they were on the wrong track."

"Are they…I mean, *were* they working alone?"

"We have every reason to think so," Paige replied to this question. "They blamed you and Jorge for the law changes, the docuseries provoking people…everything and thought if they could kill one or both of you, things would get back to normal."

"Which, of course, isn't true," Jorge reaffirmed. "This here was an old man's illusion. The old, they always want things to go back to 'the way they were' not realizing that no matter what, nothing ever can go back. We are here and now for a reason. Even if he had killed us both, it would never be the same."

Athas nodded without replying. His face showed the signs of a man in conflict.

"Anyway, it is taken care of now," Jorge continued. "You do not have to worry."

"It was," Athas started slowly as if attempting to choose his words with caution. "Very brutal."

"We need to back up a bit because he's not telling you everything," Paige cut in, turning toward Alec. "They hired the woman who used to contact me for work, back in my old life. She approached me to kill Jorge originally and when I told her there was simply no way that would ever happen, she said my only other option was to kill you."

"What?"

"This was her goal all along," Jorge took over. "She thought that the only way it would be possible is if Paige had to choose between you and me. When she still was not falling in line, they were going to threaten our children."

Athas looked horrified, his face drained of color.

"It was a way to scare me," Paige continued. "The more weight she put on top of me, the more I would likely cave and do what she wanted."

"But why....why would she even ask you," Athas asked then came to a realization. "Because you know me. Because you'd have the opportunity."

"Because I had access," Paige affirmed. "That's when things got.... messy."

Athas nodded in understanding.

"It had to be done," Jorge said with confidence.

"Ok," Athas nodded. "The police aren't reporting much back to my office but from what I'm learning, it seems like they can't get access to the cameras..."

Jorge nodded.

"No one saw a thing."

"They never do," Jorge replied.

"And there's no DNA or even a clue who could've done it."

Jorge shook his head.

"So, it's likely that it will go under the radar."

"And they think it was a robbery?" Paige quietly asked.

"Yes, that's what I was told," Athas answered anxiously. "I...that is what I was told."

"*Perfecto,*" Jorge replied and the room fell silent. "So, if that is all...."

"Is this worth it?" Athas said as he shook his head. "Is any of this worth it? The risks you take..."

"The risk we took was to save *you,*" Jorge reminded him with anger in his voice. "I would think you'd appreciate that."

"I do," Athas assured him. "But, I mean, in general. Is any of this worth it? Death threats, threats to your children, is all this worth it to you? Because I'm starting to feel it isn't worth it to me."

"Hey, hold on," Jorge said as he put his hand in the air. "You are not stepping down over this."

"I didn't say I was," Athas shook his head. "But maybe we should keep under the radar. I mean, these bills were passed but maybe we shouldn't push our luck for a while."

Jorge considered his words.

"*Amigo,* I understand," Jorge insisted. "But without making drastic and upsetting changes, then what are you doing? It is easy to maintain the status quo. That's why most leaders do not make much effort. This here, it will never make you stand out in history. You cannot submit to someone else's power."

"I'm submitting to your power," Athas calmly reminded him.

"Yes, but we work together," Jorge replied with no judgment. "I understand what you are saying but you have to think about your legacy, as I have often thought of mine. What do you want to leave when you one day retire from your position as prime minister? Do not be scared to make a difference and let me worry about the snags that get in the way."

Athas took the comments in stride, merely nodding his head. Overall, he appeared relaxed when he finally left, just as the food was arriving.

"You should stay for pizza!" Maria spoke excitedly while Cameron watched the prime minister with interest. "We got lots."

"Thank you," Athas spoke respectfully. "But I have to be somewhere. I just had something to discuss with your father first."

Turning his attention back to Jorge, he reached out and shook his hand. "Thank you for all you do. You continue to be...my biggest supporter."

"It is about making this country stronger," Jorge replied with a smirk on his face. "At the end of the day, our goals are always aligned, is this not true?"

"It is," Athas spoke with appreciation as he let go of his hand. "It certainly is."

CHAPTER 47

"Now, I shall devour you," Jorge showed no hesitation when they got into bed that night. That was, after a visit from Athas, eating some pizza and finally settling Miguel and telling Cameron it was time to go home. Their world was finally contained in their bedroom. "Let the world take care of itself for tonight."

"While I take care of you," Paige commented as she moved in to kiss him, her hand automatically trailing down his chest and into his boxers.

Within seconds, they were consumed in a naked embrace as they worked quickly to find the physical relief that both urgently needed. Jorge could sense Paige's deep longings as she rushed through foreplay as if she was about to burst with intense desires that she needed to have fulfilled. Following her lead, Jorge pushed deeply inside her, thrusting quickly as she leaned back, moaning in pleasure while she tightened her grip, making the sensations much more intense.

"Oh, *mi amor,*" He whispered, slowing down as she let out soft gasps of pleasure. He pulled back and she raised both her legs to over his shoulders, which was a signal for him to increase the intensity.

Pulling her body down, away from the headboard, he started by moving slowly as she continued to tighten her grip, moving her hips as if to experience every second of pleasure while he began to pick up the pace. Her soft moans encouraged him to move faster and faster until he was thrusting with such intensity, he feared possibly hurting her but instead, she panted, her face scrunched up as if she were overcome by pleasure. Her body started to shake, as she lifted her hips to indicate he had found that one, vital spot that needed his attention as she moaned. With one last push, he came and collapsed on top of her as their bodies seemed glued together in sweat and endorphins.

They laid in silence.

The following morning, Jorge woke feeling more alive than he had in months. While Paige was in the shower, he managed to align their meetings for the day, also checking in briefly with Athas, making sure that he was more settled regarding the events of the previous day. It was always good to sound people out, to get a sense of what they were feeling in order to keep his ducks in line.

"You're already on your phone," Paige commented as she returned from the bathroom wearing her red robe.

"Yes, *mi amor*," Jorge replied and sat it aside. "And I have figured out how to organize our day. I think we need to go to these meetings together, as a united force."

"I thought…"

"It is better," Jorge cut her off. "We were going our separate ways for weeks, trying to take care of different tasks but in the end, they are connected. We are stronger, together."

She nodded in understanding before walking over to give him a quick kiss.

The first meeting occurred later that morning at the club with Chase and Diego.

"I told her there are no guarantees," Diego was already speaking when Paige and Jorge arrived. "Just because Hernandez let you help us once and hasn't killed you… *yet*, doesn't mean you're exactly home free."

"No joke," Chase huffed from behind the desk. "I can't believe she has the nerve to think she can come back as if nothing happened."

"And that ex of hers?" Diego ignored Chase and turned toward Jorge. "Wow, I mean, she was going to kill him and his wife, or ex-wife without a second thought. Over rejection? If I killed everyone who ever rejected me."

Chase jokingly cringed.

"I wouldn't kill you," Diego shook his head. "But you know what I mean."

"Love and hate," Jorge shook his head. "It is a complicated family but do not ever think they aren't related."

"I had to hear all about it last night," Diego complained and shook his head. "Now she's staying at my house. I got the docuseries people and Jolene under my roof. Me and Priscilla might have to move in with you guys soon."

"Forget that," Jorge shook his head. "I don't need you and your dog at my house."

"They're taking over."

"Don't let them."

"I think you mean Jolene's taking over," Paige corrected him.

"She's got to go!" Diego insisted. "It's only been a day and she's *got to go.*"

"Diego, find her a place," Jorge spoke abruptly. "Problem solved. Now we got other things to take care of."

"Marco is here," Chase jumped up as if happy to leave the conversation. "I'll let him in."

Jorge and Paige exchanged looks but said nothing while Diego turned off his phone.

"So Marco," Jorge spoke in a friendly tone when the Filipino entered the room. "I understand you might have some information for me."

"I hope so sir," Marco sat down, his face still red from biking to the club. "I had a hard time learning anything but I think I might have solved at least one issue."

"Very good," Jorge nodded approvingly. "Did you find out the identity of the man who killed Tony's mother?"

"That sir, I still cannot find," Marco shook his head. "I regret that it is not so easy to figure out who it is."

"So what about…" Paige started.

"I have found," Marco cut in while sitting down. "The information you were looking for on that lady, the Argentinian."

"Like a name?" Jorge joked. "Do we finally have her name for fuck sakes?"

"We do."

"How could you work for someone that long," Chase asked Paige, "and not know her name?"

"She was always clear that I was not to ask because she would never tell," Paige said with a shrug. "She refused to share it."

"There is a reason," Marco said as he turned on his iPad. "Her name is Claudia Garcia Rodriguez and she has one hell of a reputation."

"Interesting," Jorge nodded.

"What I mean is," Marco continued as he located a document on his device. "She has been connected to some of the most powerful people in Argentina including politicians, right to the top."

"Sounds like the female Jorge Hernandez," Diego joked and everyone laughed.

"Yes, but," Marco said as he shook his head. "This woman is very evil but she shows a different side in public."

"Also like Jorge," Diego muttered.

"Let him finish," Jorge shot Diego a look but managed to grin at the comment.

"But she is very bad," Marco shook his head. "She has run an orphanage for years but there are rumors she was using this charity to launder money and in fact, that the children lived in terrible conditions but no one could prove it because when they tried…"

"People turned up dead?" Chase guessed.

"Missing, dead and sometimes," Marco made a face. "They stopped altogether. Never said a word."

"Anything else?"

"This morning I found some emails," Marco looked apprehensive. "Sir, I do not know how to tell you this but she does not work alone. In fact, according to the messages I located, she was taking instructions from someone very powerful. It was not just Melvin Gates who wanted you dead. There was someone else."

Jorge took the news in stride but sensed the concern of everyone else in the room, especially Paige, who reached out and touched his arm.

"I do not know if you are aware of this person," Marco finally continued, his face a deep shade of red. "But, I….here is his name…"

Passing Jorge the tablet, a heavy silence filled the room. With only a glance, Jorge made a face and felt rage tear through his soul. He should have known.

"Sir, do you know…"

"I do," Jorge replied as he calmly passed the device back to Marco.

"Who is it?" Paige asked as she continued to caress his arm.

"It is not important right now," Jorge replied and suddenly stood up, glancing at the faces full of disbelief and concern. "Paige, we must go to our next meeting."

"Jorge," Paige jumped up beside him. "You can't just cut this short and prepare to leave. Who is this man? Why aren't you telling us? You're scaring me."

"You're scaring *us*," Diego backed her up.

"I have to think about this more," Jorge was lost for words.

Seeing the fear in his wife's eyes, he looked away.

"Please," She sounded desperate. "You have to tell us who he is. At least do that."

Jorge considered his words carefully and shook his head.

"Is it someone from your cartel days?" Diego guessed. "Someone from another cartel? Someone in government? I didn't think you had connections in Argentina."

"I do not," Jorge confirmed that detail. "But this man, he is a man of the world. He moves frequently and although he does reside in Mexico, he has connections to many places, including Argentina."

"Who is he?" Paige continued to coax as she reached for his hand. "Please, you have to tell us."

Jorge hesitated and finally answered.

"It is a man who if he wants me dead," Jorge replied. "I will be dead."

CHAPTER 48

"Jorge," Paige rushed behind him as they headed for the SUV. "You can't say something like that and walk away! Who is this man? Why does he want you dead? Can you please..."

Turning around, he saw the fear in his wife's eyes and felt himself relent. Looking away, he took a breath and hesitated before he spoke.

"Paige, you must understand that this situation here," Jorge replied candidly, yet gently, knowing that it was important to do so despite his anxiety and anger. "It is a shock to me. This is not a man I thought would want me dead. I need a few moments to process, to understand. I am not ready to talk about it."

"But if you told me who it was," Paige attempted to calmly reason. "Maybe I can help."

He didn't reply but pointed toward the SUV. They returned to the vehicle and sat in silence while she leaned in, touching his hand.

"Paige," Jorge started before taking a moment to finish. "He is the man who gave me everything. It is because of him that I am here now."

"You mean the..."

"Yes," Jorge nodded. "You know what Claudia Garcia Rodriguez was to you? He was that to me."

Paige fell silent and nodded.

"He was like a father to me," Jorge continued. "And to him, I was like a son or, at least, this is what I thought."

"Why would he want you dead?" Paige asked and shook her head. "Maybe we should go back and talk to Marco. Maybe he made a mistake."

"No," Jorge said after some hesitation. "I do not think he would bring this to me unless he knew it was true. It makes sense that he would want to kill me."

"But why?" Paige asked with sadness in her eyes. "Why now? Why at *all?*"

"My belief," Jorge attempted to answer even though he was feeling shaky about the situation himself. "Is because he is an old man, who is probably close to his death. He does not want anything to affect his legacy. I am the *one,* the *only* person who knows how he became such a rich man. He is very powerful throughout Latin America but especially in Mexico. He perhaps fears what his family will learn once he is gone."

"Why does it matter after he's dead?" Paige quietly asked.

"Where I come from," Jorge replied. "Legacy, it is everything. You know that even I worry about such things. To this man, he comes from the old school where what others think is important. He wouldn't want his family's name tarnished if there was a chance people were to learn the truth."

"Why would you reveal anything?" Paige asked as she shook her head. "I don't understand."

"Because, *mi amor,* he knows me as a loose cannon," Jorge replied and cleared his throat. "He sees me always getting into situations here in Canada. He figures that eventually, I will get caught, and at that time, I will be forced to tell his name. That everything could come out."

"Or maybe," Paige added. "He thinks the police are already onto *him* and might offer you a way out if you sing…"

"This, *mi amor,* it does make sense," Jorge thought for a minute. "Either way, this is very difficult. It is…it is like someone hit me with a brick. I never thought he would turn on me but I always knew, if he did, I would not have a chance."

"Jorge!" Paige exclaimed and backed away slightly. "Don't say that! If anyone, can take care of this, it's us."

"This here," Jorge shook his head. "I do not know."

"I can't believe we're even having this conversation," Paige shook her head. "Who *are* you? You've never backed down from anyone before and you're not backing down now. *I'm* not backing down. I'm going to find this asshole and I'm going to kill him myself. Just tell me where he is."

"Paige, I…"

"I'm serious, Jorge," Paige continued to fume while he watched her in disbelief. "This man, he's dead. I'm one of the top assassins in the world. Do you really think I can't do this?"

"It is not that I think you cannot," Jorge insisted as he reached out to touch her arm. "This is not what I mean. What I mean is that I do not want you to get in the crossfire, the children, they need at least one of us."

"Jorge! They need both of us!"

"I know this but if…"

"I can't believe this," Paige shook her head again. "I can't believe we are even having this conversation."

Jorge was too stunned to talk. He couldn't make Paige understand that they had finally met their match. This man was too powerful, one of the oligarchs of Latin America, and could crush any man who got in his way. It was that same power that helped Jorge rise to the top in the first place.

"Now, I'm turning on my phone," Paige continued. "And I'm going to get Marco to do some research. We're handling this…*I'm* handling this. He will not get his way."

Jorge didn't argue. Stunned about what he had just learned, Jorge wanted to believe it was a mistake but deep down, he knew it wasn't.

Unsure of what else to do, he started the SUV and pulled onto the street. Paige was on her phone texting furiously, as if her life depended on it. His biggest fear was that the hit was on them both and not just him. The world would probably be a better place if he wasn't in it but not Paige. The children needed her. The group needed her. He had to find a way to give himself up in exchange for leaving his family alone. They would finally be free.

As they drove in silence, he glanced at his wife from time to time to read her face. She went from furious to anxious and finally sadness, by the time they arrived home, Paige was crying. He turned off the SUV.

"Paige, this here, I can deal with Tony and Andrew…"

"No, I'm coming too," She wiped away a tear. "It's fine. We will deal with them and sort the rest out once Marco finds more."

"Paige, I…I will contact this man later…"

"And say what?" She countered. "*I know you want to kill me.*"

"Maybe I can reason with him."

She looked away as a new flood of tears suddenly broke their way through and he moved closer to pull her into an awkward hug.

"It is going to be ok," He attempted to assure her. "What I say back there, I was upset….I will find a way to make him back down."

"What if you can't?"

"Paige, I can…we will figure this out," Jorge insisted. "Please, go to the house. Relax. I won't be long at Diego's."

"Ok," She seemed reluctant.

A heaviness filled the garage as they both exited the SUV with him going one way and her, the other.

"Make sure you have your gun on you at all times," Jorge reminded her and she nodded.

"I always do."

His body felt heavy as he walked out of the garage, feeling inside his leather jacket to make sure he had his own gun. Not that he went far without his weapons, some of which were more carefully concealed. One must always be prepared.

At Diego's house, it was Jolene who answered the door.

"These men," She spoke dramatically. "They all make me *loco*. I feel like I live with a bunch of teenagers. The bathrooms, they are disgusting and…"

"Jolene," Jorge cut her off. "I have a job for you."

"Me?" Her eyes lit up. "You have something for me? Oh yes, whatever, I can do!"

"I need you to go next door," Jorge spoke in a low voice. "I need you to talk to Paige."

"Is something wrong?"

"Well, yes…" Jorge thought for a moment. "She can tell you more. We are in a difficult situation."

"Did you cheat on her?" Jolene asked skeptically. "Because if you do, I will personally…"

"No, Jolene, not like that," Jorge shook his head and couldn't help but laugh at her passion. "It is something else. She can explain to you. I also would feel better if she had someone with her. Take your gun."

"I always have my gun," Jolene spoke to him as if he said the most ridiculous thing. "What am I? An idiot?"

"Thank you, Jolene."

After she left, Jorge made his way into the secret room where the two men were working. Andrew was the first to look up while Tony, who was wearing headphones as he stared at a screen, took a few seconds longer.

"Did you find out who..." Andrew started to ask.

"No," Jorge replied before he could finish. "We are still working on it."

"Yeah," Tony was taking off his headphones. "The picture was clear but not clear enough to tell who it was."

"Jorge has like...a magician who can figure this stuff out."

"Well, my magician," Jorge said, appreciating the lighter atmosphere. "He even has his limits"

Tony nodded in understanding while Andrew shrugged.

"What you guys got going on?" Jorge changed the subject and glanced at a frozen screenshot of a woman speaking.

"New episode drops tonight," Tony quickly replied. "And we're working on the final edits for the next one."

"We kind of jumped ahead," Andrew made a face and glanced at Tony with uncertainty. "We thought maybe with the excitement over the show, we'd do the one on Big Pharma creating those new viruses, the super viruses or whatever they're called."

"Yeah, we got someone doing a lot of talking and his story adds up," Tony said. "We have some others but everyone's face is hidden so Big Pharma..."

He didn't finish his sentence but it wasn't necessary. Tony knew first hand how these companies took care of problems.

"We knew you were talking about doing this episode later on..." Andrew quickly added.

"This here it seems like a good idea," Jorge replied even though he was still preoccupied with his problems. "I have no issue with this decision."

"We're gonna call it 'Did they create the disease that makes you sick?'," Tony said with a grin. "And it's going to blow the roof off this industry."

"And the lawyer," Jorge said as he glanced between the two. "We cannot be sued?"

"Already talked to your lawyer and we are good," Tony shook his head. "We got the people who worked in these companies. They know all their dirty secrets."

"*Perfecto,*" Jorge grinned. "This here, it is perfect."

CHAPTER 49

"Yesterday, my daughter, she says that I am never around," Jorge spoke honestly as he sat back in his chair and glanced at the phone on his desk. "She had one of her friends over and apparently, he is always at my house but me, I am often out conducting business. I miss so much and this, I regret."

"But now," Jorge continued. "I would like to think I can still make a difference, to make up for the lost time."

"It is good to put family first."

The voice on the other end of the line was that of a man who had been in Jorge's life since he was a teenager. He was the man who took over where his father had left off, attempting to guide him, to teach him the ways of the world. He was the man who made Jorge Hernandez.

"I know but it is a challenge."

"You, as they say, have too many irons in the fire."

"I do."

"You must back away and see what you wish for in the future and not what you think you *need* to do."

"What I wish," Jorge spoke bluntly as he leaned forward, closer to the phone. "Is to be alive, to see my children grow up."

Silence.

"My wish is not to have someone I have been loyal to for my entire life kill me," Jorge added. "I do not know what makes this so difficult. Is it that my life, it may end soon or the person who is going to do it, is like a father to me. Someone I thought I could trust. Someone who I thought would never let me down."

Silence.

"Did you think I would not find out?" Jorge continued. "How long were you planning this for? Was it because of something that happened recently?"

"I have been planning it for years," The old man's voice sounded distant, cold when he spoke. "It was always my plan."

Jorge was shocked and sat back. Glancing around the empty office, he leaned into his chair as his heart raced erratically. He felt a heatwave overcome him but he allowed it to pass through, finally making its escape.

"But why?" He finally asked. "Why?"

"You know everything," The old man replied. "I could not have it come out."

"But I do not understand…"

"What I mean is that it was the plan since the day I took you on," He continued. "There were times you got too close to the fire that I started to make plans but since you always got away, always made me money, I let it go. It was never anything personal. Just business."

"Just business?" Jorge couldn't help but laugh. "You are a part of my life for so many years but murdering me, it was *just* business."

"I've had a lot of hesitation over the years…"

"But you were still going to do it?"

"A few years ago," The old man continued. "I sent an assassin to your hotel…"

"What?" Jorge shot back as his heart raced. He was talking about Paige.

"Her target was someone else," The man continued as a muffled voice could be heard in the background. "But we purposely changed things at the last minute to have her go to your room. I did not count on you instead charming her into your bed."

Jorge was stunned.

"My understanding was that she would shoot not realizing it was the wrong man because this assassin, she would not deal with the cartels," He continued. "I greatly underestimated her. She not only *didn't* kill you but she *did* kill the other man."

Jorge didn't reply.

"In fairness, she did what she was told," He continued.

"You had this planned with Claudia Garcia Rodriguez, didn't you?" Jorge said as he pieced it together. "But at the time…"

"Not at the time," He replied. "She was quite angry when she realized what I had done but I managed to cover my tracks, leaving you certain that this was someone else's fault."

Jorge didn't speak.

"But later, as time went on," He paused and took a deep breath. "Claudia relented."

Jorge thought about his words.

"She saw the benefits of coming together for the same cause. If your wife lost you, chances were she would return to her assassin life."

Jorge felt his anger grow.

"As I said, it was nothing personal, just business."

Infuriated, Jorge ended the call. He sat in silence looking around the room. Glancing at the framed photos of his family on the desk, he pushed his chair out and stood up. His legs felt wobbly as he walked out of the room. His brain was spinning in every direction.

Checking his phone, he noticed a message from Diego.

We got something. I'm on my way to your house. Paige said you're there.

Walking through the quiet rooms, he couldn't find Paige. Fear caused a sharp pain in his chest and he braced himself against the wall, his head spinning for a moment. Touching the gun inside his jacket, he managed to calm down and text her.

She had already messaged him. He had missed it

Went next door with Jolene.

She was with Jolene. The two women had been discussing the Colombian's drama when he arrived home earlier. He had simply told them he was going to his office to make some calls, partially frustrated that Jolene's concern during this time was only on herself. Paige appeared troubled but listened like the angel she was, trying to help Jolene.

Going into the kitchen, he decided to have a drink to calm his nerves. Glancing at the clock, he realized that Maria would be at school for another hour and Juliana could be heard talking to his son upstairs. He knew she had a gun. It was amazing what that woman hid in a diaper bag.

He had barely knocked back his drink when Diego arrived with Marco in tow. Both were upset.

"We gotta go next door," Diego said hurriedly as he pointed toward his house. "Marco figured out something on the way here."

"What?" Jorge was dumbfounded. "What do you…"

"Trust me!" Diego insisted. "We gotta go over there…now!

Jorge didn't hesitate to follow their instructions. Locking the door on his way out, the three men rushed next door with both Diego and Jorge grabbing their guns. An unfamiliar vehicle was in the driveway.

"What's going on?" He nervously asked, knowing his wife was in the house. "What did you find?"

"Sir, I found messages," Marco spoke in a low voice as they approached the door. "This man, in the pictures from earlier, he has someone hired. They think you live in Diego's house for some reason."

Jorge raised an eyebrow but remained silent. He glanced around and peeked in the window. Nothing appeared out of the ordinary but he felt a chill run through his spine.

"Sir, do you need me to…"

"Security cameras in the area?"

"Sir, I already have them down."

"Diego, do you not have cameras in your house?"

"I do," He spoke hurriedly. "But I'm having trouble logging in. I forget my password. I had to change it to this super long…"

Jorge waved him off.

"I don't know what I'm doing wrong…"

Jorge shot him a warning look.

Walking up the step, Jorge gestured for Diego to unlock the door. He did so carefully then slowly turned the doorknob. Diego stood back and pushed the door open while Jorge automatically raised his gun and Marco stood back.

The three men walked inside with caution. No one was near but an eerie silence caused a shot of thunder to roar through Jorge's body. What if everyone in the house was dead? What if they were too late?

They moved forward, their eyes scanning each room as they got closer to the secret room where Andrew and Tony were working. Arriving at the door, Jorge swung it opened to find the two men staring at their laptops as if nothing was awry. This time, it was Tony who saw him first. His eyes widened when he noticed both Diego and Jorge were holding guns.

"We..we don't have to do that episode, you know, if…or whatever…." Tony sputtered along as Andrew turned and glanced at the two men.

"What the…" Andrew started but his eyes suddenly grew in size and his face drained of color.

Sensing that someone was behind them, Jorge turned around.

That's when his blood went cold.

CHAPTER 50

The world loves strong women. In our darkest hour, it's often the mothers of the earth that take care of us when we can't take care of ourselves. They give us comfort when we need a shoulder to cry on and lift us when life pulls us down. They're the survivors, the adapters, the healers. When the world falls on its ass, what you want, what you need, is a woman in your corner.

Paige Noël-Hernandez had often been underestimated. People thought that because she was small that she wasn't powerful. They thought that because she was quiet that she didn't have a voice. They thought that because she was calm that she wasn't thinking...or planning...or putting things together.

When Jolene arrived at the house that day, Paige had already started to research the man who wanted her husband dead. Although they played it cool when Jorge walked through the house, both were working diligently to see what they could learn. Eventually, with a few contacts from her past, Paige was able to find the name of the most likely assassin. She also learned something unexpected. The man who Jorge had long seen as a father figure always made certain to be present when he had someone killed. It was a way to make sure the job was a success since previous situations had let him down.

"This means," Paige hurriedly told Jolene her theory as she pointed toward Jorge's office, where he was talking to the man in question. "If we can track either of these men to the Toronto area, they're both here....and they're planning to kill Jorge."

Jolene's expression went from shock to sadness, followed by anger.

"We, we can stop this!"

"I know but first, we have to find out where they are....I got their names," Paige paused for a moment to take a breath and close her eyes. "I have a feeling they're close. I just....I can feel it."

"You must trust your heart," Jolene said while nodding vigorously. "Your heart, it is never wrong."

While the women worked together to find more answers, Diego and Marco were already on their way to meet with Jorge. New information had come to light as the two men sped along a busy section of Toronto, with Diego cursing the traffic.

"We must get there soon, sir," Marco sounded nervous as he tapped on his laptop. "I wish I had found this information sooner. We cannot tell them this on the phone."

"We'll get there," Diego insisted as he glared at the car ahead of him then quickly looked over his shoulder at Priscilla sleeping in the back seat. "Call Chase too. We might need..."

"Wait, sir," Marco cut him off mid-sentence. "They think Jorge lives at your house!"

"What?"

"The online map, it shows Jorge's address as your house," Marco pointed out. "This is why the message I see, they describe the house inaccurately. They think he lives at your house."

"Fuck!" Diego yelled. "You better call Paige and Jorge right away and find a way to warn them."

Marco followed his instructions as anxiety filled the car. He couldn't get through to Jorge but called Paige. As soon as she answered the phone, he carefully gave her a rundown that sounded casual if anyone was listening, warning her of the address mixup.

"Shit!" Paige started to put it together. "That's why the time Maria's friend Cameron was here, they thought he was at Diego's house. There's something wrong with the..."

"I will explain why later," Marco was cutting her off. "You must be prepared. Our…guests are on the way to the house."

"Fuck!" Paige quickly ended the call and jumped off the couch as Jolene did the same. "We gotta go next door. They're on their way, they think Diego's place is where Jorge lives…"

"What about Jorge?" Jolene pointed toward the office as they rushed to the door.

"No," Paige said and shook her head. "We got this, Jolene. I will text him that I'm just next door."

The women exchanged looks, reaching for their guns, they headed to Diego's house. Not wanting to alarm Andrew and Tony, they quietly went inside and started to look around, focusing on the back door in case they got in that way.

"Maybe we should talk to Andrew and Tony…"

"Those two *nerds,* they will not hear," Jolene said as she rolled her eyes. "They are in the secret room in their computer, weirdo world."

Paige couldn't help but grin. However, this smile quickly faded away as they made their way back to the front of the house and she noticed an unfamiliar car in the driveway. There was no one inside.

"When did that get here?" She whispered to Jolene as she clasped tighter to her gun and glanced around. The door was locked but she knew better than anyone that this was of no consequence to a trained assassin. "We should separate and look. You go upstairs."

Jolene nodded and carefully made her way to the stairs while Paige turned the corner. She was only a few steps out of sight when a cold object touched the back of the head. Closing her eyes, she remained as calm as she could, knowing that only tranquility could save her now.

"Paige Noël…or is it, Paige Hernandez, now?" The voice was deep, an older man with a Mexican accent. "I never do know what you women want these days. Sometimes you take on your husband's name and other times, you do not. It is almost as if you must destroy all traditions, everything that is moral and beautiful. You have to kill it then wonder why your men, are not happy. But we like the old ways, you know?"

Paige didn't comment.

"The fact that one of the best assassins in the world is a woman, it is surprising," He continued with laughter in his voice. "It almost seems like, you know, something in a movie. It is entertaining but yet, it does not seem realistic. Of course, this is correct because for the 'best assassin in the world' you certainly did not kill the one man I had hoped you would. You bedded him instead then weaseled your way into his life, as you women, you always do. Such master manipulators."

She remained quiet, her thoughts were processing.

"But now, you women, you want it all," He continued with a coldness seeping into his voice. "The baby, the husband, the career, then you hire someone else to look after your kids, to clean your house and turn around and say how exhausted you are but yet, you think you can run countries when most of you, you cannot even run your own homes or keep your men in your beds. Sometimes, I have to laugh…"

A shot rang out and she felt a weight falling against her body. Jumping ahead, she turned around to see Jolene holding a gun while an elderly, Mexican man fell on the floor with blood quickly filling his jacket.

"We do a *lot* of things motherfucker!" Jolene's loud voice filled the room and Paige couldn't help but giggle until she looked over the Colombian's shoulder to see another man holding a gun. She automatically recognized him as the same man who killed Tony's mother.

"Move!" Paige lurched forward, pushing Jolene aside just as the gun was fired.

It missed Jolene.

It didn't miss Paige.

All she heard was another shot ringing out as she slid to the floor. Crying, Jolene was crying. Something was squeezing her arm. It hurt. It was too tight. What was happening? She heard a man's voice. Was it Chase? She felt light as if she were floating through the air. Voices, there were voices. Jorge, she could hear Jorge.

And then she was in a room. Where was she? Attempting to lift her head, her throat was dry. Blinking her eyes, everything was blurry. And then she saw him.

Sitting across the room, the most powerful man in the world was crying.

She tried to speak but couldn't. He suddenly looked up.

"Paige!" Jorge rushed toward her bed, quickly wiping away his tears. "Paige! Oh my God. I was never so scared."

She tried to speak but her throat was too dry.

Grabbing a glass beside her bed, he maneuvered the straw to touch her lips.

"These fucking paper straws," He grumbled and she started to laugh but was quickly pulled back in pain. She glanced down at her body. What was wrong with her?

"Paige, take a drink," Jorge said as if reading her mind. "I will explain."

She followed his instructions and felt like she was slowly coming alive again.

"Paige, *mi amor*," He started as she took another drink before shaking her head. "Paige, you were shot."

Glancing back down at her body, it took a moment to realize where she had been hit. It was her arm. The same arm she was shot in when she was pregnant with Miguel.

"I am...I am so sorry this happen to you," Jorge said with emotion in his voice. "That bullet, it was meant for me."

"No, for me," Paige whispered and cleared her throat. "Or no...Jolene. It was...the other man...he wanted..."

"Paige, just relax," Jorge insisted. "You must calm down."

"Where am I?"

"I have a...private doctor take out the bullet," Jorge said with confidence. "I will explain more later."

"Am I...am..."

"You are ok," Jorge insisted. "We were not sure at the time because there was a lot of blood. When I turned around and saw Chase carrying you..."

That was when she felt light. As if she were floating in the air.

"He....was so scared when he find you," Jorge continued. "Jolene, she was frantic. She took off her top and tied it around your arm. She has been walking around in just a bra until someone make her wear a shirt."

Paige laughed. It hurt.

Jorge reluctantly joined her.

"I want to thank her," Paige said and cleared her throat, and Jorge grabbed her glass of water again. After taking a drink she continued. "She saved me. I felt a gun and thought it was over...she saved me."

"I know, she tells me everything," Jorge spoke softly.

"I know she's made mistakes..."

"*Mi amor*, I know…I agree with you."

That's when the door crept opened and Diego looked in. With relief on his face, he called out to the others.

"She's awake, guys!"

Suddenly the room was full. Diego rushed forward to give her a gentle hug while Jolene seemed apprehensive to enter the room. She was wearing a man's shirt and had tears in her eyes, her makeup wiped away.

"Paige!" She started to sob as she rushed ahead to hug her as soon as Diego moved away. "I thought you were dead! I was so scared! You save me. That man, he was going to shoot me. I am forever grateful."

"Let us, please, let us calm down," Jorge said with tears in his eyes as he backed away, noting that Marco and Chase stood back in hesitation, he ushered them in. "Please, can you shut the door."

Marco obediently followed his orders.

"Today, it was scary," Jorge started and took a deep breath as Jolene stood back up and wiped away another tear. "But we are a family and as I have said many times, it is family that takes care of one another. We may have disagreements, we have problems but at the end of the day, we protect each other. This here, it is what matters."

Paige nodded and gave Jorge a look.

"Jolene, we have had our differences," Jorge said and couldn't help but be swept up in the muffled giggles in the room. "Again and again, we disagree, and sometimes, you piss me off. But today, when we needed you, you were here. You did save my wife's life and for that, I wish you to rejoin this family. Please."

"That is so sweet but Jorge," She shook her head, her voice rising dramatically. "I never left!"

He grinned and looked at every face in the room as they did the same. He heard a giggle from the bed and looked down at his wife. He reached for her hand.

He was lucky to have these people. They were loyal to the end. And he was lucky to have Paige because as long as he was the devil, she was his angel.

Thank you for following along in the Hernandez adventure. Don't forget to go to www.mimaonfire.com to learn about the rest of the series and to keep up to date on the books, interviews and the latest YouTube videos!

Love the book? Write a review and share the love!